Mimi Barbour

I0653963

Special Agent Murphy

by

Mimi Barbour

NYT & USAT Bestselling author

Special Agent Murphy

DEDICATION

My late husband's persona is the heart and soul of Special Agent Murphy. While bringing out some of his most endearing and stubborn characteristics, his favorite cuss words, and his way of looking at the world, I found myself falling in love with the wonderful man all over again.
Together Forever, my love.

All but four of Mimi's books can be found FREE on
Kindle Unlimited!!
And those four are FREE everywhere!
~*~*~*~

My NEW Trilogy 2023
LAND OF THE FREE
Irresistible Freedom (Book 1)
Unforgettable Freedom (Book2)
Ultimate Freedom (Book 3)
~*~*~*~

The Vicarage Bench Series
— Spirit Travel at its Best! —
She's Me (Book 1)
He's Her (Book 2)
We're One (Book 3)
Vicarage Bench Anthology (Book 4 - Books 1-3)
Together Again (Book 5)
Together for Christmas (Book 6)
Together Always (Book 7)
~*~*~*~

Angels with Attitude Series
— Angels Playing Cupid! —
The Angels with Attitudes Anthology (Books 1-3)
My Cheeky Angel (Book 1)
His Devious Angel (Book 2)
Loveable Christmas Angel (Book 3) FREE
A Wonderful Life (Book 4)
Mischievous Christmas Angel (Book 5)
~*~*~*~

Elvis Series
— Make an Elvis Song a Book! —
She's Not You (Book 1)
Love Me Tender (Book 2)
Don't Be Cruel (Book 3)
~*~*~*~

Vegas Series
— Action–Packed Thrillers! —
Vegas Series – Complete Boxed Set
Partners (Book 1) FREE
Roll the Dice (Book 2)
Vegas Shuffle (Book 3)
High Stakes Gamble (Book 4)
Spin the Wheel (Book 5)
Let it Ride (Book 6)
~*~*~*~

Undercover FBI Series
— Popular & Compelling! —
Special Agent Francesca (Book 1)
Special Agent Finnegan (Book 2)
Special Agent Maximilian (Book 3)
Special Agent Kandice (Book 4)
Special Agent Booker (Book 5)
Special Agent Charli (Book 6)
Special Agent Rylee (Book 7)
Special Agent Murphy (Book 8)
Special Agent Sophia (Book 9) FREE
Special Agent Hunter (Book 10)
Special Agent Makayla (Book 11)
Special Agent Storm (Book 12)
Special Agent Jennie (Book 13)
Special Agent Walker (Book 14)
Special Agent Isabella (Book 15)
Special Agent Lucifer (Luke) (Book16 to be released in

Special Agent Murphy

winter of 2023)
~*~*~*~

Holiday Heartwarmers Series
— Truly a Christmas favorite! —
Holiday Heartwarmers Trilogy #1
Second Heartwarmers Trilogy #2
Please Keep Me (Book 1)
Snow Pup (Book 2)
Find Me a Home (Book 3)
Frosty the Snowman (Book 4)
Love of my Life (Book 5)
A Perfect Storm (Book 6)
Alone at Christmas (Book 7)
Christmas, Puppies & Romance (Book 8)
Santa's Gifts of Romance (Book 9)
Christmas is for Everyone (Book 10)
Flamingo Christmas (Book 11)
~*~*~*~

Her Sweet Revenge Series
— She's unstoppable! —
Retaliation (Book 1)
Justice (Book 2)
Resolution (Book 3
Endings - (Book 4)
Faith – (Book 5) FREE
Leni – (Book 6)
~*~*~*~

Single Title Series
He's My Baby (Book #1)
Christmas Runaway (Book #2)
Because You Cared (Book #3)
Daddy's Mine (Book #4)
Her Hero (Book #5)
You Make Me Happy (Book #6)

Sweet Christmas (Book #7)
You're the Boss (Book 8)
Young Love Strikes Again (Book 9)
Dear Hottie (Book 10)
Born a Hero (Book 11)
~*~*~*~

The Best in Romance Series
Red Hot Divas (Book #1 Box Set)
Hot and Handsome (Book #2 Box Set
~*~*~*~

Other Titles
I'm No Angel
Hotshot Cowboy
Big Girls Don't Cry
The Surrogate's Secret
Mimi's Mix (Box Set)
'Tis the Season (Box Set)
Hearts, Flowers & Romance (Box Set)
~*~*~*~

All Mimi's books can be found on her Amazon Author
Page:
http://bit.ly/MimiBarbourAmazon
OR
Website: http://mimibarbour.com

CONTENTS

Special Agent Murphy

CHAPTER 1

Murphy pulled into his driveway and saw his neighbor acting like an asshole again. It happened often, and Murphy was sick of it. He left the car, intending to ignore the fact that the kid was getting blasted.

"Little shit. You listen to me when I talk to you."

"When you make sense, maybe I will. Until then, back off and leave me alone. I'm not handing over any money, so give it up."

"I feed you, clothe you, and put a fucking roof over your head. Then… when I ask for a few bucks, you act like I'm some mysterious thief trying to steal your future. Piss on your future, what about now? What about me? I need money."

"Then get off your lazy fat ass, get a job, and earn some – like you've made me do."

"Who do you think you are, talking to me

that way." Losing his shit, the older man suddenly turned into a crazed fool. He rushed at the boy, grabbed him by his arm, and hauled back to punch. In earlier years, no doubt, he'd have connected, but now the boy was strong and filled with angry disgust. Rather than take the punishment, he yanked himself from the other's grasp, turned, and started to leave.

He didn't see his dad pull off the piece of broken fence, whip it behind his back, and swing full force.

If Murphy hadn't stepped out at that moment to haul the kid away, the board would have connected, and no doubt would have done some damage.

He pointed at his door, pushed the kid in the direction, and growled, "Get into the house. Now!"

Once Talin had disappeared, he pulled the drunk to his feet – the force from his wild swing having landed him on his ass – and shook him like a rag. "Campbell, you're a disgrace to the male race and fatherhood."

"The brat disrespe-ched… me."

"That makes two of us." He pushed the man toward his open back door, "Chrissakes, get out of my sight before I give you what you've got coming. And have a shower, you stink like puke."

***

"Jesus, kid. What set him off like that?"

"He's drunk."

"He's always drunk."

"Yeah, well tonight he was a mean drunk."

"I heard him after you for money. You working?"

Talin went to the fridge and pulled out some cheese, ham, and bread. Next, he grabbed the frying pan from the cupboard and started putting together grilled cheese sandwiches, his favorite snack that surprisingly was always available for him at Murphy's place. "You want a couple?"

"Sure. What kind of job did you find?"

Talin stopped and stared. Murphy drilled him with his no-nonsense glare. "Hey, back off. I'm helping old man Whiteland two doors down clean

3

his yard."

"Okay. Good. Don't look at me that way."

"You don't trust me to keep out of trouble? I'm hurt."

"Bullshit. There's assholes out there who'd like a youngster like you on their payroll, selling all kinds of shit. You know what I mean."

"I know. They've already approached me. I told them like you said. That you lived next door and would be on them quicker'n they could call for their mamas if they messed with me. Funny, they haven't come near since."

"Good. Keep your nose clean. Work the available jobs helping people around the neighborhood. Keep it up and you'll get to college one day."

Talin kept his head down. "I want to be in criminal justice like you."

"Not like me. It's a shit job. Most guys at work can't keep a family together and we're always broke."

"I was talking the law side, like a lawyer."

"Yeah, well before you start deciding your future, check with technology to see whether lawyer jobs will still be plentiful in your future."

"People will always break the law."

"True. Criminal attorneys might be around."

Murphy finished fixing his rye and coke and took the first swill, moaning from the good taste.

Talin watched and grinned. "How come you never get drunk from that stuff?"

"'Cause, I know my body... when to quit before I lose control. And don't say you want to be like me in that way too. It's my one vice, otherwise I'm perfect." A cynical grin broke out over a face not used to smiling."

"Last time I asked, you called it a crutch."

"Guess I'd had my second by then. Listen, squirt, grab a life where you don't need anything but brains and hard work."

"No more with the squirt bullshit. I figure I've outgrown that nickname."

"Fine, Batman, have it your way. Where's my dinner?"

Talin plated the four sandwiches and scored a big glass of milk from the fridge. "I'm staying tonight, okay?"

"Hell, yeah. I wouldn't ask a dog to go back next door the way your old man is tonight. I'll go and mess with him in the morning and see if I can't get him cleaned up."

"You're the only one he listens to anymore."

"That's because I scare the shit outta him." Murphy took another long swill. "He's an idiot, but not a complete loss. Your mom's death hit him hard."

"Maybe you should tell him what you told me."

"What's that?"

"You growled at me when I was being pathetic. You said, she'd hate to see me become a loser and use the excuse of her dying to behave like a shit. But, if I used her memory to become the son she'd be proud of, she'd be smiling with the angels. Remember?"

"Yeah. It's good advice. Don't know how I

got so smart." Murphy chuckled.

Talin pulled a funny face and took a huge bite.

CHAPTER 2

Murphy hated stakeouts with a passion. He especially hated them when he had to put up with the female yapper they'd stuck him with for this investigation. He knew bloody well why Special Agent in Charge Edna Kale made him use a partner for this job. She hated his guts and was doing everything she could to get Murphy to quit.

If his persecution complex was playing games with his head… so be it, but he didn't think so. For instance, they'd stuck him with a rookie to work with rather than a colleague from the main office… someone who knew how to behave like a pro. And as far as he could determine, she either had an in with Kale or someone higher.

The annoying woman looked to be about seventeen, played with her hair nervously and hadn't shut up since they'd parked outside the bar.

Blabberty blah, blah – on and on until he couldn't think while her soft voice drilled into his patience, making him yearn for the double rye and coke that waited for him after work.

"I need to go to the restroom." This time her words registered.

Thank God for small mercies. He'd get a few moments peace.

"So, go. Nothing's happening. I haven't seen Draper exit, have you?"

"Our perp? No. Okay, I'll head inside and act like a customer. It'll only take a few minutes."

"Hell, don't rush back on my account. Take as long as you need."

He ignored her silly chuckle and watched the slim body in tight jeans and a snug black leather jacket disappear through the double doors.

Inside Coopers, the sleazy place they were watching, their man, Ed Draper, pictured on everyone's most-wanted list hung out with his buddies. The creep had felonies for everything from larceny to aggravated assault.

Though they didn't have enough evidence to book him, he looked good for the murder of the snitch whose body they'd found recently. Playing footsies with his fellow Russians had taken Draper to a whole new level of crime.

It was the reason for the stakeout, to follow the bastard and see if he'd lead them to the major player, Vik Baranov. Something a rookie agent should be taking care of, not a ten-year veteran like himself.

Murphy rubbed the back of his neck and wondered why the hell he put up with the shit. Oh, how the mighty had fallen. A slight nine months earlier, he'd been everyone's hero. They'd acknowledged his bravery with a medal and a special ceremony after he brought down one of the worst serial killers of the century.

But all the fanfare had disappeared after one stupid mistake, one dumb move, trusting Tanner, a partner with a gambling problem. Bruce's family… a wife with no earning power who needed her husband's pension - and two kids Murphy had grown to care about – had played their part in his split-second decision.

Agent Bruce Tarner had gone rogue, involved up to his eyeballs with the worst of humanity. While Murphy'd tried to get his partner to safety, they'd shot him and almost killed Murphy.

He still got a sick feeling in the pit of his stomach at his friend's betrayal. Jesus, what men wouldn't do to feed their habits.

You'd think he'd learn. All through his younger years, he'd been played for a chump more than he wanted to remember. Girlfriend's he'd begin to trust eventually showed their worst qualities of jealousy and bad temper.

The last one having come on strong with her *I'm an innocent trying to have a relationship, but men are such morons* had turned out to be the worst of the lot. Pretty is as pretty does, and that bitch did pretty much every drug she could get her hands on.

Hid it from him by using medications from the doctor as the reason her pupils weren't regular.

Hid it until she began working on getting a discount for the crap from dealers he knew, dealers who let him know she was using his name.

Hell, he was no puritan. He'd admit to liking his one or two drinks at night, but he stayed miles away from that crazy mind-altering shit. From people who used it too. After that last breakup, he'd gone solo for months. Why give anyone else the chance to mess with his head again?

Deciding then that he needed a break from the seedy world he inhabited and backstabbing partners, he'd opted to use some vacation time. He took a long drive to Missouri to check up on his mother. Lately, she'd been pulling the good-son card – you don't call, you never visit, yadda yadda.

As a single mom after his dad died, believing in tough love, her strong personality and type of mothering had taught him his shit *did* stink just like everyone else's. And he'd learned to believe it. Not that he'd ever doubted her affection, he'd just had to work harder to earn it.

Excitement had begun building when he saw

her waiting for him on the steps of the farmhouse. Crazy but true, her opinion always did matter, and though he'd never admit to looking forward to being with her again, his heart had sped up, and a sweet excitement had made him glad he'd come.

Yet rather than hug him like he'd kind of expected, she'd shocked him by staring up at the sky, her hands on her hips, and spitting out words he had no idea where they came from or why at that particular moment they mattered.

"Bloody rain."

Taken aback - even by her standards it had been a harsh welcome. Disappointment hit hard. Though his training had kicked in, and he'd kept the expression on his face from changing, she must have sensed his shock.

Relenting, her attitude undergoing a swift about-turn, she'd grabbed him in a hard hug, pushed herself away from him, and then disappeared inside the house.

She'd remarried years after he'd moved out, and though he'd been guilted into paying that visit –

never again. From now on, she'd have to come to his place. Her new farmer husband was a prick, and worst of all, he was a dumb prick, which made the situation a hell of a lot worse. Shane caught himself several times before punching the idiot's lights out.

Driving away a day earlier than he'd planned, he shrugged off his worry. If his mother was happy, who was he to get in her way.

Suddenly, coming back to earth, Murphy noticed the door to the bar being held open by a bunch of people fleeing. That's when he saw the fight going on inside. And right smack dab in the middle of the skirmish was the yapper.

CHAPTER 3

Kayti couldn't shut up. Nervousness always transformed her from an intelligent human being into an idiot. Talking released the pressure before her brain blew up, and the pain brought her to her knees.

Not too blind, she knew it drove the man next to her crazy. Hell, it acted the same way on her… but the mouth kept working without her permission. Once she could relax in his presence, the stupid weakness would disappear. Or so it had in the past.

Another old habit suddenly appeared; her hand continually yanked at her long hair, curling strands around her finger like some nervous Nelly. Feelings of insecurity were always close. Knowing that her soft heart could be her worst weakness, Kayti tried hard to show a persona to be respected. Most of the people she worked with knew her for who she really was.

The kind who'd go out of her way to be a good person. Would sit up all night to support a colleague in trouble. A woman who always got suckered by a sob story. And don't get her started about seeing a man in tears. No way could she watch a TV program or go to a movie and sit through a male actor breaking down without dissolving into a puddle herself.

Since she'd started working for the FBI, she'd tried to reel in her weaknesses. As others told her – grow some balls, and don't be so thin-skinned – but it didn't happen.

All she had going for her could be counted on one hand. Intelligence, a mind like a steel trap for remembering everything of importance, good looks that she didn't take any credit for, and a body built to fight.

Knowing this particular talent could save her life one day, from the time she'd made up her mind to become a cop, she'd begun acing martial arts classes and honing herself – her skills and her speed.

At a bar one night, she'd sat with some of her colleagues, watching them get more and more plastered. While she'd kept up with them drink for drink, she could still walk a straight line. They'd taken their turns telling tales of what made them decide to be police officers.

Many of the stories were heart-wrenching – from watching parents getting killed, to being abused, to following in the family's footsteps.

For everyone there, cops were either involved or had made an impact. All great reasons for choosing this career. When they looked her way, expecting her story to equal theirs, she blushed and admitted, "as a kid, I liked watching Cagney and Lacey."

When the rest of them broke into gales of laughter, she kind of giggled along. Not wanting to delve too closely into the real reasons she'd made this choice, she let it drop. When the hilarity stopped, she tried to come clean. "Okay, I wanted to help people too." But it was too late. Some of the others started calling her Cagney and it stuck.

What was it about being a law officer that was so important she'd never considered any other career? She hadn't divulged her real reason and most likely never would. People just wouldn't understand her desperate need for respect.

Oh, oh. Another bodily consequence she suffered when nervous had to be the most annoying of all. Normally, her bladder could be relied on like a septic tank. She could hold on forever. But not when in an awkward situation that had her reacting like a yappy energizer bunny. She needed to relieve herself... now.

Making her excuse to Agent Asshole, she headed into the bar and straight for the ladies' room. Aiming for a stall, she barely made it before disgracing herself. Voices in the outer room suddenly came through loud and clear.

"My dad would kill me if he knew I was in a place like this, Gina."

"Jesus, Mini, just because he's a U.S. Senator doesn't mean you can't enjoy life and have some fun."

"It's Misti. Not Mini."

"Forgive me, I'm a bit wasted here."

"Sorry. Don't glare at me. I know… I know we just met. But this is really a dive. I don't think we should have let you talk our guys into bringing us here. Ryan's plastered from all the booze Alex keeps buying."

"I noticed. How about we have one more round, and then say our goodbyes. Okay?"

"If you want to stay, no problem. I know you guys brought us. I'll just call a cab for me and Ryan and leave before things get even more creepy. I've never been in a sleazy joint like this one… people vaping and smoking crazy shit. And those couples on the dance floor are all but making out. It's not my scene."

"Tell me about it."

"Like I said, if my dad ever finds out I was in a place like this, he'd take away my car, my phone, hell he'd probably lock me in my room like… forever."

Jesus, how old were these chicks she was listening to? Kayti finished her business and headed to the open area. Stained sinks, broken soap dispensers and zero paper towels for wiping her hands didn't surprise her. Taking her time to check out the other two, she had to acknowledge either Misti's ID had to be top-notch, or they hadn't bothered to check it.

The other female looked harder, more experienced, and when she noticed Kayti studying them in the mirror, she glared her objection.

What the hell are they doing together?

She examined the older one, a girl with long hair dripping down her back, colored with various shades of blonde to honey-gold but dark roots to spoil the look. Her lips were bright red, her clouded eyes bright blue, and the slinky black outfit was too lowcut, too short, and too glued to her well-endowed body.

Whatever game she played had fooled the youngster, but it didn't fool Kayti for a moment. This gal had been around the block a few times and knew the underside.

Now Misti seemed more of the next-door neighbor kind of chick if one lived in a wealthy part of the city. Since her father was a Senator, no doubt she did.

She wore her brown hair short with a natural curl and one side shaved close to her head. Plenty of cute earrings, a diamond nose ornament, and a bunch of woven bracelets gave her a look of someone popular.

Her jean outfit could be seen in any designer shop in the rich part of the city. Not only did it look modern and expensive, it was the complete opposite of sexy. Her brown eyes were clear and scared.

Kayti felt an immediate protectiveness. Misti had shown sense. They should leave. Before she could intervene, the blonde turned and opened the door.

At the last minute, the cutie caught Kayti's eyes in the mirror and smiled in a sweet way of hello – the way strangers sometimes did when they had no reason not to be friendly.

Kayti followed as soon as she'd found enough paper to dry her hands and was just in time to see Gina urging her friend toward the back of the place. Christ, was that Draper with her prompting the girl from behind? Manhandling her in a way that gave her no chance to refuse.

Stepping forward to put a stop to this bullshit, Kayti spoke up, "Hey assholes, let the kid be. She doesn't want to go with you." Not sure if she should call out her FBI credentials, they were supposed to be undercover after all, she decided to wing it and just pull a citizen's interference play.

"Go fuck yourself, lady. She's my sister. I'm taking her home." Draper spoke loudly but didn't bother to stop.

One of the other fellows at their table, more Misti's age, tried to pull himself to his feet. Either he had visions of preventing them from taking his girl, or maybe he thought to tag along himself. But his shoe got caught up in the table legs, and he fell to the floor.

Kayti saw the other chick locking arms with

Misti, hauling her out the back door. And she wasn't being gentle. It came through loud and clear, whatever was going down, blondie was involved.

Heading over to where Misti still argued, Kayti came up against a wall of men ready to stop her. Before she could even begin to talk her way out of the mess, one attacked, and the others decided to join in the party.

Out of the corner of her eye, Kayti saw the poor kid fighting to get free, then lose the battle as they dragged her out the back door.

CHAPTER 4

Murphy moved quickly. The fear of any partner of his getting annihilated spurred him on. Having to come up with explanations for the bitch-boss of why he sat outside, while an FBI agent got the shit kicked out of her didn't sit well with him. Annoyed, he rushed inside the joint to solve whatever mess she'd gotten herself into.

By the time he'd entered, many of the patrons were disappearing out the side door, a few whipped past him at the front, and still others were climbing out of an open window on the side.

Taking in the action, he watched mesmerized. Totally involved in kicking the unmitigated crap out of her opponents, and there were two of them, the yapper (best he start remembering her name) moved like a streak of beauty. The discipline in her punishment was a sight to behold.

He noticed two assailants were on the floor groaning, one holding his arm at an awkward angle, and the other rolling, grimacing while clinging protectively to his boys. Murphy found himself bending slightly forward in sympathy.

Deciding he needed to assist, but before he could intervene, his partner flipped one of the fighters onto a table full of cans and bottles. The resulting noise of breaking glass didn't bode well for the victim.

Before he could stop the one coming at her from her left, she sidestepped and grabbed his arm, swinging in a circle and landing the stranger's face against the solid oak post near the wall.

Sweet Jesus! Murphy winced when he heard the skull hit the wood. *Ouch!!* Standing and watching the action, he secretly admitted that he hadn't enjoyed anything as much in a very long time. That is until another wave of idiots thought to pay her a lesson.

A huge character moved in behind her, and

using her hair, he dragged her to him. He wrapped his bear paws around her chest, thinking to contain her arms. Too bad he hadn't controlled her legs… the ones with the killer boots at the end. She spiked his foot, slamming her heel hard enough to bring a yelp.

Murphy laughed out loud when she followed it up with a brutal kick to the fat guy's arch. When the bear loosened his grip, she drove her elbow behind her into a stomach not prepared to be hit. That's when fatso's face turned a funny shade of purple before he fell on his ass and got her boot in his face.

The player closer to Murphy who thought to get involved met up with Murphy's fist and now lay flattened on the floor nearby. It looked like all takers had disappeared, and the Yapper – *what the hell was her name* – realized he'd arrived.

Her finger pointed to the back of the place, and she ground out an order he couldn't ignore. "They have the girl. Out back. Help her."

One more idiot thought to move in on

Murphy and stop him from doing her bidding. The back of his head met with the wooden chair she flattened it with.

"Go! I'm coming."

Murphy went.

CHAPTER 5

Murphy had no idea what he was supposed to be looking for. But if someone was kidnapping a girl, he had no choice but to interfere. Yep, there in the darker corner of the parking lot he could see a scuffle happening.

At a dead run, he closed in only to see the terrified face of the teen before a fist plowed into her cheek to stop her fighting. Obviously putting up a good battle, she'd made them work hard for their prize.

He caught sight of Draper running around the car, heading for the driver's side and pulled his weapon. If he could shoot the tire, slow down the vehicle, maybe they could stop whatever shit was happening.

He fired twice but hated having wild bullets flying around in an area where too many street people hung out.

Just as he put his gun back in his holster, a vehicle pulled up next to him with the yapper behind the wheel, and the passenger window open. "Get in."

As much as he wanted to get in on the driver's side, a leftover chauvinistic tendency he couldn't seem to let go of, he did as she ordered and got in the passenger's side.

Slamming down on the gas, she aimed the car up the lane, weaving dangerously, and converged into a street, where thankfully, the normally hectic traffic had slowed down for the midnight hours.

They edged out enough to see taillights disappearing around a far corner on the left. She swung wildly, then over-compensated, which shocked two drivers in the opposite lane and made Murphy wince and brace himself.

He growled, his voice surprisingly shaky, "How do you know that's them?"

"It's the only speeding vehicle. If we're

lucky, it'll be the same one."

Since she made sense, he didn't argue. They gained on the other car, and he could see by the taillights, it appeared to be the same size as the vehicle he'd seen leaving the parking lot.

"Get a bit closer. The car we're looking for had a dented back fender."

"Okay." With her hands white-knuckling the wheel, she punched the gas. Coming close to hitting a car in the right-hand lane, they surged ahead close enough to see the damage on the car in front.

"It's the same car. Catch up to them."

"Great, a master of the obvious. Can't you see that I'm trying to do exactly that." Her sassiness shocked him.

"Don't be insolent."

She spat her reply. "Forgive my transgression... sir," her tone sarcastic as hell.

His skeptical grunt changed her snarling attitude. She backed off and explained.

"Look, that poor kid is terrified. They were hauling her ass out of the place just as I came out of the restroom. She put up a fight, but there were three of them."

"I know. I got to the parking lot in time to see her get punched… to stop her fighting. Some dude forced her into the back while Draper drove, and someone else I couldn't make out jumped in the passenger side." Murphy flinched at the memory. "How old was the girl? Fifteen?"

"Looked about that to me. I saw her in the restroom with another chick. She wanted to leave, but her boyfriend was wasted. Next thing I knew, Draper and his friends were forcing her out the back door. When I tried to stop them… well, you saw what happened."

Murphy chuckled, a disparaging sound unless one knew him and figured he'd been impressed. "Yeah, I saw freakin' Wonder Woman at work. Where'd you learn to fight like that?"

"Let's just say I didn't like being bullied in school."

"The boys give you a hard time?"

"Nope. The opposite. In my case, it was the

jealous females one had to be prepared for." With her head swinging from side to side as she checked both mirrors, her wild-looking long hair covered her face. To drag it away, she took a hand from the wheel, and the car again veered wildly almost hitting the vehicle in the right lane.

"Lady, keep both hands on the wheel."

"My hair was in my eyes."

"Hell, my stomach's in my throat. Deal with it."

She pointed ahead. "I think they're heading for the highway turnoff. Should I try forcing them over?"

Murphy, seeing her hand off the wheel again, cussed under his breath. Drivers came out of the academy with all types of abilities, from being good to great. He'd never been with one who had to have failed that course and must have passed by cheating or paying someone off.

He grabbed the handle over his head and prepared himself for a shit-show. Either they need to pull her license or force her to take more driver's training. The yapper should never have been allowed behind the wheel. But they had no time to switch places. Stopping the car ahead became more important than his comfort.

They began crawling up alongside the other vehicle.

**

Kayti knew how to handle a car in normal circumstances, Quantico had made sure they had lessons. But the training instructor had come on to her, which made her miss more classes than she should have. When the examinations were being held, she'd shown him the videos she'd taken with him acting like scum, and he'd given her the necessary pass.

Then a few minor accidents had taken away what little confidence she'd managed to achieve on her own. Unfortunately, her comfort zone had been passed miles ago.

"Step on it."

Angry, she swung his way, her hair again in her face. "You blind? I am."

"No, you're driving like a granny with bad eyesight. You're losing them."

"I know. You make me nervous."

"Oh, my Lord liftin'… He bit off the rest of his harangue. "I'm not trying to make you anything." Suddenly, he covered his eyes. "Holy, shit. Okay, okay. Don't kill us. Look, just because you're speeding doesn't mean you have to whip your wheel from side to side. Jesus, Mary, and Joseph, stay on the road."

Their tires hit the grooves of the rumble strips built into the shoulder causing a vibration. The added noise ramped up her tension. Driving turned into a nightmare she had no choice but to suffer through.

And the man next to her, his face pale, cussing under his breath, didn't help matters at all. With every hissed swearword, she felt his frustration. He clung to the handle with his right hand while his other grabbed for the dash.

Meanwhile, the car ahead took a wild turn that she tried to follow. And failed.

Shit!

They ended up in a ditch.

One too deep to drive out of.

She watched the taillights fade, and her frustration grew. She pounded the steering wheel. Dammit! Why hadn't she made him get behind the wheel? She knew her limitations, knew her skills were pathetic. She zeroed in on the man next to her and felt the danger.

His unpleasantness made her shrink. She wished herself anywhere but sitting next to a man cussing a blue streak under his breath, words spoken so quickly she couldn't tell what was said... except for the last rant which sounded very much like "silly-fuckin'-bitchy-incompetent-looney-tunes."

CHAPTER 6

The sudden silence destroyed her few remaining frayed nerves. Kayti swallowed and turned to Murphy.

Rather than act the pathetic loser she felt like, Kayti shared the information she had. "That girl is the daughter of a U.S. Senator. I heard them talking in the restroom. Her name is Misti, which sounds more like a nickname. Doesn't the Virginia Senator, Steven Bond, have a young daughter about her age named Meredith?"

"Hell, I don't know what his daughter's name is, but he's one of the good guys." Murphy put the APB out on the vehicle. Knowing they were late doing so, Kayti figured they should have requested backup just after they'd left the restaurant.

Accepting the truth, that if he'd been driving, they would have caught up to the beater they were following, didn't matter now. It was too late to cry over the should-haves and what-ifs.

She listened as he described the older dark blue Ford Focus with a dented back fender. Without any license number – they'd obviously messed with plates knowing they'd be kidnapping the girl – he didn't have much for them to go on.

Of course, calling in a kidnapping of a Senator's daughter would get his request immediate attention.

Sick inside, she didn't know what to say. Then she saw him take an empty Frappuccino bottle from the cup holder. She'd brought the drink with her on the stakeout to help her stay awake, which instead turned her into a magpie. Caffeine often worked that way.

Leaving the car, she followed him. When he placed the bottle further back on the road and broke it into smithereens with a large rock, she watched, thinking he's losing it.

Then, when he took the same rock and drove a huge piece of glass into her driver's side tire, pounding it deep to make more damage, she breathed easier, glad it wasn't sticking out of her throat.

"Okay. I know you're angry, but that's government property you're destroying. Maybe you should tell me why?"

Murphy threw the rock away and swung toward her, his thumbs in his front pockets as if he needed to keep them there rather than doing something else with his hands.

She covered her throat reflexively and forced herself not to step back from his intimidation, or from his brown eyes spitting fire.

Even in the moment of extreme tension, she couldn't stop from noticing his charisma. He'd catch any woman's eye without trying.

Earlier, when he'd picked her up at the start of the shift, he hadn't exited the vehicle, just waited behind the wheel and introduced himself curtly before they drove off.

Therefore, standing next to him now, he appeared shorter than one would think from his deep voice and strong personality. Maybe six feet... but his no-nonsense attitude, and his don't mess with me vibe intimidated. One got the feeling that the only way to stop Murphy would be to put him out of commission. Otherwise he'd keep coming.

Instincts had her wishing she could shrink smaller and become a yes-sir girl. Instead, she forced herself to stand her ground. "You spiked the tire. Why?"

"Yeah. An old trick I learned in high school. Neither one of us needs to lie. The glass will tell the story of why the car's in the ditch. And why we're not arresting that scum right now like we should be doing."

Kayti leaned over to see the tire, and sure enough, the air had leaked out, and it looked flattened. "I see. Thanks."

"Yeah. Just one question. How in God's name did you pass the driver's training course at the academy?"

Kayti cleared the fear out of her throat. But before she could start lying, he interrupted, "Never mind. Just know one thing. If we're ever partnered again, I drive."

"Deal." *Please, God, don't let that happen.*

She saw the requested police unit drive up and decided it *would* be the last time they worked together. She had pull. And she'd use it.

Right now, her only goal was finding Misti and return the poor girl to her parents.

CHAPTER 7

Once picked up, Murphy forced the summoned police unit to drive to where a sighting had been radioed in. By the time they arrived, the other cops who'd gotten there first admitted it wasn't the right car. Still in the dark, frustration overwhelmed.

They continued to drive around the area, covering every sleazy bar and motel but came up with zilch. No more sightings happened. Which meant the car with the hostage had either pulled in somewhere or the kidnappers had reached their destination and were in hiding.

Relenting, stopping the wild goose chase, they opted to be taken back to Cooper's where the kidnapping had taken place. Except now it was dark and empty... earlier police presence obvious when one saw the notice on the door.

Seeing as how their co-workers were due for a shift change, Murphy and Kayti had no choice but to get dropped off on 4th Street at Headquarters... to file their report. Before they could start, they were called into Kale's office.

Heading upstairs, Kayti appeared distraught, and Murphy couldn't stand her fidgeting a moment longer. "Jesus, Swift, she's not going to shoot you. This shit happens more than you know."

"I just hate letting anyone down. It's my fault that kid's out there going through hell. It's on me. You'd never have let them get away."

He stopped and pulled her around to face him, his hands letting her arm go as if he couldn't believe he'd purposely made physical contact. "You keep your mouth shut about what happened out there. I spiked that tire so you wouldn't have to go blabbing about the chase. Got it!" His eyes drilled into her, just a hard no-bullshit stare.

She dropped her gaze, not having the stamina to hold his. "My name is Kayti. Katherine Edwards. I did introduce myself when you picked me up earlier you know."

"Whatever. Just let me do the talking."

"It doesn't feel right."

"Take five, Katherine Edwards. Who's to know you weren't taking the ditch because of another vehicle. Look, nobody's perfect. Quit with the self-flagellation."

"Right. Okay."

They waited outside the office, Murphy leaning against the wall, his thoughts on the cold rye and coke he'd now have to pass on for multiple coffees. Why'd he ever make that shitty rule where he wouldn't drink in the daytime anyway?

Suddenly, he noticed Katherine appeared to be in a trance and left her alone, glad she'd finally zipped up, and the constant flow of blabber had stopped. Then he remembered her name, her full name, Katherine Edwards. Shock struck. He'd always had a favorite female name that surpassed any others. One he'd hoped to give a daughter one day.

Katherine.

CHAPTER 8

Waiting outside Kale's office reminded Kayti of a day a few months earlier.

Raised by a single mom, Kayti had never felt strange or that she missed out because no father was in the picture.

Spending every moment possible with Kayti, her mother had taught her right from wrong, empathy for others, sharing, caring, and instilled a sweetness of spirit (her mother's term) that often betrayed her. No matter how hard she tried to protect herself from letting others take advantage, compassion came naturally to her.

Being best friends with her mom, when the big C snuck into the picture, Kayti felt betrayed. Not so much because of the disease, but because her mother had hidden her illness. Why hadn't Norma admitted she was dying? Kayti would have gladly come home and stayed with her, helped her over those last few months.

Instead, she was at Quantico, looking forward to the Christmas holidays so she could have quality time with her mom rather than relying on their nightly phone calls.

On arrival, finding her mother wasting away, using a walker and on so many pills she had to organize them in a weekly pill container to keep them straight, heartbreak struck her hard. By this time, her mom was so far gone, she only lasted two weeks.

Inconsolable, missing her best friend, yet forced to clear some of Norma's belongings from the small apartment they'd always lived in, Kayti sifted through many heavy emotions. Anger vied with sorrow and made her grief that much harder to contain.

They'd always been there for each other. Told each other all their fears and their secrets, discussed spiritual beliefs, and romantic ideals. Though it seemed strange doing this with a parent, her mom had a way of digging past barriers, and Kayti opened up every time.

While growing through the stages of puberty and her teenage years, she'd even shared the few romantic interludes she found herself experiencing. Somehow, her mom always made her see the guys for the way they really were, not the way she'd romanticized them. It helped her understand that there was only one thing they wanted from her... and it wasn't her heart. She'd break things off and swear to stay celibate.

Even the one serious romance she'd encountered while in training had been kyboshed after a visit home. Norma had met Juan, her Mexican boyfriend, the one man who'd gotten through her defenses. Their relationship had lifted to the highest level, and she floated in her fantasies. Unfortunately, by the time she uncovered every flaw he possessed, helped by Norma, Kayti turned her feelings off. Soon after, they split.

Again, she'd relied on Norma to talk her through the pain and help her land on her feet. Her mother had always been there... until she wasn't.

While going through Norma's personal stuff, something she'd put off for a few years, another shock awaited. She discovered draft receipts from her mother's sister – one she never knew existed.

Plus curt notes that came with each proof of payment, asking after their health, sharing best wishes for birthdays, and updates of addresses and phone numbers where this person could be reached. The draft receipts showed extra amounts during holiday times.

Clearly, over the years the amounts rose, becoming more sufficient as Kayti grew older. This money – that kept them in the style they'd become accustomed to – did not come from her dead father's insurance policy as she'd been told. Obviously, those were lies.

Finally, Kayti Googled the person sending them, a person called Edna Kale. And found her at the one place she'd never have suspected – FBI Headquarters.

Seems her career with the Federal Bureau of Investigations had taken her high on the FBI's totem pole, and she held a rather esteemed position.

It also appeared that though she sent money to help her sister live decently, she'd never visited or spent any time with her. Something that Kayti found hard to forgive. After all, they'd lived a very sheltered existence and having family nearby would have given them a richer life.

Hesitating, worried because of her personal position with the FBI that she might be overstepping, she made an appointment and wondered if the woman would acknowledge her role in their lives. Pleasantly surprised by her aunt's warm greeting, she shared the last few weeks of her mother's life with the woman.

"I didn't know Mom had any family. When I asked, she'd say we were alone in the world, except for acquaintances. Are you really her sister?"

"Yes, I was Norma's sister, and I would have liked to have had more of a relationship with you both, truly. I wanted to stay together as a family, but she refused."

"Why? I don't understand."

"She had her reasons. Ones I'm not at liberty to share. Look, can we start fresh and be friends now that you're alone?"

Uncomfortable with knowing her mother hadn't wanted this to happen, though she didn't understand why, she hesitated.

That's when the woman showed why she'd risen so high in the ranks of the FBI to Special Agent in Charge of the criminal division. According to her research, Kayti had discovered that her aunt had been appointed from the ranks of her earlier position overseeing Counterintelligence.

Inflexible, even rigid, she projected a strength of will that others strove for. Her respected position and no-nonsense attitude set Kayti back in her seat, clutching her handbag.

"Understand this, Kayti. Your mother was a good person, but she had one flaw, and it's kept us apart all your life. She didn't share. Once you were hers, no one else mattered. You became her reason for living."

Not allowing any disparaging remarks or even hints, Kayti replied, "She was the best mother a kid ever had."

"Not saying any different. I wasn't criticizing, just stating a fact. But that distance wasn't healthy, and in the end, it hurt you both. Sure, I sent her money. She never could hold down a job, not when you were little. Afterward, she never wanted to work, rather she lived through you and kept the world at bay. I just thank God she didn't instill those flaws in you. That she allowed you a chance to make a career for yourself."

Relenting, Kayti admitted, "She was like a child, especially toward the last few years. I mostly felt like her mother. But a sweeter heart you'd never find."

"And that's why I didn't interfere, I kept my distance as she insisted. But not one day went by that I didn't regret our… ahh, parting. And it's not something I want to happen again. Now that we've met, thank God you reached out, I want to be in your life, have you in mine."

Kayti sensed sadness in the woman, a desperation one wouldn't expect. "Don't you have any family?"

Edna Kale folded her hands in her lap, held them tightly, her power controlled. "As you know, our parents died when we were in our teens. Norma was older by two years so she would have been eighteen. Being a headstrong brat, instead of staying with her, I moved in with a boyfriend until we parted ways."

Kayti suspected there was a lot more to the story and couldn't stand the suspense. "Then how did you know where to send her money after I was born?"

"She worked in a café in those days. After I broke it off with Bob, I cleaned up my act, got a couple of jobs, and we lived together in the same apartment you're still in now. Months later, when I started at the National Training Academy, we split ways. I worked hard, did well… probably because I loved the job."

"Didn't you ever get married, have a family??"

"Yes, years ago I did find the man of my dreams and married him. We only had one child. When our baby boy passed from leukemia at three years of age, we couldn't seem to hang on to each other… though we lived together. Years later, I lost Trevor, too. That's when my job became my main focus. It's why I regretted the missed opportunity with Norma."

Still not able to fully comprehend circumstances so intense as to keep sisters apart, Kayti delved deeper. "Couldn't you have reached out then?"

Her aunt stiffened. "Norma didn't take bad news well. At the time, that's all I had – bad news, a broken family, and a drinking problem I've since overcome."

"But you were her sister. She would have been there for you."

"She wasn't… there for me. Only one person mattered to her – you."

Kayti admitted the truth, "Mom couldn't bear anyone's suffering; it hurt her too much. I think that's why she became a bit of a recluse over the years. Hearing other's problems would affect her to the point where she couldn't sleep or eat. I guess I tried to protect her even as a child. I very seldom brought friends around or shared much of the action going on in school. The few times I did, it upset her to the point where it literally took weeks to settle her down again. I'm sorry, Aunt Edna. I'll admit I feel a bit cheated, and I'm angry that she lied to me."

Edna walked to the window behind her large desk, turning away so Kayti couldn't see her face. "I never wanted to come between you and Norma. It's why I stayed out of your lives. But things are different now." There was a pause. A long pause while Edna seemed deep in thought. Then she kind of gave herself a shake and said, "But now I'd very much like for us to be friends." As if she couldn't stand not seeing Kayti's reaction, she faced her and clung to the back of her chair.

"Not sure that's possible with me being a rookie agent, and you in your position. I wouldn't accept favoritism."

"You think I can't be impartial? Honey, I've been on this job too long not to know the boundaries or overstep them. How about we have weekly meetings to catch up on each other's lives? Say Sundays for private family times at a designated restaurant we take turns choosing?"

"And paying."

Edna grinned. "Fine. I'd like that. Since I'm the oldest, I get first pick. My selection is 7pm at Cut, Wolfgang Puck's place on 31st Street."

Kayti, reeling from all she'd learned and full of questions, agreed with enthusiasm. Before she left the room, she approached her aunt shyly and held out her arms for a hug. Not knowing if she was overstepping but having been brought up by a very affectionate mom, it came naturally for her to show her happiness in such a way.

Her aunt's face lit up, and she hugged Kayti for longer than expected. Her hand stroked Kayti's long hair in a caress. When she finally stepped back, Kayti thought she saw tears in the woman's eyes before she looked away.

Leaving the huge headquarters building, she wondered about the forlorn woman she'd left behind. Joy slowly began to seep into spots where sadness had permeated. Emptiness fled, and a tiny seed of soft caring began to form.

With a skip to her step, and her head held high, she pranced along Pennsylvania Avenue, looking forward to her future.

Because now there was someone in it who cared about her.

Someone she could love.

CHAPTER 9

Two minutes later, Kayti was brought back to the present as the secretary informed Murphy that Agent Kale would see them now. No sooner did they step through the door; the drill master attacked.

"By all that's holy, why did you two destroy a bar, put two men in the hospital, and tear away after some locals out for a joy ride?" Edna's body language boded ill for whoever answered.

Arms crossed, Murphy stepped forward and took the heat. "The girl the locals dragged out of the joint happened to be a Senator's daughter called Misti. And she didn't leave with them voluntarily. They hauled her ass out kicking and screaming. We need to question those idiots in the hospital."

Before Kale could reply, her phone rang. First she listened, and then she responded tersely. "Show him into my office." She put the receiver down very carefully, which made the nerves in Murph's stomach pay attention. *Christ, what now?*

Kale pointed at them and gave one order, "Sit!"

Then she walked toward the door and waited. The first man who stepped inside appeared to be in his mid-fifties; his hair slicked to the side perfectly groomed, his suit looking as if he'd been ironed into it, and his expensive shoes gleamed. If his tie hadn't been askew, one could be forgiven for believing this man hadn't a care in the world… other than being the textbook Washington politician.

The younger dude in his wake appeared scared, slightly high, and sicker'n a dog. He wore a dirty jacket zipped up, and if he'd mud-wrestled in his pants, it might account for the way they appeared.

The Senator shook hands with Edna and swung to the others in the room. He stared at Murphy and the power of his personality shone clearly. This man was no one's fool. He reached out to shake hands and without hesitation, Murphy stood and let him. "Hi. I'm Senator Steve Bond."

"Special Agent Murphy."

Kayti followed his example and had her hand ready. "Special Agent Edwards. Do you have a daughter called Misti?"

Murph couldn't believe she'd go against Kale's unspoken but totally understood orders to keep quiet. His new partner was cruising for a bruising. He expected to see Kale's disapproving glare and shock held him numb. His hard-ass boss wore a prideful smirk that shocked the shit out of him. He zeroed back in on Edwards and Bond.

The Senator hadn't let go of her hand. He clung to it as if she'd driven a nail through his heart, and her hand was his lifeline. Eyes determined to get a response, he answered, "Yes. It's why I'm here. She's missing."

CHAPTER 10

Kayti took her hand back and turned to the younger man standing alone by the door. If fleeing had been an option, she had no doubt his ass would be all they'd see as he hightailed it outta there. Embarrassment burned his cheeks red, and he flinched when she stepped closer.

"You were with her last night at Coopers." It wasn't a question.

"Yeah, Ryan Stover. You mean the bar where she left me."

"She left you… is that what you think?"

"Uh – yeah. Earlier in the evening, we met up with a couple downtown, Alex and Gina."

Alex and Gina who?"

"Don't know. They invited us to go to this place with them. We thought they were fun."

"Where were you when you ran into Gina and Alex?"

"A joint downtown where the kids hang out. I can't remember the name." He looked away, and she knew something was up.

"I call bullshit, Ryan. Tell us where you and Misti were. We need to talk to those people and see if anyone can recognize the couple who we believe were working with the men who took Misti hostage."

Ryan winced, then found attitude, "Hostage? They didn't take Misti. They're our friends."

"Look, bud, they were in on it. Don't kid yourself, I heard the girls talking in the restroom. Misti wanted to leave, said you were plastered, and she was scared. The other put her off. When your girlfriend still insisted she was going to call a cab, I figure it alerted Gina. She must have signaled Draper that Misti planned to leave. That's when they moved in on her."

"Draper? He's the guy who came to the table and bought us drinks."

"Draper is scum. Neither Gina nor her friend tried to stop him from taking Misti, they were in on it. In fact, the one glance at your table I had time for, I saw you being held back by the guy next to you."

"Alex." Ryan pointed at her and snapped his fingers. "You were there. Fighting. I remember thinking it was – was awesome."

Did he really say that? Kayti shook her head to clear out the urge to smack the kid's head hard enough to wake up a brain cell. "Look you, Misti is with those creeps right now. God alone knows where they're holding her, or what they're doing to her. You have to tell us everything you remember."

"That's just it." Tears filled his eyes. His Adam's apple bobbled ridiculously. Weakened, he slid to his knees, an aura of abject misery seeping from his body. "I only remember bits here and there. After she left to go with Gina, Alex crowded around me, said the girls were fine and they'd only be gone for a few minutes. He bought another round. Once I drank that, I passed out. When I came to, I had no idea where I was. Someone must have dropped me outside of an all-night service station.

One of the workers woke me up and told me to go home."

Murphy crouched down next to the younger guy and talked low, his voice like a hypnotist's working magic. "It's okay, kid. Relax. You remembered Kayti fighting. You need to man up here and help us find Misti. This is no blame game. You can deal with that shit later. We need answers now. You have them. Let us help you dig them out.

Ryan looked into Murphy's eyes and saw what Kayti did, what everyone did… a way out of the pool of shit he was drowning in. "I'll do whatever I can, man. I want to help her, she's my girl."

"Not anymore she isn't." Senator Bond stepped forward. His strong statement registered to everyone, especially Ryan.

Edna, who'd held back, took over at this point. "Senator, have you received any ransom notes, any phone calls?"

Shaking his head in a negative way, he admitted, "My wife and I were at an official function tonight and arrived home late to find this punk waiting for us." The Senator's disgust flashed over his features. "He'd been sick all over the driveway and passed out on our doorstep. I thought he was a lost drunk who'd ended up at the wrong house."

"He told you about Misti?"

"No. That's just it. He wanted to see her, apologize for getting plastered, and letting her leave alone. Or, at least, that's what he said."

Edna moved over to where Murphy had hauled the kid to his feet and placed him on the nearest chair. She stood over him. "Tell us everything you do remember."

Flinching, Ryan swiped a shaking hand over the mess on his face and took a huge breath, one soaked in tears and self-pity. "We were at the Denver; you know the new place downtown with the strippers—"

Furious, the Senator kicked in, "You took my daughter to a strip joint? She's only sixteen."

"All the kids are hanging out there, sir.

It's… I'm sorry. She wanted to go. We weren't even sure we could get in. But a group from the school planned to be there and – and I'm sorry."

Edna cut in, "Never mind about all that right now. We need you to tell us how you met up with the other couple."

"You mean Gina and Alex? When the bouncer was IDing us at the door, Alex and Gina were behind us. They jollied the guy to let us in, saying we were with them. I think some money passed hands. That's all it took to get us through security."

"So, this Alex and Gina approached you?"

"Yes. And asked if they could join us. Friends they were supposed to hang with had backed out, and they hated to celebrate alone."

"Celebrate? What were they celebrating?"

"A new job. Gina had gotten a new job and had an advance she wanted to spend on having a good time."

"Whose idea was it to go to the other place?"

Murphy spoke up. "It's that dive bar on 14th called Coopers."

The Senator roared," What?"

Ryan groaned and turned away from the Senator's glare. "Yeah, that's the place. Gina said she had a friend behind the bar who'd give us good drinks, not like the watered down kind. Said it was always a fun time at that place, and they often had live music. I'd never heard of it and neither had Misti. Gina convinced us we'd like the band. You know how Misti loves to dance. They told us to leave our car and go with them 'cause the cops were out checking for drunk drivers. By then, we'd had a few, so we agreed." He shrugged. "But the place reeked of hipster douche. You know – spilled drinks, dirty carpets, vaping, and the stench of pot. Misti wasn't comfortable, not until Gina got her up to dance. Alex kept the tequila shooters coming and pretty soon, we were both toast."

Kayti interrupted. "You were, not Misti."

Ryan shrugged, and then nodded sheepishly.

"What happened after that?" Edna's tone

held no judgement, which kept Ryan's eyes glued to her face.

"It's pretty fuzzy after that." Ryan clutched his hands together. His voice having firmed as he talked previously now became shaky. His eyes darted from one person to the next. "There was a fight. People began running out of the place. I-I wanted Misti. But she'd left me. Even left her cellphone, and like, that's a big no-no. I-I couldn't find Gina or Draper. They'd disappeared too. Alex kept talking, making jokes. I… Then I must have like… passed out."

"Jesus Christ." Senator Bond hissed under his breath; his disgust plain to see. "Way to take care of my daughter, idiot." He swung to Edna. "As far as I knew, Misti had no plans for the evening. Led her mother and I to believe she'd stay home to binge watch The Bachelor or some equally inane show."

"Yet you're here to report her missing." Edna returned her attention to Ryan, "Were these party plans just spur of the moment?"

Ryan lowered his head. "No. We'd decided yesterday that we'd go. Misti knew her folks would be out for most of the evening and figured they wouldn't even miss her." His tone became whiney. "She should have stayed with me."

The Senator made a disparaging sound, cussed, and pointed. "This mess," he meant Ryan, "scared my wife to death when he insisted he needed to talk with Misti, and we found her missing. She insisted we take steps to find her. First, we contacted her closest friends; everyone we could think of. No one had heard from her, not since earlier yesterday. My wife stayed home in case Misti called. But she demanded I come here and fill out a missing person's report. Now… you're telling me she's been kidnapped."

"Agent Murphy set up an Amber Alert after the incident at the bar. Agent Edwards here, tried to stop them from taking Misti from the bar. But she couldn't get past the gang who attacked her… to stop her interference. Eventually, they both tailed the getaway car for a short while… then had an unfortunate incident with their vehicle, forcing them to stop. Regrettably, the car with your daughter got away. Now, we're doing everything to find her as we speak."

Senator Bond shuddered, his expression darkening. "I want you to use whatever influence my position might have to find my daughter. Whatever it takes. I'll do anything you ask. She's our only child." His voice broke. The seriousness of the nightmare hit home.

"I'll have the best from this office working the case. It's top priority. Trust me, Senator, we'll do whatever it takes to bring Misti home safe and sound. Now, I want you to go with Agent Edwards to fill out the formal missing person's report. She'll have questions for you to answer."

Hanging on by a thin thread, Senator Bond's patience wavered, and his hard tone commanded. "I'm not interested in reports and papers, I just want you to do your job and find the scum who have Misti."

Edna spoke low and with the utmost

authority. "Yet we both know the information you can give us is invaluable and will be used in the search. I'll also have my agents at your home later today to see Misti's room and talk with your wife."

The Senator's gaze shifted from Edna to Murphy and then to Kayti. "This one. Send this agent. I want her on the case. She tried to protect my girl. She cares. I can see it. And my wife is fragile, needs careful handling. Agent…?"

"Katherine Edwards, sir."

"Agent Edwards will be the perfect person to handle her."

"Then it shall be so. I'll speak with you again after you've answered our questions." Edna's control of the room wasn't doubted by any of the occupants. She was boss.

"Ryan, you'll go with the Senator and Agent Edwards. There'll be paperwork for you to fill out also. And, son, you need a coffee. Agent Edwards will look after that too."

Ryan's face mirrored the color of the carpet, white with gray streaks. His trembling increased.

What had been dread earlier now became certainty. Kayti could see the shocked tears escaping and instantly felt sorry for him.

At the door, her aunt gestured for Murphy to stay. Then she held Kayti's arm for a quick consultation, "You haven't slept, have you?"

"It's fine. I couldn't rest with Misti out there."

Edna's expression firmed, and her resolve became solid. "You set up the Senator with one of the other agents who's qualified to take care of him. Go home and grab a few hours' sleep. It's six a.m. I'll expect you back here right after lunch. I want to go over a few points with you before you visit Senator Bond's house."

"I—"

"That wasn't a suggestion."

"Yes, Ma'am." Kayti had no choice. She looked down and then added, "I'll be back at one." Before she finished the sentence, her aunt had turned back into the room and began closing the door. All Kayti heard before it shut completely were words that sounded like, "What the fuck, Murphy!"

CHAPTER 11

Murphy knew he'd be sucking wind before his boss got through with him, but he hadn't expected this level of venom. He kept his arms crossed and let her rant.

"I paired Agent Edwards with you because you're the one man I knew could keep her safe. You've had years of experience with the agency and excelled during most of them. First night you work together, she ends up in a bar, fighting multiple guys who were trying to kill her, then in a car chase with her driving... Lord above, man?

"I know! Holy Hannah, have you driven with her?"

Edna stalked up to him. "Don't push me, Murph. You're that close to walking out of here without your badge."

"Okay... ok-ay. She's a good detective...

just needs more training. Maybe start her again, and make sure she gets her driver's ed redone." Murphy heard the threat in Kale's growl as she strode around the office and eventually returned to stop in front of him again... this time real close.

"She aced her training, came up within the top five highest scores, and impressed her instructors with her abilities in all aspects of the academy. I'm thinking it's you who's losing it, Agent. What were you doing while she was in there trying to save the Senator's daughter?"

"Enjoying the quiet...? That girl never shuts up."

Anger flared in Kale's narrowed eyes.

"Right! Look, she went into the bar to use the restroom. We'd been watching for Draper and had been there a few hours."

Edna nodded tersely.

"Well, then I saw a bunch of customers scurrying from the place. It looked like trouble, so I entered to see Agent Edwards embroiled in a scuffle, which I then proceeded to assist. Until she ordered me to go after some girl who'd been taken against her will. I ran out the back to see a young girl fighting with her abductors. I tried to intervene, but they pushed her into a vehicle and drove off."

"And…"

"That's when Agent Edwards drove up in the SUV, picked me up, and we followed. Only to lose them after driving over a Frappuccino bottle and our tire became flattened, which put us in the ditch."

"How the hell did you know it was a Frappuccino bottle?"

Murph hesitated before he replied. "Because I saw a portion of the label on the scattered glass. I'm trained to take in details like that."

"Right. So, the glass cut the tire and forced you into the ditch – at high speed."

"Yep, that's about it."

"No brake marks, no gravel scuffs, nothing."

"She didn't have time to hit the brakes. It happened too fast. One minute we'd gotten close and the next… ooppss."

"Right. You're a liar, but we'll let that pass. You know I've been in your corner, Murphy."

He lowered his face so she couldn't see the sneer. This woman had ridden his ass like he'd just started his career rather than a veteran with ten years of experiencing some of the worst jobs the company could pass out.

He'd been involved in more undercover assignments than any other detective, and many had been rough, dangerous, and dirty. Then one partner had betrayed his trust, died on the job looking like a hero while Murph wore his treachery, so the widow and her children never had to know the extent of their man's disloyalty.

Would he change roles again? Probably. Being a sucker for hero-worshipping kids who adored their fathers had worked against him. He found himself wearing the crime, being the loser, and paying for it by hanging on to his job by a hair. And... having to eat all the shit Kale wanted to pass out.

Edna continued, "So you understand, I kept

your ass out of the sling it was in with the superiors after your recent lapse. Talked them into letting me have you, letting me work with you rather than kicking you out of the Bureau. It was me who pointed out your past, how many times you shone. I wanted your expertise, Murph… knew you hadn't lost it. And you let me down."

"Yes, ma'am. Guess it's time for me to look into getting a PI license." He started to walk out of the office, sick of being the scapegoat. Tired of feeling like the loser, he'd reached his shit-eating limit."

Her voice rang with authority. "Get back here you idiot. I'm not letting you off the hook that easy. You need to find this young girl, Shane. You're one of my best men. I'm not letting you go until you do."

"If I'm so important, why'd you stick me on a crap detail of surveillance with a rookie that any first-year agent could do? And why have you pulled both me and Agent Edwards from the field office to work for you directly from Headquarters?" His arms lowered and his hands slid into his pockets. Somewhere in her speech, he sensed a compliment. "Something else is going on."

Edna settled back against her desk, her slim hip pushing aside the calendar that sat in a position where most people kept family photos.

Through the grapevine, he'd heard she'd previously worked her way up the ladder, ending with a high position in Counterintelligence.

An accidental meeting at a bar on the night when he'd felt as low as a man could get stuck in his memory. She'd miraculously appeared and bought him more than one drink. That occasion, they'd shared stories. He'd almost come close to telling her the truth about what had gone down with Bruce and caught himself at the last minute. Then he'd turned the tables on her. "Why're you here, drinking ginger ale and nothing in it.

That's when she'd admitted to it being the anniversary of losing her only child to cancer. He'd commiserated and asked about her husband. "Yeah, well he took the easy way out, died a few years later."

Not that those life traumas had turned her soft. Cemented in place by all her years as a leader and boss, this woman's spine had no give. She reeked of discipline and toughness.

Returning to the present, he held her stare and gave back the same. Finally, she sighed. "See, that's why you're still on my employee register. You have the balls of a stallion, and the stamina of a man who knows his worth. I trust you, or I did. There's something else you're not telling me about last night. And I doubt you'll share, since you're a stubborn jackass. Okay, keep your secrets. But I will share mine. And it stays in this office."

"Right. Got it."

"You're probably already aware that some Russian oligarchs are laundering money by buying up a lot of property in the U.S. and have been doing so for some time. They're using illicit funds… but if it's done legally, through proper channels, we can't do much other than keep track and watch for when they cross the line. Now, we've encountered information that there's political bribery and corruption involved with some of these sales. One is happening in Virginia. And that's where Draper comes into the picture."

"Draper, the man you had us watching earlier?"

"Yes." She went over to her desk and lifted a file folder to retract some papers from inside, then handed them over." Here's a picture taken in Chicago last week with Draper and Oligarch Viktor Baranov seen lunching together. We have very little intelligence on these men, other than two corpses we believe belong to Draper. But we have no proof, or we'd have arrested him already."

"Two dead? Who?"

"One was a snitch who must have pushed some buttons. The other was a reporter that broke the story about the conflict of interest where Russian money made its way through our system illegally. We're talking hundreds of millions."

"Understood. But what's that got to do with Senator Bond?"

"There are plans under way to pass new legislation restricting certain major purchases from out-of-country buyers, Bill 539. This would put an end to any legal way they can launder their illicit funds here. Many of the Senators are coming around to seeing it as a good bill, and it sounds like they might be able to pass it in the Senate.

"And Senator Bond designed this bill."

"Yes. Him and the Senator from Massachusetts, Linda Nelson. They're the key architects. We've notified the field office in Boston to put protection on her. Sadly, they informed us that Senator Nelson had a freak car accident last night. She's in the hospital for a long-term recovery.

"Then it all lands on Bond's shoulders."

"Exactly. Others would support the bill, but no one has the pull these two have. Without their leadership, it'll be crushed before they can even get the voting started.

Murphy began putting the pieces together. "Doesn't look good for the US, does it?"

Edna shook her head. "Since Bond's the

person who drew up the document, without him, the Bill will die before it ever reaches the floor."

"And we both know; the Russians need to end it."

"Exactly. Which means they take the Senator's only daughter, blackmail him to stop what he's doing, and Bill 539 disappears."

"Does the Senate Committee Chairman know about this?"

"Who knows what that man is privy to, or what he cares about? All I know is this. Whatever laws they figure on breaking in this state ain't happening, not while I'm in charge of the Criminal Division. And kidnapping definitely falls under that umbrella."

"You still haven't explained why you're handling this investigation at Headquarters. Why not through normal channels?"

"Again, it's a need-to-know basis, and Murphy, you don't need to know why. You just have to keep your mouth shut and do your job."

"Fine, what do you want from me?"

"It's a delicate operation. I can trust you. I want you to find that girl and get me all the shit you can dig up on this Draper asshole. Who working with him, and what they plan next?"

"And Edwards?"

"Right now, she'll be busy getting the information about Misti Bond, let her handle the Senator and his wife. That should keep her out of trouble for a while."

"Okay, fine."

"And Murphy…"

"Yeah?"

"You deal directly with me."

Ain't that just peachy! Yes, ma'am."

Son of a bitch!

CHAPTER 12

Kayti wasn't happy with the directives given to her from her Aunt Edna, not at all. But the woman was her immediate superior and had to be obeyed.

Even though her chief had insisted that she let another agent take the senator's information, she hung on a few minutes longer and got the specifics from the man herself. Letting someone else deal with young Ryan Stover didn't bother her, but an anxious father couldn't be pushed aside. Besides, her questions were ones that only a close family member could satisfy; things that brought the girl alive in her mind.

Rereading the information, she admitted to requiring those answers for herself as much as having the basic details for the missing person's report form. A picture of Misti had begun to take shape: the pretty girl she'd connected to in the mirror loved to swim in summer and ski in the winter. She took ballet lessons for years and then switched to basketball when she started senior high school. As far as her father knew, she was well liked, popular, and aced her grades. And absolutely no drugs.

Ok-kay.

Sure.

***

Having slept for maybe four hours, and still nestled under her warm covers, Kayti reviewed the night before. Enduring a fiery hell might describe how it felt locked in a car for three hours with Agent Shane Murphy.

Not that he was ugly, far from it. She remembered watching his hands on the steering wheel and thinking about how strong they appeared... and capable. He'd worn a darkish gray shirt and had rolled up his sleeves partially so the digital hands on his watch had glowed in the dark.

Remembering him in Edna's office, the

obvious chip on his shoulder evident, she chronicled his description in her mind. Not too tall yet appeared so because of the way he carried himself. He'd worn jeans, tight and washed-out, low on his hips which showed off a nice ass. His black hair had been short on the sides and kind of messy in front which would make any woman he was with want to run her fingers through it to see if the slight curls wound around a finger.

He'd needed a shave, his beard dark, appearing thick, but not long enough to have been there for more than a day. Kind of like a five o'clock shadow. Finally, she zeroed in on his face and that's when her heart sped up.

Brown eyes penetrated, no expression other than boredom, until he'd worked his magic with Ryan. Then they'd softened with understanding and male tolerance, sending a shiver over her just thinking about the change from soulless to caring.

Yep, his face was all male, thick eyebrows, lush lips over a strong chin. He could easily play the male star in a cop show where the hero worked miracles with his fists and his sex appeal. That actor would never have trouble getting a woman, and no doubt, Murphy didn't either. His attraction radiated and would suck in any female within his radius.

It was this maleness, this charisma that had stressed her, turning her into a gibbering idiot. Lord Almighty, looking back, shame flooded so she pulled the covers over her head and groaned loud and long. He must think her a naïve whack-job.

And then driving the car into the ditch. *Seriously?* Where were her skills? The ones that had put her at the top of every Quantico class. Even Roberts, her driving instructor, though not impressed, had passed her. Of course, it was only after she'd blackmailed him.

No one understood. And she'd never shared. It was the one fear she'd agonized over – being behind the wheel and having a motorized vehicle in her control.

No one knew about the many accidents her mother had gotten into while Kayti had been a kid, confined in her child seat in the back, terrified from every honking horn, skid sounds, and many times the inevitable crunch.

Terrorized by the time she'd reached ten, having had a broken arm, stitches in her forehead and other places from broken glass, multiple wounds, gashes, bruises, whiplash… all leading to nightmares. Self-preservation finally kicked in and made her stubbornly refuse to get into any car her mother drove.

And now you're the same.

Seeing the similarities in her own skills, she promised herself she'd fit in more driving instruction as soon as this case finished. No doubt, Edna would be after her about the car incident when they met up for dinner on Sunday, and she couldn't lie. But then, she couldn't get Murphy in trouble either.

Frickin' fu…dge!

Not sure what she'd do, she changed direction and began revisiting the case, going to the last time she'd seen Misti. Their eyes had caught in the mirror, and as it happens sometimes with strangers, they bonded for a few seconds.

She recalled the way the girl had dressed, like one of the monied teenagers of today, with her styled hair shaved over her left ear, jewelry dangling, and makeup applied so she looked like a movie star rather than the defenseless young girl she was.

Her clothes resembled a safari-style in the taupe tones, sleeves rolled up to show her bulky bracelets taking up a good section of her wrist. And... hold it! did she have on a Fitbit under all those junky accessories?

Kayti flew out of bed and ran to her tablet. She'd emailed a copy of the Senator's information to herself, his address and phone numbers. Within seconds she'd gotten through to him. "Are there agents there with you now in case the kidnappers call you?"

"Yes, they arrived a while ago. Though I haven't heard anything more from Agent Kale. What are you doing about finding my daughter?"

"My supervisor will be following every lead

they have, no doubt she has people questioning those who were at the bar last night to see if anyone knew Gina and Alex. The Amber Alert is set up and every police officer in the city is on the lookout for the vehicle. Sir, the reason I'm calling… did Misti have a Fitbit?"

"I don't know. Hold on, I'll ask my wife."

Kayti waited. Her heartbeats doubled, anxiety ramped up and her fingers crossed as she held onto her cell. Please let her be wearing one.

"Yes, my wife says she does have one."

"Does she know if Misti was wearing it yesterday?"

"She wears it all the time. She's a fitness freak and has to get her minimum fifteen thousand steps every day, or she goes to the gym downstairs and works out before bed."

"Okay, I'll be right over. Can you find the information on it? She'd have it set up in her phone. We can check it there."

"Her cell is password protected."

"Of course, it is." Kayti knew it would be,

but hopefully, they could figure out the password. Maybe it was a blessing after all that she'd left it behind at the table with Ryan when she went to the restroom. It would have been the first thing the kidnappers looked for. They'd have either thrown it away or shut it off to make it useless.

"Think about it. I'm on my way."

She whipped around her apartment, getting dressed and gathering items she'd need to do her job. She rifled through her variety of holsters and grabbed the hip device she preferred, then retrieved her weapon from the gun safe. Once she'd slid into her favorite black leather jacket, tied back her hair, and found her last clean white T-shirt, she felt ready to face the day.

Before leaving, she made sure she had her car keys and driver's license in the small bag she normally left in her car. That's when memories of last night's companion spiked.

Was Murphy still her partner for this case? They'd been paired up for the surveillance duty, but did that automatically lead to Misti being a joint assignment now? Edna hadn't been clear when she'd passed out her duties earlier.

Fu...dge!

Rather than pissing him off in the event they were supposed to be working together, she pulled out her phone, hesitated, bit her lip, strode around the couch, kicking away the clothes strewn nearby, and finally used the private number to call her aunt.

"Yes, Kayti."

"I'm sorry to take advantage with this number, Edna. I promise it won't happen all the time. But I just remembered something, and I need to know if I'm still working with Murphy on the Bond case? Something came to me just now."

"What have you remembered?" Her aunt's voice thawed slightly.

"Misti was wearing a Fitbit. I remember seeing it in the mirror when we were in the washroom. She had it on the same arm as a bunch of other bracelets. I called the Senator, and they confirmed she wore it all the time. I'm just on my way over there to try and get the Fitbit data from her phone. I'll call it in as soon as I find the serial number. No doubt our people can track it as long as she's still wearing it."

"Right. Get over there and get us the data. I'll let Murphy know. He'll meet you there. We'll catch up after you've followed this lead. And Kayti. Call anytime you feel it's appropriate."

Wow!

That blew her mind. "Right. Thanks, Edna."

CHAPTER 13

As she turned onto his street, she noticed how the Senator's house perched higher than others nearby and showed beautifully. His home was the type every American dreams of owning, yet very few do. The colonial style with white columns on the front gave the porch a spacious look, which presented the appearance of a large estate.

As she slowed down to pull into the circular driveway, she noticed a car parked a few feet further up the road with a full view of the Senator's house and entrance.

Because she was on alert for anything unusual, seeing a person behind the wheel on a perfectly nice day, no rain or reason why anyone should stay in their vehicle, she continued around the block so she could pull up behind it.

Being paranoid about anything out of the ordinary, she wasn't going to let this get past her.

Considering his daughter had been kidnapped the night before, having someone possibly watching the Senator's house could mean nothing, or it might be problematic.

Before she exited her car, she tried to read the license plate so she could phone it in, but the numbers were fuzzy, probably mucked up from the recent rain. She'd need to get closer to read them. Instead, she pulled out her phone to take a picture.

Unexpectedly, a force backed into her car and the impact whiplashed her head, making the phone fly from her hand.

A screech of the tires could be heard as the car ahead of her sped away. *What!!*

Twisting the key, she threw the car into drive, slammed her foot on the gas and whipped the wheel to follow the vanishing car. A sickening crunch kyboshed those plans.

Instead, she glanced up to see a really pissed off Murphy exit his SUV, check the scrape on his front passenger bumper, and then approach. The gritted teeth and clenched hands gave an indication that his mood might not be the best.

Her instinct to roll up the window and pretend she was a very small child fled as soon as it appeared. Instead, she waited, breath abated, her knees tight together. *I'll need to find a restroom real quick.*

"Lady, you are the worst menace in this city. They ought to paint hazard signs all over your car to let the rest of us poor schmucks know you're on the road."

"God, I'm sorry, Murphy. There was a car parked here with someone sitting inside. I kinda thought it was strange, so I pulled in behind. I wanted to take a picture of the license plate. I couldn't read it. I wanted to call it in, but they backed into my car. Smashed it really. Before I knew it, they'd raced off."

Lifting a trembling hand to her neck, she added, "I think I got a slight whiplash." Not seeing any sympathy, she admitted, "I'd decided to follow him. Just as I pulled out, you appeared out of nowhere and…."

"Shit, lady. Take five. Your face is red. You gonna pass out?"

"No. But, I-I need a restroom."

"Jesus, Mary, and Joseph, you shouldn't be let out without a handler."

Kayti got a sudden urge to giggle, another of her silly habits when under stress. Instead, she reached over on the floor for her phone. "I hope I got the license number before he bashed my car." Her hand shook so badly, she couldn't work the phone.

"He… it was a he?

"Yes. I didn't see anyone else. And I never got a good look at him either."

"Right. So he backed into you?" Murphy stepped forward to see the damage which freed her from being imprisoned inside. She quickly stepped out; her phone still clutched in her hand.

He came back to her and said, "It's not as bad as the one you have on the other bumper." He watched her struggle with her phone. "Here give me that thing. What's your code?"

"Eleven forty-seven. It was an old post office box number when I was a kid so I can remember it easily."

"Good to know." He scanned her face, obviously paying attention to her leaning against the car for support. "You going to be okay? Maybe you need to go home and rest up for a few weeks?"

She heard the hopeful note in his voice and knew it was her sign to pull herself together. "It's just that a girl doesn't often get into two accidents within a matter of minutes and be expected to deal with it like water off a duck's back.

"Maybe not normal girls, but you're in a bracket all your own."

This time she did giggle, then stopped as he stared her down. He checked her phone, but the latest photo showed a small slice of the sky and the roof of the car. Glancing over his shoulder, she felt frustration over the missed opportunity. Doggonit, she needed to get her act together. He must think her a real number.

Trying to explain, her tone stronger, "I'm a

bit shook up, but I'll be fine. Get your car out of my way, and I'll pull into the driveway."

"Helluva good idea. Will you do me a favor? Wait until I've driven in and parked."

Ha! Not funny.

Kayti pulled into the circular driveway behind him and let out a sigh of relief. Why other cars seemed to continually bash into her vehicle still didn't make sense. She followed the road rules, drove slow, and careful. But it never failed that some asshole in a hurry either stopped too late or turned without paying attention. She only hoped that was the case earlier, and she hadn't let a suspect flee.

Leaving her black sports model with numerous scrapes and dents everywhere, she walked up the steps and waited for Murphy before ringing the bell. Glancing to the side where the attached garage had three entrances, she saw two other police vehicles parked. Good, the others were here to protect the Senator.

When Murphy stepped up behind her, she

stiffened her shoulders. No more bullshit. She was a good agent, had aced her classes, came out on top of others in competition, and her colleagues had a healthy respect for her accomplishments… and abilities. No way, this crusty son of a bitch was going to make her feel less capable.

CHAPTER 14

Murphy hadn't had more than a couple of hours to snooze before Kale called to tell him about Kayti's memory of the Fitbit. After the meeting in her office, he'd spent time the previous night hauling the bar owner's ass from his bed and pelting him with questions about what had gone down in his bar earlier.

The man didn't share, even after Murphy told him about the kidnapping. When he tried to threaten him with all kinds of bogus crime and got cranky enough to put the fear of God into his captive, he still didn't cave.

The man remembered nothing, bragging how he kept his nose clean, paid his taxes and called the cops when anything bad happened in his place. Like the famous three wise monkeys, he knew how to play stupid. And Murph couldn't arrest a man for that crime. If that were the case, they'd have to build a lot more jails.

One thing he'd dug out were names of others who hung out with Alex. The bar owner had never seen the teens, Draper, or Gina before… swore on the soul of his dead mother, but Alex he knew. The kid lived nearby and ran with a local gang.

After a bit more persuasion, noting the broken bylaws his bar faced if a cop wanted to play dirty, he spouted off more facts. The guys Alex hung with could often be found at a pool hall not far from this place. Which gave Murph a lead he could work with.

He just had to wait until the hall opened later this afternoon. Then he'd start questioning the clientele about their buddy.

Needing a photo of the dude, following protocol, he'd decided to fetch Ryan Stover back to the office to try and pick out Alex from the database of lawbreakers around the area. No doubt, they had a long list. It wasn't the worst part of the city, but crimes were rampant, and hopefully, Alex had a previous record.

They already had a good image of Draper; one his boss had shared taken during Draper's lunch with the Oligarch, Viktor Baranov. He'd flash that one around too and see where it took him.

Stunned from exhaustion, he'd headed home to catch up on some sleep for a few hours. Finding the kid on his couch, Murph's favorite place to rest if he only had a short time, he'd been too wired to go to bed right off the bat.

Instead, he'd gone into the kitchen and headed for the easiest cupboard to reach. Hesitating, holding his rye bottle, he wavered between heaven and retaining his badge. An image of Kale lodged itself in his conscience which cemented his decision.

Swearing, releasing his building frustration, he threw the 48-ouncer of Canadian Club back into the cupboard and grabbed the milk carton from the fridge. Lifting it to take a swill, he sat on a stool by the island in the kitchen, his newest addition to the renovations he'd worked on for the last few years. Reaching for his laptop, he opened it.

It hadn't taken long to find information about Viktor Baranov. The man had history. A close associate of Putin's, he'd made a few billion dollars from oil and who knows what else.

Hiding his wealth from a money-grubbing wife who'd decided since he'd cheated on her, she deserved for him to pay up, he refused to share his moola. In order to keep his bank account secret, he'd been making enormous investments. One type was buying up large properties in America. The perfect way of keeping everything to himself.

Not that Murphy didn't sympathize with his predicament; a man worked hard for his money. And in this case, he doubted the spa-loving, model-type wife lifted a finger to help. But breaking other country's laws didn't cut it with him either, especially if they were American ones. He lowered his head into his folded arms and dropped off. When the phone rang, he almost fell off the stool.

Listening to Kale's instructions, he grabbed a five-minute shower, one he'd perfected over time. Then dressed in his street clothes of jeans, a navy sweatshirt topped with a navy jacket. Better to keep a low profile. They didn't want to announce the FBI's presence in the house to others on the street.

He liked these assignments best when they didn't demand he wear the official dressy monkey-suit he'd begun to hate. Undercover worked better for him.

He whipped up two eggs with a bit of butter for the microwave and spooned them right out of the large heavy measuring glass he used onto a slice of toast. Slugging down more milk, he eyed the amount and then stopped, leaving enough for the kid's cereal.

***

Walking toward the Senator's house with Katherine, he still couldn't comprehend his bad luck in meeting her in the street. She'd smashed into his SUV, the new ride he'd put off buying for years until he could pay cash. Only had it for a few months. He'd kept it pristine, didn't have so much as a scratch.

Jesus help him!

If she hadn't looked at him with those big brown eyes all globby with tears, and her hands shaking so much she couldn't even use her phone, he might have lost his shit.

Nah... that wouldn't have happened.

One thing he knew about himself, whether it was a good trait or not, little things irritated the hell out of him. But the big stuff didn't faze him. He'd feel himself settle into the let's-just-deal mode, and he'd fix things the best he knew how.

He remembered the year after he'd graduated and started working to save money for college. His mom had won a trip for two to Miami and having no one in her life to go with, she'd guilted him into taking her. They'd been at the beach and the waves had been high and so strong they ripped a loose ring she cherished right off her finger. He'd never seen her so frantic, diving to find it, had him search too, but the water gods only laughed at their pathetic attempts.

She'd cried for hours, and as much as he'd tried to soothe her, take her mind off her loss, make stupid jokes to bring a smile back on her face, she'd stayed sad.

Finally, she'd admitted that his father had purchased the golden Sluice Box ring in the Yukon and had given it to her out of the blue. "I asked him why he bought it for me, Shane. And you know what he said? It's not for any special occasion other than I love you." The love ring became her most treasured possession.

That's when he took on a second job, working nights delivering food, and used the money to order her a new ring made at the same Murdoch's gem shop. He'd found a photo on their website with the exact design.

Christmas had been nice that year. He'd felt like a good son and the feeling had stayed with him for a long time, until she'd remarried and replaced his old man with the idiot... and his ring with a cheap diamond.

Now, waiting with Katherine for the Senator to open the door, he watched his companion for any indications that she needed to step down – any signs of stress. After all, as she reminded him, a girl didn't get into two car accidents in a matter of minutes and go unscathed.

She'd noticed his attention and smiled at him in the way a woman does to a man she trusts to understand her personal signals. I'm fine said her eyes.

And I'm hooped said his heart.

Jesus!

The yapper?

CHAPTER 15

Stepping inside the Senator's residence, Murphy shook off his ridiculous reaction to the woman at his side. Instead, he scanned his surroundings, and his first impression of the house screamed opulence. Then he reconsidered. More like comfortable opulence.

The Senator appeared relieved to see them and anxious to assist in any way he could. Politicians he'd known normally wore an aura of calm, polite interest. It became a manner they all perfected over the years of being in public service. Senator Bond was no different. Except now, he resembled any man in fear for his daughter's life. A man on the edge and helpless to take control.

After shaking hands, Murphy didn't dodge the questions over what was happening to find his daughter. Once the Senator realized the answers were the same, he backed off. "Sir, every cop in the district is looking for the vehicle, and we're scouring the city looking for Gina and Alex. We've pulled every video from the surrounding area, and nothing gives us a facial description we can use. Every lead we have is being followed, even to putting out a request over social media and TV for anyone who'd been in that bar last night to step forward. No matter how small the tip, we'll jump on it. But until you hear from the kidnappers, know their demands, there isn't a lot more we can do that isn't already being done."

Senator Bond's face fell, his expression of grief seeming to deepen until Murph had a hard time keeping eye contact.

"How's Mrs. Bond? We'll need to talk with you both."

"Yes. I know. But she's ahh… fragile. Her imagination is working overtime, and the stress is driving her mad. Come with me. We're just having coffee in the den."

Murphy, appreciative of Katherine's instincts to let him do the talking, waved her before him. They followed the Senator into a smaller room, one decorated as a family area – a television with a huge screen opened over the fireplace and pearl gray leather couches in front with comfortable lounging spaces so a family can be together while being entertained.

A woman curled in a fetal position hugged a pillow at one end of the closest sofa, her luxurious dressing gown wrinkled, and coffee stained. At the other end of the room, their officers had cleared a section where they'd set up their equipment on a large table, and the two were quietly discussing something as Murphy and Katherine appeared.

"Hey, Black."

Nodding at the one who'd used his nickname, Murphy questioned him with a raised eyebrow, got the negative shake he'd expected and ignored them for now. Instead, they moved over to where the Senator's wife waited anxiously.

He saw Katherine give a small wave to their agents and wondered about that. Then shook off the interest. None of his business. He didn't exactly know why his mood soured, but he didn't have time to look into it either.

Katherine took the chair closest to the woman, reached out her hand to touch the other's arm, and spoke, her voice soft and encouraging. "Hello." Only one word but it seemed to wake the woman from the coma-like state he'd noticed.

The Senator quickly stepped in to make the introductions. His voice took on the quality of a parent talking to a child, seemingly frightened to push her buttons. "Darling, this is Special Agent Murphy," he motioned to Murphy. Then he gestured to Katherine. "And this young lady is the one I told you about, the one who last saw Misti, Agent Katherine Edwards. This is my wife, Francine." He reached down to touch her shoulder. "They're here to question us about Misti."

The pathetic lady seemed to shake off whatever spell had overtaken her. She went to raise a hand, but as if it became too heavy, she let it drop before Murphy could shake it. "How do you do?"

Then she turned to Katherine, stared until

her eyes filled. This time she reached out for comfort. "She's my only baby."

He watched Katherine move closer so she could make a connection. "I'm so sorry, Mrs. Bond. Your daughter is very beautiful. She caught my eye in the mirror in the restroom and made a huge impression on me."

A sob broke loose. The woman nodded. "People like her. I never had that ability. People just make me nervous, make me want to hide. So, I do. I drink." She lifted the full wine glass she'd kept lowered and slurped at the side of the glass, making some of the liquid trickle over the side.

Murphy's shock at the woman's raw honesty stayed hidden. He had the ability to conceal those feelings. He also realized how very precarious her grip on control was, and sure as hell didn't want to be the one to make her lose it.

He'd leave her to Katherine. Moving toward the Senator, he asked the question they needed answered.

"Sir, can you please show us your

daughter's phone?"

"Yes. It's here. Ryan brought it with him last night when he came looking for her." The Senator rushed over to a table where the phone waited, it's pink rhinestone cover sparkling. "We've wracked our brains for the password and gave up. I hope you can break in without it."

Katherine looked over and asked, "Did you try the house number?"

The man looked at his wife and then shook his head. "No. We didn't."

Mrs. Bond's expression looked hopeful. "She wouldn't forget that one, would she?"

"We tried birthdays, and variations of her phone number, anything that came to us. How could we have forgotten that?'

As if terrified of the reaction from one more failed attempt, his hands shook. He passed the phone to Murphy and seemed dazzled by the competence of one who handled the item constantly. When he saw the window open, his nod of affirmation to his wife made her cry out. She'd have spilled her drink if Katherine hadn't grabbed for it.

It didn't take long for Murphy to access the Fitbit app, find the Bluetooth link, and get the info they'd need to find the apparatus. He passed it over to the pros who'd been watching them carefully. Within a short time, using the up-to-date equipment so easy for those in the know, they found the address that showed the watch's location.

Hurrying from the room with Katherine right behind him, he spoke quickly to the officers. "Get us backup and have them hold up in the next block. Tell them to contact me when they're ready to move. We're not far away and should be there in ten."

Senator Bond followed them to the door and grabbed Murphy's arm, the question on his face not needing to be asked.

"Sorry, sir. This could be dangerous. I'll get back to you as soon as we can."

Deflated, the Senator let go and even gave the arm a push. "Right. Go. Bring her home."

CHAPTER 16

Kayti hadn't expected the level of understanding her partner had shown the Senator and his wife. He'd been kind but firm, and no one with any brains could fault his demeanor nor his ability to make miracles happen. The trust inspired by his self-confidence gave no room for any doubts.

Following him to his vehicle, she watched him handle the monster as if born to do so. Nothing fazed him as they raced to the address he'd delivered to the GPS. Not only did he drive like a pro; his strong hands whipped the wheel with perfect timing for every corner. He looked at her trying to appear nonchalant when her innards were wanting out.

"You okay?"

"Sure. No problem. I hope this is a good

lead. I want to find this girl. She seemed like a nice kid and must be terrified out there alone with those weirdos. She—"

"Then why are you gripping your door handle like that?"

Not realizing what she'd been doing, Kayti sat back and shook off her unease. "Must still be reacting to the accidents earlier. I'm fine. Why did the agent back there call you Black?" Murphy's quick grin made her even more curious.

"It's an old nickname not many of the guys know."

"It's a strange nickname. Is there a reason for that particular word?"

He didn't answer. Silence not suiting her, she continued. "I have a nickname too. My real name is Katherine but most everyone calls me Kayti. I like the shorter version. My mother always used Katherine whenever she got angry with me, so now it makes me uncomfortable."

Ignoring her yattering, Murphy checked the estimated time of arrival and got them there just as the others were seen a block over.

He drove past the address, and she saw an empty lot where an old, unpainted shed sat near the back, locked up tight. Silver foil and cardboard window coverings gave the place an appearance of down-and-out slum.

Taking lead, Murphy called the others to be ready to move in. They parked the car a few doors down. He stepped out in front, and she followed. Like him, she had her gun in her hands but held low.

Once they were in position, four other agents, all wearing FBI vests started forward and surrounded the small boarded-up building. Within seconds, using hand signals from Murphy, they'd breached the door and were inside.

The old lady sleeping on a cot against the far wall arched herself into a ball at the end of her bed, her hands clutching rag covers up to her face, her screams unbearably loud.

Kayti pushed aside the store cart and got close enough to see the fancy black band on her wrist and her wildly beating heart stalled before it started up again in its regular beat.

Calming the bag lady and reassuring her they wouldn't steal her belongings, Kayti asked the question, "Ma'am, where did you get that Fitbit?"

Looking completely out of it, her eyes darting everywhere, never stopping long enough to make contact, the woman whined, "Didn't do nuthin'. Finders, keepers. Maddie didn't do bad."

Kayti soothed the poor old skinny female. Heartsore for the wretchedness of another human being in such shape, she started over. "Of course, you didn't steal it, Maddie. We just want to know where you found it." She pointed at the Fitbit and shock hit when the old tramp tried pulling it off, scratching at her arm and leaving gouges from her dirty long fingernails.

Kayti, sensing Murphy's anxiousness, was thrilled that he'd stepped back and let her handle the situation.

"Maddie, please. Let me help you." A sudden thought snuck in, and Kayti decided to go with it. She pulled a twenty from her pocket and held it out. "Did you know there's a reward for the watch?"

Money might be the root of all evil, but the old lady knew the worth of a twenty and it stilled her craziness. A crafty look appeared. She held her arm out in Kayti's direction with an unmistakable invitation.

Gently, Kayti removed the Fitbit while asking again, "Maddie, where did you find this?"

Staring at the money on Kayti's knee, her eyes never leaving it, she mumbled something.

"I didn't hear you, Maddie. You need to speak up."

"I says I found it dis morning in front of da store up the street. Vinnie's place. It's on the ground outside. I never stole it."

"What time did you find it?"

"Don' know."

Passing over the money and having it snatched from her hand, Kayti moved out of the way as Maddie, remarkably spry, lunged from the bed and began gathering her belongings. Muttering constantly, the old woman in men's clothes, her white hair streaming in a matted mass down her back, stumbled around the small space before she pushed her way past the others milling around outside. With her cart in front of her, she hurried away.

Murphy stood aside and nodded to let her go. "She's got nothing to hide. We'll go to Vinnie's place and check it out. I'll just let the others get back to their desks."

***

While Murphy did a surveillance of the outside area, Kayti walked into Vinnie's convenience store. Christmas lights hung around each of the aisle ends and in both the front windows. The place was chockablock full of everything most of these stores sold, but Vinnie had piled it all into a smaller, more crowded space than usual.

She spotted a mirror over the door and wondered why they bothered. It wasn't like you could see anything with aisles loaded almost to the ceiling. There were coolers along the wall where a short counter had been installed. The fellow sitting on the stool behind the counter looked at her, waiting with a grin. He winked. "Hey, sweetheart. What can Vinnie do for you today?"

Kayti took a liking to the older man, and his gentle smile. His coffee-colored skin was the perfect setting to make his white teeth shine and his green eyes startling.

She showed him her badge and smiled back. "Do you know an old bag lady called Maddie?"

"Sure. Everyone around here knows her. Just saw her this morning. She stays in the old shed on the vacant lot a block over. There's a few of them take turns using the bed in there. Her time is mornings. Is she okay?"

"Oh, she's fine. Did she tell you she found this Fitbit outside?"

Vinnie leaned over and checked it out. "Nope. But I saw her rummaging around on the ground by the gas pumps before she left. Probably about eight this morning."

"It belongs to a missing girl. She must have been here at some point during the night. What time do you stay open till?"

"Twenty-four seven. I work dayshift from seven to seven. I like my bed at regular hours, we usually have another person who works the nightshift."

"So, you weren't here last night?"

"Not saying that. The kid quit two days ago. I had my son come in for a few hours last night so I could catch some sleep. But until I find a replacement, it's mostly old Vinnie who'll be looking after the joint."

Murphy had stepped inside, showed the badge at his waist, and picked up the conversation. "Do you happen to have surveillance equipment, Vinnie? Any cameras with views of the gas pumps?"

"Sure do. But they don't work worth a damn. Bin meaning to change them. You can take the tapes from last night, but I bet they're empty.

Damn new-fangled thing doesn't turn on like the instructions read. My son says I need to spend money and get the better brand. Guess I will one day."

"Thanks, Vinnie. Do you remember anything at all about a car this make and color turning up here? Has a dent in the back-right fender?" Murphy had found a similar model to the one they were after, saved it and now brought it up on his cellphone to show the old man.

"Sorry, I'm color blind so that don't mean anything to me. It was busy last night. There may have been a car like this one, I can't say. The folks… they fill their cars nowadays using cards. A few come in to buy stuff, but not often enough. How old is the girl?"

"Sixteen. She was snatched at a club on Fourteenth. Her father is frantic. You might know him. Senator Bond?"

"Sure, I voted for the man. Wish I could be of more help."

Murphy answered, "If you think of anything

that might help, here's my card. Call anytime."

Kayti handed over hers too and smiled when the old man took her hand and gave it a squeeze. "I hope I do remember something so I can call you, pretty lady."

CHAPTER 17

Murphy saw the way the old man held on to Katherine's hand and her sweet reaction. The woman was a puzzle to him. If he hadn't seen her fight the night before, he'd never believe she had the killer instincts she'd exhibited... to his delight.

She joined him in the car and asked, "What now?"

"I'll drop you back at the Senator's house so you can check out Misti's room and get a list of her friends. We'll have to question them. See if any of them were at the strip bar last night and can tell us about Gina and Alex. Maybe someone took some photos, selfies, whatever. We need to gather any info we can on those two."

"Okay. You're right. I meant to ask. When they left the club, Gina was with Misti, but you never mentioned seeing her at the car. Only the two men. One that pushed her into the back and went in with her and Draper who drove, right?"

"Yeah. I can't say if Gina did go along. I didn't see if the other passenger was the girl, but it would make sense."

"Except nothing about this case makes any sense."

"What do you mean?"

"Well, why would two perfect strangers woo two kids out for some fun with their peers. Take them on, buy them enough drinks to get them plastered, even drag them off to another bar and then kidnap the girl? Oh yeah, and not bother to ask for any ransom."

"Oh, it'll happen. They're just stirring the pot, driving the parents crazy with worry so they'll be more apt to pay without making waves."

"The waves have already crashed the shore, bud. When I was occupied in the bar, I have no doubt my badge was in full view of anyone who was watching."

"What're you getting at?"

"I'm thinking of Alex. According to Ryan he stopped him from getting involved with them taking Misti. I figure Alex will be letting them know the FBI became involved that night."

Murphy took his time to answer and finally admitted what he'd been suspecting all along. "Which could be the reason why they haven't asked for ransom. Kidnapping's a felony with a huge penalty, like jailtime until one's Social Security kicks in... and then some."

"Exactly. What if they're rethinking their plans and just decide to cut their losses and kill her? Dump the body so it's never found?"

"Okay, now you're switching the endgame. Fuck... and it's making sense." Murphy clutched the steering wheel tighter, sad that she'd connected to his own earlier deductions. He growled his frustration, "Son of a bitch."

"I know. Right? Did you find out anything from the bartender or any of the waitresses from the club on Fourteenth?"

Murphy gave her his look that usually made

people uncomfortable and realized it didn't faze her at all. Not knowing how to take that, he ignored the slight rise in his interest and decided to answer, "Yeah, I talked with the owner. He tended bar that night and was a bit helpful. Didn't know where Alex lived. Did give me an address where he often hung out. A poolroom in the area where a lot of gang members gather."

"Oh, good. I imagine we'll be visiting the place later?"

"Not we. Me. You'll be more help with the Senator and his wife. Keep them calm and get names of her classmates so we can start a sweep of her friends."

Murphy saw the look she flashed him, the one that said you're an asshole and liked that she let her feelings be known. But he still wasn't about to include her in an action that could be dangerous to the extreme. If she'd have been a male, it might have made a difference. Call him a chauvinistic old dog, but for some crazy reason, he wasn't about to explore, he'd rather she be safe.

Plus, being a loner after the shit show with his last FBI partner was safer.

CHAPTER 18

Misti woke up in a dark room, her body feeling heavy, and her head reeling from a hangover of all hangovers. The harsh, disgusting taste in her mouth reminded her of the anesthetic sourness after her appendix operation a few years ago.

She moaned and found it difficult to swallow. Wetting her chapped lips, she felt the bleeding cracks, and her mind screamed for water.

Moving took forethought; it didn't come easy. She soon realized it was because she'd been tied down to a bed of sorts. It felt small, like a cot, and the room she sensed around her seemed confined too. Once her eyes adjusted to the little bit of light that came through the window near the ceiling, what felt like her cell looked to be about the size of a bathroom.

She turned her head slightly and realized it

was a bathroom. One where they'd added her bed. A sink and toilet totaled the rest of the furnishings.

The heavy beating of her heart increased during her inspection to where the screams in her head became nightmarish. Everything inside her wanted to release her fear by voicing it as loudly as humanly possible. But her brain told her to shut up. Don't bring those monsters back.

As long as she was alone, she was safe. It was only when the others were with her that she had something to panic over.

She pulled her numb arms out from under her and saw the ties on her wrists were actual chains that were attached to a ring in the wall. She had one blanket covering her. It smelled faintly of vomit and musty odors that made her worry she'd soon be making it worse. Throwing it to the floor, she shuddered... thoughts rampaging.

Daddy help me!

Her first clear thought went to her father, the man who'd always been there for her during the worst moments of her life. When she'd come to in the hospital, he'd been holding her hand, whispering about how strong she was, how beautiful his little girl was and how much he loved her.

The intensity of her craving started a sob building way back in her throat, reminding her of how she'd fallen asleep the night before. After they'd dragged her into the room, slapped her to stop her arguing, and warned her she'd be toast if she said one more word, she'd finally collapsed in a pitiful state.

It took both men to pick up her off the floor where she'd slumped and lift her onto the bed. The needle she saw coming towards her sent her screams to a new intensity. The resulting blow stopped that nonsense.

Praying, pleading with them, she tried to explain she never did drugs, hated them. Imploring them not to inject it went unheard. Last thing she remembered was being released from all her worries while floating away on a cloud of pure joy.

Now apprehension returned and with it came

sheer terror. What happened? Why did they want to hurt her? Cowering into a fetal position, she let the tears flow. As she agonized over her prospects, she prayed to be left alone, but knowing she couldn't survive unless someone saved her.

Time passed and the call of nature woke her from her fitful naps. Sitting up, ignoring her body's trembling, she lowered her feet to the floor. Don't make any noise. Carefully moving the chains around her ankles, she crept the couple of feet to the toilet and closed the top rather than flushing. Then she made her way two feet over to the sink for water, thankful that it worked.

Taking a few minutes, she saw the only items left for her use – a facecloth that she wetted and washed her face with, a bar of soap like the kind hotels doled out and a small towel that looked frayed. It was the pitiful sum of the articles for her use. Not even a glass to drink from. Instead, she cupped her hands and eventually gave up this method to get her water directly from the tap. She wetted an edge of the towel and scrubbed at her teeth and then surveyed the space.

Dim, no light other than what seeped through the blinds at the meager window above, her disgust with her surroundings increased. With no way to get close to it, she couldn't even look out and try to see around the area.

Inside, the glossy green paint on the walls had peeled off in spots and the gray tile flooring had certainly seen better days. Remembering her own delightful white and lime green bathroom with its wide mirrors under the crystal lights, heated floors, and walk-in shower with a rainforest faucet that gave one the feeling of being under a waterfall, another sob broke loose.

She'd never appreciated her luxurious existence before; her loving family, and the lifestyle she'd taken for granted. Suddenly repenting her selfishness, a yearning grew, and a promise took shape. She'd never again accept her blessings with such an immature, entitled belief that they were her due.

Dear Mother Mary, please help me. I

promise I'll never be a spoiled brat again. I'll use my brains to help others. Like my dad, I'll care about people, do my best to make the world a better place. The prayer became her mantra and helped her settle when she curled into a fetal position on the bed, hoping no one would enter. Unless a miracle happened, and they were there to save her. A pathetic sob hung at the back of her throat and tears leaked down her cheeks.

***

Again, Misti woke to voices. Gina! She remembered her. Had she come to help? No! Coming back to the reality of her fate, she knew Gina was an enemy. Her and Draper both. They wanted to harm her. It was the other man, the one who'd held her in the back seat of the car, and whispered for her to be still, not to be scared.

That devil had put the first needle into her arm.

What had they said the night before? She wracked her brain trying to remember the words screamed behind the closed door.

Yes, she remembered. Gina had been frantic because an FBI agent had chased them to the car and then had followed them for a while before they'd lost him.

The girl in the restroom at the bar. Filtered memories started to take shape. A female had come out of the stall, and when she'd washed her hands, she'd twisted to throw the towel into the bin. They'd caught eyes in the mirror, and Misti remembered seeing a badge peeking from the waist of her pants just under the jacket.

She'd been drawn to the woman and had the strangest premonition she'd wanted to stay with her. When Gina'd tried talking her into going out back, she'd hesitated, even began fighting to stay with Ryan. That's about the time she'd seen the same female agent battling to help her.

She shook off her memories and listened carefully to Gina's shrill voice as she let off steam.

"You promised this would be an easy crime, non-violent, a quick way to make ten thousand. After a few days, we'd take the girl back, walk away, free and clear."

"Yeah, missy. We all wanted that result, but shit happens. Things don't always turn out the way it's planned."

Well, now the FBI are involved, and kidnapping can draw a sentence of up to thirty years. You guaranteed there'd be no danger, no chance of getting caught. I'm outta here. You can keep my portion."

"Yeah? I don't think we can let you do that. Either you're in or dead."

"You can't threaten me, dude. You know I won't reveal anything, or I'd be an accessory and end up with jail time. Like I'd want that to happen, man? Just let me leave and you'll never see or hear from me again."

"Sorry. No can do."

Suddenly, the horror of what happened came back to Misti. How Gina's screams were cut off, the muffled sounds of a human in the throes of being strangled.

The unmitigated terror of knowing she

might be next… hit her hard. So hard, she'd pretended to be blacked out when the shadow had entered, checked her, and administered another dose.

The last words she'd heard were, "She's out cold. We're good. The original plan will work. Let's just stick with it but wait a while before contacting her family. Let them stew. Then the Senator will be more likely to do whatever we tell him."

"What should I do with this body?"

"Put it with the old car, in the trunk. They haven't found it yet."

"That's over a three-hour run."

"You got a problem with that?"

"No. Of course not. Where's my gloves? I'll be glad when this is finished."

"Da, me too."

"Then we return to Moscow."

"Da, and never return to this crazy America."

CHAPTER 19

Just after four-thirty, Murphy walked into the poolroom and took a table at the back. He wore an old, tattered Redskins cap, a favorite he'd used while painting his house.

Surveying the place, he saw a rundown yet comfortable establishment with a sign over the crystal-studded black granite counter saying it opened in 1938. Multiple beer advertisements lit up the wall and made the display of mugs and glasses sparkle. No doubt, many generations had sharpened their baby teeth in this place where society's underdogs could feel relatively safe and be with others of the same ilk.

For years, he himself had spent hours and all his spare cash in a similar joint and had become a good pool player, one good enough to hustle others into paying a lot of money.

He and another buddy worked to suck in the

losers. The games and resulting extra cash had given a lift to many of his days when he'd been working bullshit jobs for minimum wage.

As the hours passed, he saw the eight pool tables begin to fill up with customers. He even stepped up when one of the others asked him to make up the fourth. Though he played, his shots wowing his loud-mouth partner, he never lost sight of the reason for being there.

Thanks to Ryan identifying a mug shot of Alex taken after he'd stolen a car five years earlier and got off with probation and a fine, he had a good idea of what the guy looked like. They'd texted the image, and he'd memorized it.

Suddenly, he noticed a female, dressed in a black leather jacket – her long dark hair streaming in waves down her back almost to her waist. She headed over to get a beer, strutting like she owned the place. Leaning on the bar, she downed half the bottle in one gulp.

Lord love a duck!
Katherine…?

He was *not* happy.

It was his turn to shoot, and he had to take his eyes off her long enough to win the game and nod when they racked up the balls for the next team to step up.

What the hell? His pool partner and others had organized a round-robin competition without him paying attention. Suddenly, he was involved in a tournament with a bunch of money as the prize. Others had begun watching, and mouthy, his partner, hadn't stopped bragging since they won the third round.

Watching for the person he wanted to talk to, he now had to worry about what's her name – right, Kayti – not to get into trouble. And from the looks of her, with a pool cue in her hand, dusting the end, she knew what the hell she was doing with it. He wished he'd have given into the urge to drink rye and coke rather than sip on a warm beer.

As the evening slowly passed, he listened to the raucous laughter coming from the table near the door, the one Kayti had joined with another female, a chick who'd obviously been around the block a few times.

They'd teamed up and seemed to be making a run on the table, which shocked the shit out of him. Christ if he'd have figured she'd be the kind to play this game! Then again, many at the training school had frequented a nearby place where pool tables were a draw.

Teach him to slot people into types. Although, his ability as a judge of character - honed over time - meant he seldom made a mistake. He'd learned early never to trust anyone until they gave him good reason to do so. And for many, he didn't care enough to stick around and give them that chance.

To his regret, when he did wait, he'd found most people were flawed. Since he didn't have the time or the stomach to deal with that type, he cut them loose.

He guessed people picked up on his lack of interest and tended to give him a wide berth. Those he liked; they became friends. To his surprise, they never wavered. If their constant invitations to hang out were any indication, they seemed to like being with him.

What most people never knew, except the few he let in – he was a nice guy. It was a fact. Problem was, he hated liars and cheats and most of all bullshitters – weak-kneed assholes who thought themselves better than the average hard-working joe. That kept a lot of people off his radar.

Playing by reflex, watching but not really involved, he spent more time paying attention to the goings-on two tables over. Especially to the bearded, greasy-haired freak who'd sidled up to Kayti and put his hand on her hip, then lowered it to her ass.

An atomic bomb detonated in his gut. Before Shane could step in, and he had full intentions of doing so, he saw Kayti's pool cue being driven into the guy's lower stomach. Curled over with no breath to cuss, the prick now used the offending hand to clutch himself.

Murphy watched as Kayti, all apologetic,

helped the fellow to a chair and pushed his head down over his knees. She knelt beside him like she was apologizing.

What the hell?

As if she sensed his stare, she glanced his way and winked. That's when her partner won the game, and it soon became clear the winning females were heading over to his table.

Kayti sidled over to him, her bared shoulders gleamed under the lights above, her tanned skin soft and supple. She'd removed her jacket, revealing a tiny, black, body-hugging T-shirt with thin straps and no sleeves. Hell, the bloody thing barely covered her chest.

The urge to caress her arms to see if they truly felt like silk, caught him unaware. He shook off the vision before he embarrassed himself.

The fact that he'd been staring only hit him when her tentative smile faltered from his glare, and she quickly looked the other way.

Then his eyes were drawn to her… ahh, assets the same as most others standing around. She was built. And there'd be piss-all he could do about it. Being that he worked with her meant she was off-limits.

He knew others in the department played around with relationships, and some got caught and had to change jobs. Others stayed under the radar. But he'd never imagined being in that kind of a situation.

Buddy wake up... it ain't happening.

Lord almighty, some days were better if one didn't get out of bed. Where the thought came from, he had no idea, but it was a sentiment he fully agreed with.

In minutes, after a lot of discussion that he ignored, her friend set up the rack, and Kayti stepped forward to break. Leaning over to take the shot, Murphy's inner cussing started a burn low in his stomach.

Sweet Jesus! The lady had an ass on her that drew every eye in the vicinity. Encased in tight jeans only sensationalized it. No wonder so many males had been watching their earlier games.

Instincts to throw her jacket at her with instructions to use the bloody thing had to be stomped on. He knew it. But he didn't have to like it.

Soon, the game kept every person motionless, it was that close. Murphy came up for the final shot, and it was a doozie. He figured Kayti had set him up, and so did her partner. The chick was pissed. He didn't blame her. But he had a partner too and a couple hundred bucks rode on the outcome.

Sinking the black was a tough one, but he'd made it before. Though the angle, just slightly off, happened to be enough for him to fake a loss. He pointed to the left-side pocket. Then sidled up to the table, bent down to see the best shot, and saw her waiting next to her partner. She bit her lip and caught his eye. They stared across the table at each other for seconds before he stood and sauntered over near her to take the shot.

Seconds later, his partner jumped, pumping his hand in glee. Kayti's grin flashed, and then quickly disappeared. She offered to buy her pissed-off partner a drink and he could tell Kayti'd schmoozed her enough to see the other shrug and accept the loss.

He stepped over to hang up his cue, his partner still slapping his back when he recognized Alex. He'd been one of the watchers.

CHAPTER 20

Kayti saw many of the spectators waiting to shake Murphy's hand. And, at first, he took it in stride, but after a few rowdies began fawning, he stepped aside and looked her way.

At once, she sensed a change. He'd suddenly become a cop on the job. She followed his gaze to see who'd caught his attention.

Ahh, the man they were here to find, Alex. She'd noticed the guy earlier hovering behind other onlookers and hoped he didn't recognize her as the FBI fighter from the night before.

She'd purposely worn her hair down and had dressed in a totally different way than she'd normally ever appear in public, certainly while on the job.

She'd changed her make-up from low-key warm tones to the in-your-face movie-star look, which meant red lipstick, heavy mascara, and sparkling shoulder-duster earrings to complete the new look.

Dressed so males would be more interested in her body, she kept her head down so her hair covered her face as much as possible without it getting in the way when her turn with the cue came along.

Murphy didn't want her there; she knew it. But it was her place to be with him. It wasn't right for any partner to leave her out of a possible arrest.

What if he needed back-up? That job belonged to her. According to her aunt, anyway. She might not have come right out and said they were working together, but she'd insinuated it when she'd promised to send Murphy along with her to see about the Fitbit at Senator Bond's place.

Therefore, Kayti took it to mean they were working the case as a team. If the man didn't like it, he could lump it.

Besides, she'd followed his instructions earlier. Had done what he'd asked. It hadn't taken her long to get information from Mrs. Bond, though she wasn't in too good a shape to do much but point Kayti to Misti's bedroom and give her permission to look through anything she wanted.

She stopped to get a printout of all Misti's cellphone contacts from the officers still waiting for a call from the kidnappers. Then she asked about her text messages, Facebook posts, and other social media sites where all the kids her age appeared. The officers kept shaking their heads, meaning nothing new or unusual to report.

These were different from the men assigned there the last time she'd been to the house. She didn't know either of them.

Finding no secrets in the girl's room, no diary, no hidden drugs, she contacted Ryan to get names of any possible friends who'd been with them at the Denver strip club the night before.

"There was only one other couple." His voice sounded rough, as if he'd been crying.

"Yet, you led the Senator to believe a bunch of your school pals were going to be there."

"They all planned it. I swear. But I guess no one other than Misti's friend, Allie, showed up. And I didn't even know that until Allie told me. We spent all the time with Gina and Alex, so I never really paid attention."

Kayti called the number for Allie Williams, Misti's best friend, who admitted to being at the Denver and seemed willing to talk to her.

Kayti walked the block to her house and was pleased when Allie's mother allowed them to talk privately.

"You and your date were at the Denver last night."

"Yes, but don't tell my mom, or I'll be grounded until I leave home.

Kayti grinned, nostalgia materializing, reminding her of her many dilemmas with her mom, then got back to her questions. "You saw Misti and Ryan there?"

"Yes." Allie held out hands that were as shaky as her voice and admitted, "Ryan called me earlier and said that Misti was in trouble. That I needed to talk with you and tell you whatever I could to help find her."

"Good. Is there anything unusual you remember from last night?" Kayti saw the girl swallow, and then tears gathered in her eyes. "You say your boyfriend was with you. What's his name?"

"Coleen Stubbs." Once the name was whispered, Allie broke down and begged, "Please don't tell my mom. She doesn't know."

"That you date girls?"

"Yes."

"Honey, that's your business. If you want some unsolicited advice, don't let her find out from anyone else, or it might be harder for her to accept your truth." Kayti put her arm around Allie's shoulders. "Are you okay?"

Pulling herself together the girl nodded and wiped the tears away with shaking fingers. "I can't tell you much. Ryan and Misti were in the lineup outside before us. An older couple joined them and got them in. From what little I could see, they seemed to be having a great time, laughing and drinking. Ryan appeared as if he knew them, and so we figured they were friends and didn't want to intrude. We stayed away and kept to ourselves."

"Were there others you recognized? Someone who knew Misti too?"

"There was supposed to be a group of us from school, but I don't think any of the others got in. As far as I know, it was only the four of us."

"Did you take any photos, or selfies with your phones? Maybe some where Misti and Ryan's table would be shown?"

"Oh, no. We didn't even take our phones out. The place was too noisy and kind of terrifying. We didn't stay very long. Just ordered one drink so we could say we'd gotten in, and we didn't even finish them. Just left."

"Were Misti and Ryan still there when you left?"

"Yes. I wanted to go over and say something, but Coleen didn't want to go past the table next to them filled with obnoxious drunks.

After we left, I texted Misti wc were going to a nice restaurant up the street, and for them to meet us there. But she never answered."

"Can you give me Coleen's number?"

"Yes. I wrote it down for you. She said if you want to talk to her, she's working for Subway at the American University. If you call first, she'll be able you meet with you outside."

Kayti did and it only took a few minutes with the girl to see she had the exact same story as Allie. Right down to the table of drunks and feeling uncomfortable enough to leave without finishing her drink.

By then, close to her own apartment and after Googling poolhalls in the area near Coopers' bar, Kayti made up her mind.

Now she was glad she'd made the decision. Alex had no idea who she was; she sensed it immediately. No wonder... since the dude had been pretty wasted the night before and was close to being in the same condition right now.

Time to make a move. Obviously, Murphy

felt the same way. It took only a few minutes to convince the idiot to come quietly, and she trailed them to be sure no one followed. When Murphy led Alex to his SUV, Kayti followed, watching him cuff the drunk. Taking directions from his nod, she got into the front seat.

Murphy forced Alex into the back, and it was when arms suddenly tightened around her neck, the cuffs choking off her air, that she panicked.

"Don't say a word. Pass over your gun."

Forcing back the natural urge to release her bladder and do something stupid, she nodded slowly. Speaking would be difficult with her windpipe feeling the pressure of the chain pulled tight. But she knew once Murphy got into the driver's side, her being victimized might force him to do something that might get him killed.

She lowered her hand to her waist where her gun was nestled by her hip and slowly withdrew it. Then she lifted it, forcing Alex to lean over in order to retrieve it. That's when she dropped the gun. Using the momentum of him diving to catch it, she grabbed the cuffs and leaned forward, forcing him to come half-way over the seat. Able to slide down and pull her head loose, she drove her knuckles into his face.

That's about the time Murphy arrived at the driver's side, noticed her predicament and cold-cocked the bastard. Pushing the slumped figure backward to land half on the floor and over the seat, he turned to her.

Not that she expected any soothing, or a commiserating reaction, she kind of thought he might have come up with something better than… "you finished messing around with our suspect now?"

Turning to give him what for, she saw the unholy twinkle he didn't try to hide and nodded instead. "Yeah, I've had my fun."

"Lady, you sure as hell keep things from getting boring." He got out of the car and headed into the back where he lifted Alex to the seat and put the handcuffs around the door grip so he couldn't make any more stupid moves.

Kayti couldn't resist croaking loudly, sarcastically, "No worries. I'm okay." She coughed without any real need to do so. "Getting choked isn't as bad as they say." She rubbed her throat to enhance her victim ploy.

After Murphy returned to his seat, he pulled her to face him and gently, ever so gently, his hands surprisingly warm, he rubbed the skin on her neck and whispered, "The prick left scars. He'll pay for those."

Mesmerized, she answered, her voice weak but not from the earlier punishment. "He already did. You hit him."

"Not nearly hard enough." Their eyes connected. She couldn't look away. His deep brown pools suddenly beginning to fill with questions made her shiver, made her want more, his lips, his arms, a naked body… a-a bathroom.

Oh, Lord, not now!

***

Once they had the perp at headquarters, Murphy passed him over to an officer saying, "put the son of a bitch in an interrogation room. And find a paramedic to check Agent Edwards. She's been choked and should be examined in case there's damage."

He strode away from her as if she wasn't even there.

Hey!

She hurried to follow. No way he was leaving her out of the fun part, watching Alex squirm while being interrogated. She loved this part of the job. Took it personally when a criminal thought they could outsmart the officer who had the upper hand and was privy to a lot more information and technical advantages.

Murphy suddenly stopped.

Not realizing his intention, she ran into him and would have knocked them both over if he hadn't of stood firm and held her up. "What are you doing?"

"I'm coming with you."

"You're getting checked. Your neck is red, there's a cut and it looks sore."

"I'll get to it later. Right now, I want to hear the BS what's-his-name has to say."

A grin appeared and faded as fast. "What's his name?"

"You forgot it? Alex. Alex Traver."

"No. I didn't forget it." Murphy's hands went to his pockets, and he leaned in close, eyes flashing. "You did."

"No, I didn't."

Did he roll his eyes? She could have sworn he did just that. A bit incensed, she gave him back what-for. "You just said what's-his-name."

"I was quoting you."

"Oh…" Realizing that their conversation had sunk to a real low, she admitted, "That's just a term I use sometimes. Like a thingamajig or a doohickey."

First, he stared. And then his eyes lit with a sparkling glow, and he actually laughed. It was low and husky and the pleasure of hearing it traveled over her whole body to settle into her tummy… where tiny butterflies were floating everywhere in a cloud of softness.

It was when he turned to continue down the hallway, muttering "Who's on first? I don't know's on second," that she caught on and knew he was making fun of her.

Shouldn't she mind? Trailing behind him, she decided she didn't. In his own way, he was teasing, and she deserved it. Why the hell she shared that silliness with him, she had no freakin' idea?

Besides him making her get the urge to use a restroom more than she'd ever figured would be possible, he also made her want to taste his mouth and take off her clothes.

Oh, my. What a mess!

CHAPTER 21

Murphy took it for granted he'd be the one to do the talking, that Kayti would back off and leave it to the pro.

Yet in no time at all, he could see his demands weren't being answered. Alex wanted nothing to do with him. Maybe the fact that he'd punched the asshole was playing against him. No matter which direction he came at, Alex shut down.

The question of Gina especially created a response. A tightening of lips, and his hands gripped till they showed white knuckles. But Alex's silence didn't waver.

Not until - in a long lapse - did Kayti step forward from where she'd been leaning against the wall and ask the magic question. The one that broke his restraint.

"Alex, I'm worried sick about Gina. What's going to happen to her now that the FBI are involved with the kidnapping? Have you heard from her?"

As if on cue, Alex's head dropped into his hands. His shoulders stiffened. His voice broke as he muttered low, "I'm sorry I hurt you." He looked up. "Your neck is still red. I've never hurt a woman in my life, but I had no choice. I had to get loose."

"I'll accept your apology if you answer one question. Why?"

"Because, I haven't heard from Gina since last night. I sent her a text to meet me tonight, and I have to be there.

"Look, you two are involved in kidnapping a United States Senator's daughter. That's huge, my friend. On the other hand, if you answer our questions and help us to get her back, it will go a long way in lessening your sentence."

Alex looked first at Kayti and then turned to Murphy as if he knew who to convince. "I have no idea where they planned to take Misti. Neither did Gina. We were only supposed to have her in that nightclub to meet up with Draper."

"Except, Gina went with them." Kayti's certainty let him think they knew for sure she'd done so, yet it was still something they had no proof of.

"They made her."

Bingo! One loose thread tied.

"She sent you a message?"

"Yes, last night she texted me. Said she was terrified and would make a deal with Draper."

"What kind of a deal?"

"To walk away."

"Did you hear from her after that?"

"I wrote back. I said I would meet her at our place tonight."

"Your place?" She noticed the understanding on Murphy's face, and it clicked. "Ahhh, the pool hall."

"Yes. See, they paid Gina extra to coax Misti outside to the parking lot. Said the others would take it from there. They'd promised us it would be all over with by this morning. They'd blackmail the Senator for whatever it was they wanted from him and let Misti go. And we wouldn't have anything more to do with them. Draper even paid our ten thousand early."

"Did Gina text you back about the meeting?"

"Only a short yes – okay – late. It's all she replied. No hearts, no nothing. And that's so not like her. She loves overusing those fucking emojis." Alex lifted his hands toward Kayti pleadingly. "I need to be there. She's scared. Something's wrong."

CHAPTER 22

Kayti followed Murphy into the small observation room. Together they watched Alex fold up into a sorry specimen of abject male misery.

Kayti spoke first. "I believe him. He's terrified. And I think he cares about Gina."

"Yeah. I got that too."

"You think those texts came from Gina?"

"Nope."

"Think they'll show unless Alex is there?"

"Doubt it."

"And other than Draper, we have no idea how many there are and what they look like."

"Yep. We're royally screwed without him."

"So, we set up a sting."

"Looks that way. I'll have to pass it by Kale, but I doubt she'll put up any roadblocks. The Senator has a lot of pull with the Bureau."

Kayti had a slight problem thinking of her supervisor as someone other than her aunt. As Murphy suggested, they'd need her permission. After all, they might be putting a man's life at risk as well as their own.

In a short time, getting authorization and working with another division where the S.W.A.T. team joined in with the code name Eight Ball, they had Alex adorned with implicit instructions.

In the special vehicle that looked like a travel van, the officer in charge shook hands with Murphy. "Hey, Black. Good to be working with you again."

"Hey, Frank. How's the gout?"

Frank's grin widened. "I don't have gout, and you know it."

"You will if you keep eating that sweet shit you love."

"Man, you're the one could use more sweet shit eating. It might lighten your disposition." Frank turned to Kayti and shook hands before he scrutinized the perp and got serious.

"We have you covered, Alex." He handed him an ordinary looking black hoodie similar to the one he wore and gestured for him to put it on. "There's a video camera in this zipper catch. All you have to do is make sure to scan the room constantly giving us a good view of who's there, and how we can get in should we need to move fast."

"If she comes, what will happen?" Again, Alex asked Murphy, automatically accepting his command.

"We'll take her back downtown with us to bureau headquarters. Hopefully, she'll be able to give us more information, even the location where they're keeping Misti. That intelligence would work in your favor." Alex seemed uneasy with the proposal.

Kayti kicked in before he could change his mind. "You're doing this for Gina's sake as well as Misti Bond's. Working with us will go a long way to righting some of the wrong that's happened."

Alex's eyes grew larger, even more

protruding than they were normally. He reached to touch Kayti's arm until Murphy's growl let him know it wasn't such a good idea to lay his hands on her. "We just needed the money so badly. I lost my job at Walmart a while ago, and Gina just lost hers. The bills were piling up. We didn't know where to turn."

"Maybe by looking for another job." Murphy's no bullshit attitude had Alex bristling. "I did, man. It's not so easy when you got a record. And when you get fired for standing up to a prick boss who thinks he's Napoleon, and you're his serf. I put up with the asshole for as long as I could take it. But he got worse. Others quit, and it made things even harder for those of us left behind."

Kayti stepped in to smooth ruffled feathers. "What about getting retrained?"

"Sure. Sounds easy, but it takes money. And we were looking at getting evicted. You can't know what ten thousand bucks could do for us."

"Yeah, I know exactly what blood money does for you." Murphy's non-existent sympathy reared again. "It gets people in trouble with the law and in jail for the second time. Misti is a sixteen-year-old who never hurt anyone. She didn't deserve to be kidnapped. Not for a day, not even for a minute, and bloody well not for ten thousand dollars."

Kayti didn't know if she agreed totally with Murphy's harsh reality check, until he reminded them about Misti. Then her bleeding heart froze, and she flipped to his point of view.

"Alex," Murphy sat across from the culprit and made sure he had his full attention. "I'll be on you every minute. If Gina shows, things should go smooth. But if not, we'll hang out until it looks as if there'll be no one coming before we shut it down."

Alex looked perplexed. "Who else would come?"

"Who has her phone?"

Alex's face tightened and fear began building in his eyes. "You think she's in danger."

"You did earlier."

He nodded. "I'll do whatever I can to help

her."

"We know that. Just give us a signal if you recognize anyone you either met or even saw hanging around at Coopers."

CHAPTER 23

When Kayti entered the bar for the second time that night, her pool partner's face lit up. She approached. "Wanna play some more, maybe make a few bucks?"

Kayti could see this girl had been through the ringer more than a few times. Her appearance and her attitude made it plain her hard exterior covered a battered heart that wore a very thick shell.

Not wanting to seem like a chick playing games, she shook her head and tried to look sorry. "Can't, I'm here with a friend." She pointed at Murphy.

"Got it! Asshole beats you at the tables and gets you as the prize." Kayti didn't like the sneering comment, not at all. Considering their situation, she had no choice but to let it pass. Deciding to smear some salt in the other girl's obvious wound, she grinned nastily. "He isn't only a pro at pool; the dude has a lot more going for him."

Her bitchy pool-partner glanced over to
where Murphy leaned against the bar, waiting for
their beers. The man reeked with sexy vibes.
Feeling their eyes on him, he glanced their way and
winked cheeky-like at Kayti whose heart flipped
over and had her stuttering a quick goodbye.

Glancing over at Alex who sat at a high
table alone with a bottle of beer in front of him, his
eyes glued to the door, she went to Murphy's side.

When his arm went around her waist to pull
her in close to the stool he now occupied and
snuggle her between his open knees, she thought
her legs would give out.

Her bladder tried to rear its ugly head, but
she ignored the signal. *Sweet Lord, not now.*

Instead, she burrowed in and caught a faint
scent of the soap he used. It was nice, not stinky.
Putting her hand on his knee to stop from landing
on her butt, she closed her eyes to memorize the
intense moment.

"You okay?" His voice sounded in her ear,

his breath fanning through the wisps of her hair, making her shiver.

"Umm. Fine. Good. Perfect."

His deep chuckle broke the silence. "Tell me something about yourself."

Kayti looked up at him and saw his eyes passing over the room, checking each person there. Thankfully, because it was late, most people had either left, were too drunk to do much but sit and nurse their drinks, or were swaying to the music… if one could call clinging to each other, hands groping and kisses getting wilder, dancing.

"What do you want to know?"

"Do you have a big family?"

"Just my mom. She passed a couple years ago. My father was never in the picture. And I have an aunt I recently just found out about."

"Excuse me? How did that happen?"

"Mom was a bit of a recluse, didn't like to share. I'm still upset with her decision."

"Ye-ah. I'd be pissed too."

"No. You don't understand. I'm not so

angry as I am hurt. I thought she only wanted the best for me. She encouraged me to go to the academy, to become an agent. Yet all my life she let me miss out on the attention and affection from another family member."

Murphy's hand stroked her hair, smoothing it as if sharing her sorrow. She didn't dare to look at him, afraid he'd see the adoration building. She had to force her knees together even harder.

Suddenly, he leaned closer. "Alex is agitated. He's seen someone."

Both her and Murphy scanned the room and other than a black-haired guy, sporting a scruffy beard and dark-rimmed glasses who just entered the bar, nothing had changed. This man wasn't Draper, they both knew that for sure.

Kayti questioned, "You think this guy was at the bar the night before, and Alex recognizes him?"

"Don't know." Murphy opened his mic and spoke. "What's up, Alex?"

Faintly, she heard him reply, "Nothing. Going to the men's room. Be right back."

Kayti thought about heading in that direction herself, but it would take a lot for her to leave the comfort of Murphy's body. Unfortunately, she sensed a problem and looked to see where the newest customer was. "Where's the new guy?"

Murphy moved quickly, heading for the bathroom, Kayti trailing him. Then Frank showed up behind her, a sign that something had spooked him.

They both rushed for the room only to have Murphy turn around, push past them and head to the back door. Once he'd moved out of their way, they saw the body, the knife still embedded in Alex's neck, blood beginning to seep everywhere.

While Frank checked for signs of life, Kayti drew her gun and followed Murphy. Catching up to him, she saw the body of the S.W.A.T. guy Frank had assigned to cover the back.

Rushing over, she checked for signs of life and was thrilled to find a pulse. Following her, Frank dropped to his knees too, his expression worried.

Kayti relieved his fear. "He's still breathing. No gunshot wounds. I think they just knocked him out."

Calling into Command for an ambulance, Frank took over the care for his man.

She surrendered her place next to the fallen cop and went to Murphy. "He's alive."

"Good. You know they had this planned in advance. Someone must have cold-cocked him knowing the killer would be leaving from the back." He re-holstered his gun.

"Where did he go?"

"I have no fucking idea. He just disappeared. Probably ran over to one of the streets nearby and was picked up."

She scanned the area and saw why Murphy hadn't followed, defeat making his face livid. In all three directions, a path or a lane joined a main street. Who knew which one the killer used?

***

Hours later, after getting all the evidence together and watching the video from Alex's hoodie, all they had was a dark-haired man, thick glasses and obvious fake beard hold up a phone, making sure Alex paid attention and then angle his head to the restroom.

When Alex stepped through the door, the man attacked from the side before he even knew what hit him. Then the camera went black.

CHAPTER 24

Hours later, after the crime scene technicians had scoured the place for any kind of evidence, they found piss all. Murphy, Kayti, and the team questioned the other bar customers.

With nothing to show for their efforts but a bunch of drunken grumps not impressed with being involved in a criminal investigation, they finally shut it down.

By this time, tempers were badly frayed, especially Murphy's. Losing a suspect sucked big time. But when that same person agreed to work with them and then got killed, it sucked worse. The earlier reprimand he'd taken from Kale was only a prelude to what he had coming.

Fed up, Murphy insisted he drive Kayti home. He led her to his SUV and helped her in as if he feared she might jerk away.

She argued and tried to pull away. "No need.

My car's outside."

"And you're exhausted. Having you in traffic isn't great at the best of times, but right now, with you being so tired and all, you'd be a road hazard with a high possibility for disaster."

"Don't be silly. I wouldn't hurt myself." Weariness had her being slightly testy.

"I was thinking of the other drivers."

"You're *so* not funny."

He grinned in her direction, and before he shut the door, he added, "Who's joking?"

By the time he'd gotten behind the wheel, she came up with another reason for her to drive herself. "My car will be here overnight."

"So, get it in the morning. Trust me, with all those dents and crushed fenders, nobody's gonna steal it."

"Ha. Ha. Still not funny. I'll need it to get to work."

"I'll pick you up early and drop you off here so you can pick it up then."

Before they pulled away, one of the

uniformed policemen rushed up to Murphy's window. "We were checking the bins and found this."

His gloved hand held the same cell phone the killer had shown Alex in the video. "It's the one... right?"

"Yep. Tell me it's functional."

"Nope. Everything's missing in the back."

"Figured. Okay, good job. Bag it for evidence. Thanks man."

CHAPTER 25

Kayti had noticed as the night passed that Murphy always praised others, and they treated him with respectful deference. It mattered. Made him a better agent, and one day, a good boss.

She stared out her window, saw they were passing Vinnie's store and noticed something strange. The Christmas lights weren't lit and the enter sign had been turned off, yet the store lights inside glowed faintly, revealing his shadow behind the counter. Strange. She definitely remembered him saying they were open 24/7.

Not willing to have Murphy rolling his eyes over her wild hunch of something out of order, she asked, "Can we stop at Vinnie's? I need some ground coffee for the morning."

He didn't say anything, just pulled into the parking lot and sat waiting behind the wheel.

"I'll only be a moment." She stepped into

the convenience store and sensed instantly that she was right. Earlier, Vinnie had called her sweetie, and his welcoming wink had cheered her so much. Tonight, he did neither. Sweat rode his cheeks and dripped off his chin. She could smell his fear and wasn't sure if it was for him or her.

"Shit, Vinnie. Sorry. I left my wallet in the car; I'll be right back."

Now totally convinced there was trouble inside, she grinned, winked and turned to leave.

That's when the gun in her back pushed into her ribs.

"Jesus, kid, take it easy before you hurt someone." She could see the menace in the mirror over the door, and her stomach dropped. He couldn't have been more than thirteen or fourteen. Nervous as hell, the red surrounding the pupils in his eyes made her wonder if it was fear, or some crap he'd used to muddle with his reason.

Could be his brain cells were occupied with a high so crazy, he ran on adrenalin fired by some shit he had no business even knowing existed. "I'll do whatever you want." She slowly raised her hands so they could be clearly seen in the window.

"You tell that old fuck to give me his money, or I'll shoot."

"Shoot who?"

"Whaddaya mean, who?"

"Well, if you're going to shoot me, I might have to stop you. But if you want to shoot him, I'll get you the money and wave you on your way."

She couldn't believe the ruse worked. The kid was loco. He stepped to the side of her and aimed at Vinnie, leaving his gun exposed and close enough for her to reach out and pull the rubber toy out of his hands. "Sorry, kid. Real guns don't bend when they're shoved in someone's back."

Before she could add more, another voice interrupted. "Then it's a bloody good thing this baby is real." She looked into the eyes of a real killer, and her heart wriggled inside, trying to find a hiding place.

"Ahh, sending in a kid to do a man's job. Not smart."

"Yeah, well they won't throw him in jail if he gets caught, will they. Stupid shit never could do anything right." He slammed a kick in the kid's side, driving him to the floor. Twisted into a fetal position – no doubt a position he spent a lot of time in with an old man like this lowlife – the youngster began to beg. "Ow, Dad, don't."

Vinnie spoke up, his voice wavering at first and then strengthening. "Leave the kid alone. I'll give you the cash. Then the both of you get out."

Suddenly, the thief with the gun spotted Kayti's phone held in her hand and hissed his command, "Give me that."

"What?"

"Don't play bullshit games, lady. Give me that phone."

She handed it over, hoping the 911 call she'd been placing had been the right numbers.

He snatched it from her hand and stuck it inside his jacket. Then he turned to the boy. "Get up, you idiot. Grab the cash."

Maybe if she hadn't seen the bruises already

decorating the boy or heard the hiccup that broke loose, she'd have played it safe and waited for Murphy to get through from the back.

But this kind of abuse from a father to a son burned away every bit of her training. Just as the foot came back for a second aim, she grabbed the six-pack of Diet Coke on a rack close by. Grasping the wrist holding the gun – to make sure his aim, should he pull the trigger, wouldn't hit Vinnie. Then she swung. When the Coke hit the side of his head, he shook it off.

When she went to deck him again, he pushed her so hard, he drove her against one of the displays, and she landed on her backside.

Grabbing the kid's arm, he dragged him off the floor. Kayti tried to stop him from taking the kid, and his fist connected with her ribs. That's when father hauling son flew out the front door.

Vinnie swore, but not louder than Murphy, who'd taken the time to break in through the back. Not wanting to threaten the perp into doing something drastic, like shooting Vinnie or Kayti, he knew getting the drop on the guy was the best plan, until fucking Superwoman pulled her stunt. He rushed over to Kayti, his furious expression scary.

"Are you hurt?" He lifted her up as if she weighed less than a kitten. "Lady, you're a disaster just waiting to happen. No matter where you go crazy shit follows."

Almost in tears, bruised and feeling sorry for herself, she weakly hid her face against his chest.

"Don't you be mean to my little friend," Vinnie broke into Murphy's scolding. "She saved my life and tried to protect the boy from getting kicked again."

Oncoming sirens screamed as backup approached. Seconds later, flashing lights appeared outside the building. Murphy looked over at Vinnie. "You got an alarm button back there?"

"Nope, but now I'm serious about following my son's advice and get proper security. Today's modern toys scare me, but I guess it's time." Vinnie pointed to Kayti and in a boastful way he admitted, "She called 911 before that bastard took her phone.

I saw her fingers push the buttons when she had her hands up over her head."

CHAPTER 26

Kayti was still arguing when they pulled into his driveway. She'd become the yapper once again, and he wished he knew where her off switch was.

"Why won't you listen to me? I want to be at home... my house. Where I have my things."

"You brought your things." He pointed to the backpack at her feet.

"You rushed me so fast; I forgot pajamas."

"How could you forget pajamas if you sleep in them every night for Chrissakes?"

"Because I don't. Sleep in them. They're just what I wear before bed."

The vivid image of her sleeping naked messed with his head and made him even grumpier. "Look, darling, I'm losing my patience with this whole scene. You gave the creep your phone. He has your address, and… he has a gun."

"I didn't give him my phone. I told you –
it's new. I didn't get around to setting it up with a
password."

"Uh huh."

"He took it. You make it sound like I wanted
us to trade numbers or something."

"Yeah, well, we're not that lucky. He was
smart enough to shut it off. Now, we can't trace it. I
added a tag so as soon as he does open it again,
we'll be able to locate it."

"Not if he changes the sim card."

"Without needing a password, he'll have
time to get your info before he changes it over. That
only takes a few minutes." He saw her beautiful
face and the understanding beginning to dawn on
her. "Come on, we need some down time. You can
borrow a T-shirt to sleep in for what's left of the
night."

Murphy hoped she'd stop being stubborn
and let him help her until they find the prick who
laid his hands on her. He'd sure like a few minutes

alone with the bastard before hauling his ass in. The thought of her home alone and having the sicko find her, hurt her, maybe kill her, had only risen for a second before he'd found it so unbearable, he'd squashed it. And forced her to do things his way.

CHAPTER 27

Kayti's first impression of Murphy's home stunned her. His kitchen was immaculate, roomy, and filled with new appliances. The bedroom he showed her was equally neat. But the shocker was the living room where a young person lay nestled under a comforter on his couch.

She entered the kitchen, wearing the T-shirt he'd passed over to her after dropping her gear in the bedroom. She'd grabbed a quick hot shower and felt better for it, though her thigh and side still stung from when she'd been brutally shoved to her ass in the store.

"Murphy, there's a body sleeping on your sofa."

"Yeah, it happens, more than I'd like. Not because I have a problem with the next-door kid being here, but because whenever he is, it means his old man is out-of-his-mind drunk."

"There's a story in there somewhere, right? You let your neighbor's kid sleep here to get away from a drunken father?"

"That's about it."

"Does he assault the kid?"

"He's spiraling. Before, he'd just get obnoxious and pass out. Lately, Talin, who's going to turn fourteen this Christmas, is pushing back, and that's making Rob worse. I haven't wanted to get involved, but it's getting to where I'll have to step in."

"Can't you call family services? Or arrest the father for assault?"

"Sure. I could. But I won't. Rob, the old man, used to be like family before his wife's death sent him into this spiral. And Talin, the kid, he matters."

Kayti didn't understand the reluctance but sensed there was more to the story. "Tell me. Why aren't you being the hard-assed cop everyone has warned me about?"

"Who's warned you? About a nice guy like me? Give your head a shake."

"Seriously! A few of the others I've worked with sent me texts and emails about your reputation for being tough."

"Okay, I'll accept that. I am tough."

"And…?"

"And, what?"

She looked away, embarrassment coloring her cheeks.

"Come on. They gossiped that I got in trouble for letting my last partner get shot, right? For getting us into a shootout with drug traffickers while they were making a big sale. Most agents figure I got him killed."

"Did you?"

"That's what they say."

"I'd rather know what you have to say."

Ignoring her invitation, he pulled out a couple of beers and led her into a family room where the two major pieces of furniture were puffy armchairs facing a big screen TV… which he switched on.

"Hang in here and wait for me. I'll go check next door and make sure it isn't a crime scene." He grinned so she knew he was kidding.

"Okay. I'm too wound up to sleep anyway."

While alone, she checked the room and noticed the corner where a small Charlie Brown tree had been assembled with a string of multi-colored lights and a few cheap decorations that looked sad and yet kind of heartwarming.

She wondered if it had been his idea to decorate, or if he'd just gone along with the plan? Too shy to ask and show her nosiness, she remembered the chat she'd had with Bud, Agent Fowler, at Senator Bond's house.

Bud had been a good buddy when she'd been in training. She'd often run into him at the pool hall close to the academy, and they'd hook up for a game. From the beginning, his interest in dating her had been obvious. Gently yet firmly, she'd pushed back until it became more of a running joke.

He'd beg her to go out with him, tongue in cheek. "Baby, you need to give me a break and save my heart." Her kiss on the top of his head and her pretended heartbreak over having to refuse would leave them both grinning and enjoying their bantering. It had been Bud who'd seemed more familiar with Murphy and had called him Black.

"You know Murphy, Bud?"

"Yeah. He's a good guy, sweetheart. You're lucky to be working with him."

"Yet I've been warned by others to be on guard."

"Yeah, well, ignore those nosy assholes. The man's a star and has been many times over. He has eyes that don't accept bullshit. He sees right through it and kind of pins you to the wall. I'd rather have him by my side than most of the others who believe the crap about him."

"The crap... what actually happened that day?"

"No one really knows but him. And I wouldn't be surprised if he's taking the fall." Bud,

good-looking and clean-cut, shook his head sadly. "Poor bastard would do anything for his partner."

The other agent listening kicked in, "And Tim knew it."

She turned back to Bud, "You're making him out like he's some kind of giant."

"I know, right? Yet the man's shorter than me, maybe six feet... if he's stretching, but you'd swear he was another five inches taller and a hundred pounds bigger. There's a charisma about the prick that makes a person watch their words and tow the line."

She'd laughed. "Yet you call him Black."

Bud chuckled, "It's to mess with him. I went through the academy with Murph. In fact, we lived in the same building. Another guy there, a real show-off prick didn't like the way Murphy had no time for him or gave any credence to his bullshit. Said whenever Murph entered a room, it was like a black cloud forming overhead. The nickname stuck; we just shortened it to Black."

She smiled with the other two and added,

"I'm not sure why they picked me to work with him, but I'll put up with anything if in the end, we find Misti."

Bud sobered. "That culprit Draper better be prepared to either kill Black or give up, because our guy never will... not if he figures he's right. And he's seldom wrong. He gets in a fight, or trails a killer, and he's in all the way."

"You know, you talk about him like he's a legend. He's not that old."

"That's the thing, he's only in his thirties. The legend began when he was a rookie and grew."

A smile still on her face, her eyes closed, she jumped when Murphy, who'd been leaning against the doorframe watching her, stepped into the room. "Sure would like to know what you were thinking about just then. Did anyone ever tell you that you have a very expressive face?" He picked up his beer and sat beside her in his chair.

"I know. It's a curse, one I try hard to cover up. This career doesn't bode well for a cop who's an open book. Everything okay next door?"

"Yeah, I got him into bed. Looks like he'd tried to stand and just slid off his chair instead. It's a bloody shame to see him like this. He wasn't always a drunk."

"What happened?" Kayti snuggled into her chair, folding her knees under her, and turned his way so she could watch his face.

He shrugged as if to drop the subject, but thinking better, his deep voice told the story. "Before Mary got killed, Rob was a good cop. Put his life on the line more then once to save others and never bitched about everything the way the rest of his squad often did. He'd invite me over to play poker with them even though I was younger and in training. Never looked down on me, treated me with respect."

"Yet he's a drunk today."

"He blames himself for her death and drinks to forget. A few years back, he tried to help a kid out. When he busted him with a small bag of weed, deciding to be magnanimous, he gave him a warning and let him go. It was their anniversary, and he'd made plans to give Mary a special treat, a date to make up for all the overtime he'd been working."

Her stomach dropped from expectations of a bad ending to Murphy's story. "What happened?"

"Kid followed him home. While they were out, he broke into the house. They'd left to take Talin to the sitters, but Mary had an earache. Deciding she couldn't enjoy the evening in pain, they turned back. She caught the kid who'd found Rob's gun in his night table, and he used it to shoot her before Rob brought him down."

"Oh my God, the poor man. Did he kill the kid?"

"Almost. After hearing a gunshot, I arrived a few seconds later. He had the weapon pointed, his finger on the trigger. It was shaking almost as much as the druggie pissing himself and begging for his life. Took me forever to talk him down. Only by bringing up Talin, and how much he'd need Rob, did I get through to him."

"Poor, poor man."

"Mary's sweetness kept them grounded and happy."

"What made that kid come to his house?"

"Turns out, he was after a gun. His supplier promised him free weed if he stole a weapon they could use for a holdup on a rival grow-op. He died in prison after serving six months."

"Oh Murphy, that's a sad story. What a terrible waste. I'm so sorry for them, but for you too." She wanted to go to him, comfort him, but being intimidated by his attitude, scared she'd be rejected, she stayed where she was.

***

He heard a definite sniff.

"What are you doing?"

"Nothing."

"You're crying."

"No, I've got a cold."

"Bullshit, that was a definite sniff." He heard it again, this time with a soft sobbing sound.

"Leave me alone. I feel for your neighbors."

"You're a cop for Chrissakes. Cops don't

cry."

"Do so."

Muttering blasphemies, he stood, came over to her chair and picked her up in his arms. Then he returned to his own place and lowered them both. He felt the satin softness of her naked thighs before nestling her in his arms.

"Shush, Darling." He crooned low while she let loose all the frustrations of the last two days. He'd known her fears for Misti Bond's safety had been eating at her. For old Vinnie being terrorized. The cherry on top had no doubt been the horror of seeing a dead man lying in his own blood in a poolhall bathroom.

Any one of these atrocities could put a kind-hearted soul in jeopardy. He knew it. Sensed her tender persona wasn't cut out for the job she'd landed and made up his mind to get Kale to pull her from the case. Hell, pull her from active duty and stick her in a safe desk job.

Right – because she didn't have the balls to play the game with a solid steel heart and an I-don't-give-a-shit attitude.

It had nothing to do with the fact that just the thought of her in danger was unbearable and could rip him apart at the thought of anyone getting to her as easy as they'd gotten to Alex.

Without any intention of going further, he kissed her forehead, smoothed back her damp hair, and gently rocked her. When her lips searched for his, what could he do? Never in a million years did he have it in him to reject the only female who'd broken through his defenses and made his heart wake up.

He let her kiss him, soft lips gentle, and her sighs sexy as hell. Being a man of the world, having had a lot of action with women who loved being with a handsome man, and showed their appreciation, he understood her desperation. Her need to feel anything but sadness.

This was her way to… ahh, sweet Jesus, he tasted her tears. Like nectar from cupid himself, the emotions they set loose came straight from his deeply hidden mushy heart. The very organ he'd been protecting since around the time his mom had brought home a craved-for puppy right after his dad died.

His arms tightened. Cautiously, he returned her kiss, devoured her mouth, and knew he'd never, ever... *ever* tasted anything so wonderful. She opened her lips for him, and he carefully entered, unwilling to frighten her with the greedy neediness that instantly attacked, leaving him shaken.

While every nerve ending in his body zinged to attention and gave him hell, she lifted her arms and wrapped them around his neck, her bottom nestling against the very part of him he couldn't control.

Lord, give me strength.

His hands lowered to lift her away from him, to stop the train wreck. After all, they were partners. He wrenched his mouth from hers and looked into her drenched, sultry eyes. His hands somehow landing on a smooth, warm thigh. "This can't happen, doll."

As if she didn't hear him, she smiled and

brushed her lips over his chin, her hand caressing his cheek. 'You're not such a meanie after all."

"Of course, I am. Stop that."

"No. I like it." She kissed his mouth and moaned when he let her. He got caught up in the rioting sensations for a few breaths. Before sanity surfaced yet again.

Unfortunately, by this time, his hand had strayed from her thigh and traveled up her hip, his T-shirt rising with it. When she winced, he saw it. "What? Did I hurt you?"

"No. Don't stop. Please… it's just a bruise from where I fell earlier."

He looked down, and there on her beautiful body, the discoloration had already settled in. The black and blue area on her skin ripped him to shreds.

Rage at the animal who'd laid his hands on her, marked her, rampaged his system, and he had to fight back the incredible urge to go out now, find him, and kill the bastard.

"You need to go to bed. I can't keep my

hands off you, and we have a lot to do in the next while. Go to the other room."

"No. I'll be good. I promise. Let me stay here with you." He had a hard time believing she could stare him down without flinching from his eyes drilling her to stop it. Behave.

Losing the battle, he lifted the wool cover his mother had crocheted for him, the one he always kept folded in the basket by his chair and covered them both.

While she cuddled her face into his neck and relaxed like a trusting child, he held her close. Settling comfortably, he watched her as she dozed. Her childish trust spiking his role from a dude slightly interested to a man caught and accepting the new status.

He leaned his head gently over hers so as not to wake her up. He closed his eyes and planned the next day, a custom he'd had since he was a rookie.

The first item on his agenda was to contact Kale and advise her he needed a different partner.

CHAPTER 28

The next morning, Talin stood at the doorway looking into the room and jumped back when Kayti popped her head out from under the blanket covering them.

"Holy shit!" were the words that roused Murphy. Glaring his dislike of being awakened in such a way, he helped Kayti to stand, and then handed her the blanket to cover her bare legs that had drawn Talin's eyes.

"Good morning, Talin." Her voice seemed a bit husky. It was either the beginnings of a cold or self-conscious shyness. And she never got colds.

The boy looked at her and then a grin broke out as he caught Murphy's warning glare. "Hi." He stuck his hands in his back pockets and aimed his question toward Murphy. "Want me to take the truck and go get some milk for breakfast?"

"Considering you're fourteen, don't have a driver's license, and asking's your way to con me into going and buying you milk, I'd say nice try." Murphy headed for the doorway and stopped in front of Talin, his shoulder nudging the boy in a friendly kind of way. "Eat toast and eggs. They're good for you and make some for Kayti too. Introduce yourselves. I'm grabbing a shower."

Kayti grinned at his terse way to handle the awkward moment and turned to the boy watching her closely. She held out her hand. "I'm Kayti Edwards. I work with Murphy."

Talin's eyes grew round from shock. "You're with the FBI?"

"Guilty."

He stopped shaking the hand he'd held too long and added, "I'm Murph's next door neighbor, Talin Campbell. He lets me crash here sometimes."

"That's nice of him."

A hero-worshipping look appeared for seconds before he laughed and added, "He's a nice guy. He tells me that all the time, even when he's being a jerk."

Laughing, she nodded. "Funny, I know just what you mean."

"You up for eggs and toast. Might even have some orange juice."

"Sure. That would be great. I'm starving."

First, he passed her over a cup of the delicious coffee she'd been aware was brewing since she entered the room and her taste buds flared with joy. Sipping it, she watched Talin organize the meal, which only seemed to take a few minutes.

"How do you want your eggs and how many?"

"Just two and scrambled. It's the only way I can make them without them either turning crisp or all runny. Don't like them either way."

Talin seemed to enjoy her confession. "Yeah, I know what you mean. When I first began coming around, Murph made a rule – no kids in the kitchen. Later, he'd allow me to mess around in here if I let him give me lessons. He's a great cook. You should taste his lasagna. It's my favorite."

"Quit bragging me up, brat. Have you fed her or just talked her ear off?"

"Stop badgering the chef, Black. He's creating."

Before Murphy could take offense at Kayti's teasing, other than a lifted eyebrow, Talin slid a platter in front of her that looked good enough for any restaurant to serve.

He'd even added hash browns that Murphy kept in the freezer. With orange slices and bacon on the side, the eggs and toast filled the dish, and the smells filled her head. Wonderment flashed that she didn't try to hide.

"OMG, you're a genius. If you ever want to leave old grumpy here and move in with me, I have an extra key."

"Yeah, no one's going to be living in your place until we catch the bastard who stole your phone."

Kayti, loving the idea of boarding with him, slyly winked at Talin and ate her breakfast.

CHAPTER 29

Murphy dropped Kayti off to get her car as he'd promised the night before. It almost killed him to drive away and leave her, even though they planned to meet up at the Headquarters' office Kale had assigned them for the case.

His plan was to get to Kale before Kayti arrived. And to make it happen, he drove like a fiend… took shortcuts, drove faster than normal, and got in to see her as planned.

As he walked into her office, she stood and approached him unsmiling. "I've just read the report on the murder at the poolhall, Agent Murphy. Alex Traver, the only reliable witness we had, is dead."

"We took every precaution. Didn't Frank add the details in his S.W.A.T. report? We had no way to identify the killer. All we do know is that it wasn't Draper. We'd have recognized him."

"Murphy, I'm not blaming you. You set up

the sting exactly as per policy. Shit happens. But I'm thinking if they killed Alex, it was to tie up loose ends. Most likely, Gina's already dead."

"I agree, but I don't figure they'll kill Misti, not yet anyway. She's their golden goose. If it was a purely for-money kidnapping, and they got spooked by the FBI suddenly being involved, I wouldn't give the kid a chance in hell." Murphy just knew it to be true. It made sense.

"Right. My thoughts exactly. Those Russians want something worth more than money from the Senator. Now, I want you to find out exactly what he'll be facing in the Senate when those bastards hit him with an ultimatum."

"So you believe the same as I do. They'll keep her alive to bargain with, and then she hasn't a rats-ass chance of coming out alive." Disgust echoed in Murphy's words.

Kale didn't disagree, she couldn't. But she did push her shoulder-length dark hair behind her ear, a move she often used when she wanted to think before answering. "Okay, yes. I believe you're right. But there's still a chance. Until he gives in to their demands, we have time. Use every FBI resource available to find that poor girl."

"Right, I'm on it. We had Gina and Alex's apartment closed off. I want to check it out and see if we can find anything to connect them to the kidnapping other than just a sad couple in need of money. There might be friends who can share some insights into why they were the ones picked out and approached to work with Draper."

"Figured you would."

"I also wanted to find out how Draper met up with the Russian bastard. I sent for the files from the Chicago jurisdiction where they ran Draper through the FBI N-DEx system and came up with nothing. It's like he appeared in the states, probably on a false passport, and we swallowed him whole."

"So, it's not just me. There're so many loose ends to do with Baranov, and others like him, I can't begin to count them all. No wonder the Senator and his colleagues decided to put a stop to their money laundering."

"By the way, what's happened to Viktor Baranov? Is he still in Chicago?"

"No. He left on a private flight to Vancouver, changed to Air Canada and flew from there to Paris. We lost him after that. But he's no doubt back home in Moscow right now waiting for news that they killed the Bill."

"But you don't know that for certain?"

"No. According to sources, who wish to remain anonymous, he's hired agents to buy two floors of apartments in the new condos being built downtown."

"Not too shabby. Real Estate is one of the rich man's ways to hide income from tax collectors. Using Shell companies works for them."

"And without the Bill, it's legal. Look, the Senator called a few minutes before you arrived, and he's frantic. They haven't been notified, and his wife's thinking the worst. Poor woman collapsed and is under a doctor's care."

"Jesus. Look, I'll try my damnedest to get some answers, but this won't end soon."

Kale rested her hip against her desk and changed the subject. She considered her words in a weird way that had him watching her closely. He'd never seen her wring her hands together or flush and look away. "Tell me what went down at the convenience store."

He gave her a brief outline of the events. And she became even more serious when he added, "I meant to talk to you about this. I'd like you to move Agent Edwards to another case. Maybe Intelligence or Surveillance. A job where she isn't expected to drive... or be under fire."

Kale glared at him before she answered. "I did put her on surveillance. With you. Your orders were to watch Draper, follow him, then report back. Not get involved in a dangerous kidnapping of a Senator's daughter. Not to have her up to her neck in a case with one dead and how many more to come before we get this one tied up. What? You don't like the way she drives. You want I should pull a highly thought of agent, one who ranked in the top five in her class from working with you?"

Fuck! Murphy watched her reaction and was stunned. Her voice rose with each new sentence, her tone dripping sarcasm.

Not intimidated, he answered in a similar tone, "Yeah. That's about it." He glared back before he added, "She's a softie. Those Russians will eat her up and spit her out. And I can't be watching her every move."

"Is that so? Well, I'm here to tell you right now. You'd better watch. And you'd better keep her safe. Or I'll come for your badge, your gun, and your ass. Got it?"

Pissed and showing it, Murphy sauntered to the door. He opened it and stopped. "Yes ma'am," was all he replied.

He reiterated it again when she added, "Keep me in the loop." This time, he didn't grind the words through bared teeth.

CHAPTER 30

Kayti arrived at the office later than the drive called for because of a detour around the main streets, and a traffic pileup as a result.

Murphy came at her snarling, "Where have you been?"

She played it cool. "There was a traffic jam. You must have gotten caught up in it too."

"No. I went another way. I've been here for almost an hour."

Kayti checked her watch and knew he'd exaggerated. They'd separated merely forty minutes earlier. Rather than argue with a man whose pissy attitude appeared filled with frustration, she changed the subject. "Did you talk with the boss?"

"Yeah. Hell of a lot of good that did me."

"What do you mean? She shouldn't have taken it out on you for what happened at the poolhall last night. God knows, we did everything by the book."

"Nah, she's good there. Look, we need to get over to Alex's apartment and see what we can shake loose there. I have his phone contacts, a pitifully small list, but we'll pay them visits too."

Minutes later, driving with Murphy, Kayti tried to cheer him up. "I liked Talin. He seems like a good kid, and he adores you."

"Whatever."

"No, seriously, he told me you taught him how to cook."

"Had to. The kid was starving, living with a drunk who didn't care enough to look after him. His choices were to survive on junk food or learn to fend for himself."

"Yet he eats at your place."

"That's because I buy groceries." They stopped in front of a run-down duplex with yellowed sheers hanging lopsided in the window. "Here's their place."

"It's a rental. According to Alex, they'd gotten their eviction notice. I checked after he mentioned it while we were interviewing him. They were broke… up to a week ago. Then ten thousand dollars miraculously got deposited in their bank account."

"The money from Draper."

"Yes. Cash. No way to follow any trail."

Kayti met him at the cracked sidewalk leading to the front. When they went to open the door, the lock held. "Damnit. I had one of the secretaries, Helen I think was her name, get in touch with the landlord to either meet us here or leave the door unlocked." Disgust rippled through his words.

"Maybe he's just late."

"No, we are by five minutes."

"I'll check next door and see if he left the key with them."

"Fine," Murphy had the phone to his ear, and as Kayti walked away, she heard him ask for Helen.

Disappointed to report that the neighbors weren't answering their door either, she admitted. "No one seems to be home on that side. Look, the owner gave us permission to enter, I'll just open it myself."

He swiveled as she headed for the door and followed close behind. "Say again?"

"I'll open it. It's easy. Watch." She removed a small pick-like instrument from her bag, grabbed the door handle, poked the device inside the lock and jiggled a few seconds. The knob turned, and they were in.

Not wanting to preen, she ignored his hum of appreciation and stepped inside a messy place filled with gloom and poverty. Clothes were strewn over the room, empty beer bottles, dirty dishes, and a stained rug that hadn't seen a vacuum in ages.

They began a systematic search and soon gave up. Nothing appeared incongruous. No drugs, no weapons, only a tablet that took Kayti seconds to open and read files that held utter garbage, even spam. She checked Gina's Facebook stream and found excerpts where she mentioned they had a recent bit of luck and things were looking up.

"Anything worth following up there?"

"No, I'll pass it on to the IT department, but nothing jumps out at me." She noticed a vehicle pulling into the driveway next door. "They're home." She pointed to the window.

"Good, let's go."

Kayti walked beside Murphy and had the weirdest impulse to reach for his hand. Shaking off the ridiculousness, she stepped forward to knock at the door only to have him step in front of her. *Dammit!* The man was pushing her buttons.

Saying nothing, they waited until the door opened to a young woman who showed insolence, which meant she'd made them as cops.

"Yeah? You guys again? Tell the asshole I paid my child support yesterday and to leave me alone."

Kayti spoke first. "Good for you. I'm sure it wasn't easy with prices being what they are. We're not here because of that situation. We just wanted to ask you some questions about Alex Traver and Gina Cummings, the couple who lived next door."

"What about them? They kept to

themselves, and so do we."

"Did you hang out with them at all?"

"Nah. She's a real douchebag, and he isn't much better. At least, my boyfriend works."

Murphy spoke up, "Who's your boyfriend? Is he here?"

Suddenly, the blonde whose roots showed half-way down the straggly hair to her shoulders stiffened. "He's out."

Kayti knew that was crap. She'd seen the bearded bum in the driver's seat and stepping out of the beat-up old truck when they pulled into their yard.

She argued, "I don't think so. I saw him arrive with you a few seconds ago." Out of the corner of her eye, she saw a shadow in the door's window and knew the creep was listening.

"You want to step outside, ma'am." She reached for her gun just in case she'd be needing it.

Before she could release it, the blonde got brutally pushed at them, and it was all Kayti could do to step aside and let her fall onto Murphy.

Hearing the brute running through the house, she took off and followed.

Heading for the back door, when he tore around the corner into the kitchen, she launched herself and caught him by the legs. Scrambling over him to control his flailing arms and stop his oncoming punch, she straddled him and pulled her gun. "Stop it, man. Don't make me shoot you. I will if you keep acting like a dumbass." Once he saw the gun pointing at his forehead, he stopped struggling.

Keeping the gun aimed at his beady eyes, she slowly stood up and made way for Murphy, who'd bolted in behind her.

His strained voice would scare anyone with a brain. And even though this maniac looked strung-out, he was no idiot.

Murphy took over manhandling him. He ground out words, showing no tolerance. "Turn onto your stomach, numbnuts, and put your arms behind your back."

The creep did as he was told and yelled at the screaming blonde nattering in his defense.

"He's high. But he didn't do nothing. Leave him alone."

"Stop it, Maggie. Keep your mouth shut."

Kayti put her gun back into her holster and approached the plump twenty-year-old who's agitation had gotten ridiculous. Watchful, she saw the girl's intention before she acted and found it was easy to stop the swinging arm from making contact with a simple move that had the woman in a hold she couldn't break. "Settle down, Maggie. We're not here to hassle you about drugs or anything else. Our intentions were to simply ask a few questions. You really want to turn this meeting into a crime by attacking an FBI agent?"

She could see Murphy calling it in, and knew he wasn't in any mood to be forgiving.

She led Maggie back into the first room, a place surprisingly tidy, and let the other woman go. "Look, Maggie, I know you can't afford to be in jail. You were just looking out for your boyfriend and lost it for a few minutes. I understand. I'm not here to arrest you. Just please, let me know if there's anything you can tell us about your neighbors. Alex was killed last night, and Gina is missing. We're trying to find her, and we need help."

Crying now, Maggie nodded and rubbed the arm Kayti had locked in a hold behind her back. Obviously shocked by the news Kayti had shared, she stared straight ahead, her lip wriggling with emotion. Then she reached out, her hand trembling. "I'm sorry. I didn't know. They weren't friends, but we sure as hell wouldn't want them dead."

Kayti took the hand and led Maggie to the sofa so she could sit next to her. "Can you tell me if you saw any strange people around their place, say in the last week or two?"

"No, but I sleep on and off during the day. I have insomnia so it's a real struggle to get more than a few hours in total. I work nightshift at the Best Western Plus on 5th."

"What about social media? Were you friends on Instagram or Facebook?"

"I did see her last Facebook comments about

things looking up, and that they intended to blow the city. I just figured it was booze-talk. If the number of empties in the garbage every week was any indication, they drank a lot."

"Would you know their friends? Anyone we can contact to get information about them?"

"I only know that she worked at the hairdressing place on Atlantic Street. Maybe someone there can help you. We never spent any time with them."

"What about Alex? Do you know where he hung out?"

"Seriously, I don't think the bum had a job. He'd come and go at all times during the day. But I never saw him with anyone else." Maggie's eyes kept shifting to the kitchen. She finally broke and asked, "What about my man? Are you going to charge him?"

"Agent Murphy's called for backup. The officers will arrest him for domestic disturbance. He'll be released by tomorrow. Just get him to stop being so jumpy when he sees law enforcement. This could have all gone differently if he hadn't of shoved you and ran."

"He didn't mean to hurt anyone. He's not a bad guy. He just uses pot sometimes, and it makes him jumpy."

The knock at the door signaled the arrival of the squad car, and in a few minutes, Murphy and Kayti were driving away.

***

"Domestic disturbance? Look sport, the guy would've decked you if you hadn't of shoved that gun in his fuc… face. Why'd you tell the officers you weren't charging him for resisting arrest and assaulting an officer?" He sounded grumpy as hell.

Kayti shrugged. "Because he never actually assaulted me. I didn't call out, and I had him on the floor before he could try anything."

"Doesn't mean he wouldn't have if you hadn't been smart enough to pull your weapon."

"Who knows. I wasn't about to take a chance. Besides, Maggie didn't deserve more hard luck. From the look of things, they're barely getting by. Yet she kept a clean house, and there were even homemade cookies on the counter. It doesn't hurt to give people a break when it's possible." She closed off the discussion right there by changing the subject, but a tremor ran through her body. She'd seen the look in that wild asshole's eyes – the second of indecision before Murphy arrived. And she had to ask herself one question. Would she have pulled the trigger?

They spent the rest of the day on wild goose chases, going from one lead to another, asking questions and having to deal with cranky fools who either clammed up because they had nothing to say, or other's who never shut up and added zero value.

Kayti sat quietly most of the time they drove from place to place. From Murphy's terse answers, she sensed her earlier chattering had annoyed him, but she had an idea. "I'm thinking we should ask some follow-up questions at Coopers."

"The bar?"

"Yes. On Fourteenth."

"I know where it is." He flashed her a glare

meant to put her in her place. Instead, it earned him a huge innocent smile that made him shake his head and groan.

He gave in and asked, "Why? We had agents checking them over, and I visited the owner the day after the kidnapping. He's the one who gave me the poolhall."

"I know. But I've been thinking. We have Draper's picture with Viktor Baranov. What if we flash it around? That's the kind of place where regulars tend to hang out. Maybe some of those customers, or even the bartender will remember seeing him."

"Okay. You're thinking Draper maybe hung out with the other kidnapper, and he'll be recognized."

"It's worth a try, right?"

"Yeah, it's a good idea, doll." He swung the vehicle around and headed in the other direction.

"Doll. I've never heard anyone use that term before. I like it."

He turned her way and smiled. The

unexpected gentleness made her weak.

He hesitated, but she waited until he finally spoke. "My dad called my mom Doll until the day he died from cancer."

"They were happy together?"

"Very happy. Mom adored the old guy right up till the very end. He told me he felt like the luckiest guy in the world. After he passed, she picked up the pieces, sold off the big old barn he'd refused to leave and bought herself a smaller, newer rancher. Rather than grieving herself silly, she made a new life, even built up a business, became a blogger that many people followed. She had skills... the motivational kind. Making people see the ridiculousness of wallowing in a lot of angst and grief while their lives wasted away. I guess she wanted to help them. She called it, *Live Your Life*. It had a huge following."

Amazed, almost speechless, Kayti turned to him and stared. "After a friend of mine passed from cancer, I used to read her blog all the time. It was refreshing and filled with good advice. I loved it."

"You and a few thousand more. I called it simple, common sense, and she'd laugh and agree. But people ate it up."

Kayti noticed the frown starting to form. She felt him distancing himself both in body and spirit. Not wanting to lose the closeness she'd worked so hard to form, she forced herself to question him more, thrilled when he hesitated but accepted her questions. "What happened?"

"She remarried."

"That's good. Right?" Then she saw the sneer on his face and added, "Or not."

"Not. This time she ended up with a control freak farmer who had a strong back and no brains."

"And you haven't forgiven her for that."

He yanked the wheel and spun around the next corner. "You don't know what the hell you're talking about."

"You love her."

"I fucking adored her. She meant everything to me, and that slimeball is hardening her and slowly breaking her spirit."

"Does she know?"

"What do you mean, does she know?"

"That you're worried about her? And you truly dislike the man?"

"If she doesn't, then I'm a hell of a lot better actor than I believe I am."

"Right. She knows."

CHAPTER 31

Sitting in the SUV before they entered the bar, Murphy checked in with Bud. All day, he'd hoped for a message and felt his bile rise when the news hadn't changed.

"Nothing from the kidnappers?"

"Nope and the ongoing stress has reacted on Mrs. Bond. She suffered a small stroke about an hour ago. The doctor just left. The Senator won't leave her side, but he wants to see you."

"Which is probably why he hasn't returned my earlier call. I'm sorry, man. Tell the Senator we're heading there right now."

"Will do. He's torn apart with this ongoing mess, Murph. I'm feeling for the poor guy. It's the not knowing that's the hardest."

"No doubt. I'm thinking the kidnapping might be over the upcoming Bill the Senator wants to get passed in the Senate at the end of the week."

"Holy shit, I never thought it would be about anything but money."

"Not this time. I want to speak with him about his proposals before anything happens. We need to make plans on how to handle their demands when they appear."

"What a bloody shame!"

"Yeah. We're on the way."

Kayti had listened to his side of the conversation. "What's happened?"

"It's Francine Bond. She had a stroke a while ago."

"Oh, no. That's so sad."

Not liking to hear her distress, he quickly added, "Bud led me to believe it's not too serious. The doctor was called, and she's resting."

"I assume we're going there."

"The Senator wants to speak with us. I've been trying to get hold of him for the last few hours. Now I know why he never responded."

"You think there's some sort of Bill in the Senate that he's involved with?"

Remembering that his earlier conversation with Kale had excluded Kayti, he laid out what he knew. "Two Senators, Linda Nelson from Massachusetts and Senator Bond, are the main designers. I've recently been told that Nelson is in the hospital fighting for her life after a recent car accident."

"Goodness. Now we have Misti being kidnapped. It can't be a coincidence."

"You think so too?"

"Of course. Isn't it significant that both those government employees have been targeted?"

"Kale seems to believe it, and so do I. She pointed it out at the beginning of the investigation."

"Not with me."

"No, we were alone. Now I know we're working the case together, it's best to bring you in the loop."

"I should think so." Kayti huffed, which made a grin form that he couldn't hide. "I'm not deep into politics so I haven't heard about this particular bill."

His voice teased, "Don't you carry out your civic obligation?"

"You mean, do I vote?" She grinned, "Sure, for the party I like. I'm certainly not hooked into the constant reality-show baloney."

"I know what you mean. It's mind-boggling." He did keep track of most of the breaking news, but by using his phone with apps to all the major news outlets.

"Are you a Republican?"

"Does it matter?" The question lingered, waiting for an answer.

"I don't know. I guess it's an insight into what matters to you."

If anyone else had asked him this question, he'd have told them to mind their own fucking business. With her, things were different. "Nope, but I'm not a Democrat either. I'm a guy who votes for the best candidate with the platform that makes the most sense. And in case it matters, I was brought up as a good Catholic boy."

Kayti laughed and the sound went straight to

his happy place. "Me too. Not that my mom ever took me to church. When I have kids, I'd like them to be part of a religious community." He stiffened when she veered off on her plan for kids and realized the idea of her as a mother sat fine with him. He liked the thought of her with children to love.

She continued, returning to the original topic. "Mom was a staunch Republican, but not me. Before I vote I research both sides and make my choice based on what I've read. Lately, I'll admit it's been difficult to choose."

"Yet it's a pivotal moment in history we'll all look back on. Pray we don't find we've made the wrong choice."

"Amen." She nodded in agreement and sat quietly for a few seconds before asking, "What controversial proposal are the two Senators working on to create this situation Mist's caught up in?"

"According to the boss, in a nutshell, they're striving to close off the loopholes where money from other countries can be legally laundered in the states. I'm guessing this includes shell companies, offshore accounts, smurfing, and fraudulent record keeping. How many rich bastards are involved in concealing illegally obtained funds, transferring money in elaborate and complicated financial transactions that make it difficult to identify the original party? The whole system reeks of corruption."

"And if they're able to pass this law, will there be more accountability, more regulations to impede these players?"

"It's a start. But unless we save Misti in time, there won't be anything done. And that will be a shame because from what I've read, they've assembled a bipartisan majority willing to pass it."

He pulled into the Senator's circular driveway and stopped the car. Turning to her, he encountered a soft smile that hit him square in the lower regions. A tide of pleasurable reactions overcame him. Without stopping to think, he reached toward her face, his hand caressing her soft cheek while she lowered it into his palm trustingly, like a child would do for a beloved parent.

Though her eyes questioned, he didn't speak. As if stunned by emotion, the long lashes lowered, and she gently kissed his palm.

Sweet Jesus! Buddy, you're a goner.

Shaking off the effects, he lingered for a second and then retreated, exiting the car and waiting for her to walk ahead of him to ring the bell.

Bud answered and led the way back into the room where the two agents had spread out. Murphy followed with Kayti. "Hey snowflakes, what's the news?"

Bud grinned at him, but his eyes swung to Kayti whose expression appeared befuddled. Murphy could see his puzzlement, and when Bud approached her with a nudge, she came out of the trance, grinned easy-like and spoke. "Hi Bud. I'm so sorry to hear the news about Mrs. Bond."

"I know. It's been a hell of a couple of days around here. There's so much tension, you can chew on the stress. We've been researching every app on Misti's phone and every place this girl has ever spent time – Twitter, Instagram, Facebook, you name it."

"Nothing?"

"That's right. She's clean, and so is her boyfriend, Ryan. Just two entitled kids out for some excitement."

Murphy broke in. "Can you let the Senator know we're here to ask more questions?"

"Sure, be right back." On his way past, Bud patted Kayti's arm in a familiar way not used by casual colleagues. Flames of jealousy exploded inside Murphy. Knowing he had no right to those feelings, he pushed the chair in front of him a bit too hard, gaining no satisfaction or relief.

"Agent Murphy, Agent Edwards, thank you for taking time to stop by." The Senator looked as if he'd aged ten years. His pallor could be mistaken as being the patient who'd suffered the stroke.

He led them into his office and closed the door. "I've been on the phone with Special Agent in Charge Kale. She's filled me in on the FBI's supposition that they've taken Misti to stop me from presenting Bill 539."

"Yes, it's what she warned me they suspected from the start. You and I both know this will put a real kink in the ability for a lot of foreign rich pricks to take advantage of the open loopholes there are now."

"It's why we've worked so hard to prepare it. There's a huge need to stop the unlawful behavior and clean up these rampant criminal actions. Linda and I have collaborated for months, streamlining this work. It's been approved by the House and is on the calendar to be presented to the Senate for a final vote. In fact, I've been trying to reach her to explain about Francine. And why I won't be able to make the presentation personally. She'll have to take over."

Kayti leaned toward Bond to answer. More than happy to let her step in, Murphy said nothing.

"I'm so sorry, sir. We've been informed that Senator Nelson is in the hospital after a car accident. She's in critical condition and won't be able to appear on your behalf at the reading."

Senator Bond sat stunned. If his complexion grew any whiter, Murphy'd be performing CPR and calling an ambulance.

"Oh, my God!" The Senator dropped his face into his hands. "I can't bear much more." The entreaty came out in a voice filled with pain.

Murphy instantly suspected there was more going on between the two Senators than a friendly collaboration of co-workers. Considering it to be none of his business, he asked, "How long before your Bill is called?"

Senator Bond overcame his shocked anguish. "It's on the calendar for the day after tomorrow."

"Then I suspect we'll be hearing something from the kidnappers very soon."

"And what do you expect will happen?"

"They'll want your assurance that you don't intend to present the Bill for a vote, and that it will falter and fade away like a lot of others."

"But how will I know they'll let Misti go free if I promise to follow their instructions?"

"That's just it. You have to insist you want proof of life, and you want it by speaking to her."

"But there's no guarantee they'll let her go, right?"

Murphy watched the other man's eyes, and knew he'd figured the answer out himself, he just craved reassurance. And there was no way Murphy could promise this would all end with no more lives lost.

All he said was, "I want to be notified the minute you hear anything from them. Let Agent Fowler guide you through the call. He's one of the best and will know exactly how you should handle it. In the meantime, Agent Edwards and I are out there working the angles and doing everything we can to find her before it comes time for you to do anything too hasty."

"You mean like canceling the presentation? What if I called a press conference and crushed the Bill right now?"

"Then they would have no need to make any deal. They could walk away, and you'd never know what happened to her. Like Agent Kale notified you earlier, they've already killed our only witness. They'd have no hang-ups about doing so again."

Tears appeared in Senator Bond's eyes and slowly trailed down his cheeks. He stared at Murphy beseechingly. "I couldn't bear it if my beautiful baby girl died because of my insanity at believing we could overcome this evil. You must save her. I'll give you anything."

"Sir, we'll do everything in our power." Murphy didn't get choked up about much, but he did have to admit to feeling sorry for this poor, broken man. Maintaining his FBI poise helped. When he glanced at Kayti to give her the hint they were leaving, he had to look away. Her sad, globby eyes did have an effect, and his throat jammed before he could stop it.

He stood to leave and knew she'd gone to the Senator to give him her Kayti-style sympathy; a warm touch and a few soft-spoken words before she joined him to leave.

CHAPTER 32

Misti had no idea how long she'd been chained to the cot in the stinking bathroom. All she could go by was the number of times the man came to give her another shot of joy.

She'd drank water as her only form of sustenance. They hadn't passed over any food, and hunger pains were beginning to keep her awake.

When she heard the door being unlocked, she begged the masked man, "How long have I been here? I'm so hungry. Can I have something to eat?"

"I'll see. You've been a good little girl, not making any noise. You be nice to me, and I can be nice to you, sweetheart. Maybe next time I come to visit, I'll bring you a hamburger."

She didn't answer. Just turned her head and let him plunge the needle in so she could escape from the terror his meaningful words had produced.

She barely heard the yelling from the other

side of the wall that provided her a hint of solace. "Knock that shit off, lover boy. The boss says she's to be left alone."

Could she believe that?

"So… who's going to know if we have a little fun?"

Dad-dy?

CHAPTER 33

Kayti had watched Murphy with the Senator. She'd seen his compassion for the man before the cloak of indifference appeared. The one that all FBI personnel were trained to perfect.

And no matter how hard she tried, that was the second failure she suffered in the job. Somehow, she just couldn't maintain the distance they were all expected to uphold.

She'd always known she could take extra driver's training to correct her worst hang-up but had no idea how to fix her soft-hearted deepest instincts.

By the time they'd returned to the SUV, she had some controls in place and could talk without embarrassing herself. She waited until Murphy had read his incoming text.

"We need to get to Misti before they make

contact and deliver the ultimatum. We both know the Senator will do whatever they ask. What we don't know is if they'll kill her when he does."

Murphy looked her way, his mouth hard, his eyes cold. "They might have already killed her. I just got a text that they've located a young female body in the same car we've been searching for. They found it in an underground parking lot in the north end of the city. Let's go."

While they drove, snowflakes drifted past, which reminded her that in a few days it was Christmas. The lights on the houses that flew by were pretty and helped to alleviate her abnormal depression. Thank goodness she'd already ordered Edna's gift. But now she had Murphy and Talin to add to the shopping list.

To move the slow traffic along, Murphy flipped on the switch in the SUV. Sirens screaming and lights flashing, she tried to concentrate on anything but what might be waiting for them. The thought of finding that beautiful young girl's body made her sick inside. "It could be Gina."

"Between us, that's who I'm expecting to find."

Not wanting to feel relief, knowing the death of any innocent girl was a tragedy, she let her mind wander. If rich Russians were responsible for the kidnapping, they'd be pulling strings behind the scenes with a good chance of getting away scott free. How disgusting to think they could come to her country, wreak such havoc, and not rot in jail.

"You okay?" Murphy's voice broke into her painful thoughts and pulled her from the labyrinth of disgust she kept having to push past. "I'm thinking the men in charge of this fiasco will be the ones to get away with it because they'll just leave the country."

"You mean Viktor Baranov? Not unless we get to him first and lay charges. But we need evidence. In the meantime, he's under surveillance, and we know every move he makes."

"And shit happens."

"True, people have been known to slip through the cracks. We can only do our best."

"I know. But him and the rest of the slime who have too much money and no honor should be indicted, charged, and jailed to show those other ex-pat money-baggers we have laws."

"Calm down, tiger. We'll get him."

"Yeah." She let out an unladylike snort. "Maybe this time."

Once they arrived at the underground parking lot, they both put on gloves and approached the vehicle where the body still rested in the trunk.

From the first glance, seeing the neck abrasions, death had been by strangulation. The coroner's assistant had arrived only moments before they did and could add very little other than an approximate time of death.

"There isn't a lot of deterioration to the body because this parking lot isn't heated. Plus, the outside temperature the last few days has been just above freezing and the nights even colder."

While Murphy talked with the crime scene investigators, Kayti wandered around the scene. What struck her instantly was the mud-like substance pooled around the driver's side. She opened the door and checked on the floormat to see more of the claylike muck.

Calling over one of the technicians, she requested them to send a sample to the lab and let her know as soon as possible if they could identify a specific area where the substance would most likely be found.

Before she could mention her notion to Murphy, he started walking to their vehicle while listening to his cellphone. He turned back to see if she was paying attention and following.

She hurried after him, waiting to find out what was up. When she saw his expression, she moved closer. If she'd of had the right, she'd have rushed into his arms.

CHAPTER 34

"Murphy, he's gone plum loco." Talin's voice broke.

"What's he done?"

"He's gone after Neil Somers. I couldn't stop him. He took his service pistol."

"Slow down, sport. Who's Somers? Why would your old man chase him?"

"He found weed in my closet. I wasn't going to smoke it."

"On my way. Get over to my place and stay there."

Murphy's heart rate doubled. Anger suffocated, so he had to slow-breathe deeply before he could answer the questions in Kayti's eyes.

Blasted woman didn't do anything that would have put him off. The contrary. She followed him, got in the car, and waited for him to answer questions she hadn't asked. Now how bloody great was that? He'd ponder her behavior another time. Right now, he had to get to the kid.

Finally, taking pity on her curiosity, he spilled out his angst. "Rob Campbell, Talin's dad, took his service weapon and is going after some kid called Neil Somers, one of our local drug traffickers."

"Ok-kay…"

"That's a cheap, sneaky way of keeping me talking. You know that right?"

"Right. And…?"

Murphy loved her way of handling him. Again, he'd store these memories for later. "And… he's probably drunker than a skunk. An incendiary bomb with a short fuse."

"And drug-selling ignites that fuse?"

"Only as it pertains to Talin."

"Talin uses?"

Murphy ground his teeth hard, his way to stop words he hated to say. Or was it more that he hated to hear. "Christ, I don't know. Kids will be kids comes to mind, but he's not just any kid. He's lived with addiction for years and saw what it's done to his old man."

"You know that's not a detriment for everyone. Sometimes, it's just the opposite. Didn't you ever do drugs?"

"Sure, who hasn't?"

Kayti didn't respond at first. Her hesitation lasted long enough that Murphy knew her answer before she gave it. "You. Chrissakes! You've never done any kind of drugs?"

"Of course, I have." Again, she didn't elaborate.

"What? Cough syrup?"

"I've used Tylenol and even Ibuprofen at times." When he swung her way, he saw the cheeky grin. "Jesus, you had me scared there for a minute. I'd have to ask what nunnery you came from?"

Still grinning, she changed the subject. "Will he know where you can find his dad?"

"I bloody hope so. These creeps tend to hang out in the same places. He should be able to give us directions."

They arrived at the house and Murphy shoved the gearshift into park, pushed the button to turn off the motor and was out of the car in seconds.

He left the house door open for Kayti to follow him in and went straight to the kid. Talin looked terrified. Smudged tearstains marred his cheeks, and his clutched hands covered the trembling at his mouth.

Eyes, mirrors of apprehension, were so filled with fear, one could almost smell it flowing in waves.

Murphy had known this kid since he'd worn droopy diapers. No way he could withhold the craved solace, especially when Talin rushed into his arms, his voice filled with relief. "Murph, you're here."

"Where the hell else would I be?" He wrapped the terrified boy in a bear hug and held tight. "Hey, kid. It's going to be okay. Tell me, what set him off this time?"

"He's never been like this before, Murph. I've never seen him so furious and weirdly focused."

Worries shimmered inside, ones Murph couldn't shake off. As a drunk, Rob could be ignored, but a Rob focused and pissed created a nightmare scenario. They wouldn't easily kick that man to the curb.

Fuck! "Tell me."

"I had some weed sitting in my closet for months, maybe even longer. You remember Toby? The kid who overdosed. The night that happened, he'd left his jacket here and the bag was in the pocket. I had no one to pass it to, and so I buried it in the closet and forgot all about the shit. Until Dad found it earlier."

"Why did your dad go rummaging in your stuff?"

"He figured I had some cash lying around. Said he needed cigarettes. Figured I wouldn't mind if he only took a few bucks."

"Yeah, right? Was he pissed?"

"No. That's just it. He must have hit a low point yesterday. I've never seen him in worse shape.

I know you put him to bed, but this morning I found him on the bathroom floor, naked and… a-a real mess."

"I'm sorry, sport. He'd have hated you to see him like that. Last night it became apparent that he's tumbling down a slippery slope and needs intervention. I figured to get him into a rehab place I know where the percent of recoveries is higher than most."

Kayti broke into their sudden silence. "You need to tell us where he'd go to find this Neil Somers, Talin."

"That's just it. Somers surrounds himself with a gang of armed assholes and calls them his guard dogs. Dad'll walk right into his nest of vipers, and they'll gun him down. Especially since he's carrying. Or… if they get any inkling he has anything to do with the law."

"Tell us where this slug hangs out."

Minutes later, Murphy hit the gas and they were speeding along the back streets that would lead them to the park where Talin figured they'd find the dealer.

***

Kayti decided to break the deadly silence. "Do you think Rob will know where these characters are?"

"I doubt it. At one time, he'd have had firsthand information from his old partner, but as far as I know, she's on medical leave right now. And... I don't think they've kept in touch. She used to try to get Rob sober, help him over Mary's death but eventually, she gave up."

"Unless he already knows where these druggies hang out, he'll ask for a favor. I would."

"Yeah, me too." Murphy used the call-in-car device and had connection with Officer Dell in a surprisingly short time. "Hi Sophy, it's Shane Murphy. By any chance, did you hear from Rob tonight?"

The speakerphone came through loud and clear. "God, Murphy. I'm glad you called. I've been sitting here with my son of a bitchin' leg in traction and wishing I had your number. Was just getting ready to call the FBI to connect with you. Rob called me. First time I've heard from him in years. He sounded deadly calm, almost like the old days."

"He wanted to know the whereabouts for a certain drug dealer named Neil Somers... right?"

"That's right. And I know those boys. They're as mean as any of the caged killers we're holding in the state pen. I could only tell him the last area they've been servicing. You know the Deanwood area?"

"I do."

"Marvin Gaye Park?"

"Right."

"We've busted them a few times at the steps by the bridge. The boys congregate there around ten to pick up their product and then spread out. It would be a good place to watch for them. And Murph...?"

"Yeah?"

"That's what I told Rob. You'll most likely find him there."

"Thanks, Sophy. Talk soon." Murphy pulled

a perfectly executed U-turn, and they were only five minutes away.

Kayti checked the time. "It's quarter to ten. We've got time."

"Unless they got there earlier."

"Murphy, don't be such a naysayer."

"Hell, slick, I'm a realist."

"Well, stop it. We'll get there in time. I'm praying."

"Funny thing, when you were driving, I was doing the same thing."

CHAPTER 35

Vests on and weapons ready, Murphy led Kayti through the park to the bridge and gave her hand instructions to circle one way while he did the opposite.

Dark had descended, which gave them cover. They moved around the various bushes carefully so as not to attract attention, but with the sole purpose of stopping Rob Campbell from getting himself killed.

Kayti came in from the top of the steps and saw a group of people on the right, through evergreen bushes that screened exactly who they were.

She sauntered closer, as if she were a walker out for a stroll, and overheard words that chilled her to the bone.

"Gramps, you'd better put that Goddamn

gun down and do it now or you *will* die. There's two guns to your one, so even if you get a shot off, you're fucking toast."

"Okay, I can handle that. But can you? See, you stinkin' piece of shit, my gun is pointed right at your head."

"Maybe, but your hand is trembling so much, I doubt you'll hit the target."

Kayti stepped into the light. "He might miss, that's true. But there's nothing wrong with my aim." She faced the three men, two with their guns aimed at Rob, and the one disagreeable punk who scared her stupid. That bastard had no fear of dying. Or at least, if he did, it sure as hell wasn't apparent. His sarcastic rambling could be believable if she didn't know one thing. If he was so cool, why'd he hire two bodyguards to save his punk ass?

As trained, she took in the full scene. Two of the schmucks were scrawny white boys with arrogant attitudes because of the weapons. The other was overweight, black and had a spaced-out look that made her decide he used too much of his own product.

The fact that their adversaries were a skinny female, and a weak old man didn't put much fear into them at all.

The standoff continued until she added, "I'm Agent Edwards with the FBI. Throw your guns to the side, get face down on the ground and place your hands on your heads."

Suddenly the mood changed. All three punks stiffened.

Unfortunately, Rob now deciding he had a sidekick turned her way so quickly, he stumbled and would have gone down if not for her hand grabbing his arm to hold him up.

That's all it took for Somers to reach out and slap her gun away.

With no time to help Rob further, Kayti released her hold on him and backed up to bring Somers to her. When he rushed her, she dropkicked the son of a bitch; one heel smashing into his stomach and the other into his thigh, bringing him down.

Seeing his boss in trouble, one of his guardians decided to come to his aid. She let him approach and swung her elbow at the last second to connect with his unprotected chin. Hearing his teeth crunch, she did a circle move with his arm laced through hers and over her back he went.

Stunned by the speed of events, prone on the ground, his gun flying some feet away, she followed up with a kick to his head and put him out for the count. Taking only seconds to deal with him, she was ready for Somers to come back for more.

Without taking her eyes off her opponent, yet checking her peripheral, she saw Rob getting pistol-whipped by the third loser and made her decision.

Charging over to give him a hand, she got close to the poser he was fighting. In a split second of time, she wrenched back the arm of the hand wielding the weapon and drove her fist into the armpit to stun and weaken the limb.

It was that moment that Somers came up behind her, wrapped his arms around her body to lift her away, and got back-kicked in the crotch for his trouble.

An enraged growl sounded from the left, and she knew Murphy had joined the fun. He rushed forward, stopping Somers from making a comeback. She wheeled aside without a split second to spare.

Watching Murphy in action had become her favorite amusement. Effortlessly, he drove the loser so hard, the force lifted him plumb off the ground to land about four feet away.

Somers, seeing Murphy approach, squirmed wormlike, trying to wriggle backward. Following, Murphy used the prick's hair to hold him up while he slugged him again.

Grunts sounding nearby broke into her gleeful satisfaction. She could watch Murphy all night. He moved like a well-oiled machine, a sight to behold.

Dragging her gaze away, sensing Rob had lost control, she headed over to stop him from slugging the hell out of the punkass now under him.

"You ever sell shit to my kid again, and I'll break every bone in your fucking skinny-assed body, you got that?" Kayti stopped his next downward thrust and held his arm from making contact yet again.

"That's enough, Campbell. You've made your point."

He pushed the bleeding face away and slowly rose to his feet, wobbly… painfully. "Who're you?" Suddenly, he noticed his neighbor approaching. "And Murph? How the hell did you know I'd be here?"

Kayti dragged the half-witted, bloody-faced kid by the arm to the other felon still in dreamland. She used the zip-ties Murphy handed her to bind them together, then checked on Somers, who hadn't moved.

Not wanting to intrude, but curious, she gave Rob Campbell a once over. How did this broken soul deserve to have his kid still care after years of drunkenness and bad behavior? And the respect Murphy had maintained even through the bad times. She marveled at how the disheveled, unkempt figure, trying to stay upright could earn such loyalty.

Then she moved closer and looked into blue pools filled with sadness so deep, if one had a heart, one felt instant empathy. If a person believed in such things, his aura was pure, unrelieved grief. He'd suffered terribly. And it showed.

Holding out his unsteady hand toward her, he stared until she looked away out of deference to an old cop. Then he mumbled, "Thanks, darlin'."

Murphy interrupted, forcing Campbell to sit on the top step nearby. "Hey old man, what the hell were you thinking? Coming out here alone to deal with these bastards."

"Watch who you call old, Murph. I could still take you."

"Maybe if I had both hands tied behind my back and my feet were chained."

Campbell's chuckle became a cough and had him writhing for a few seconds before he wiped his mouth and turned to look at Kayti. She'd finished the call-in for backup and stood silently nearby. "Who's Wonder Woman?"

"She's Agent Kayti Edwards, my partner."

"She's a slick fighter, never saw better."

"Get's her ass into all kinds of trouble." Murphy's disgruntled tone had her paying attention.

"Well, I owe her. She saved my bacon."

"Yeah, and from the looks of you, I'd say she didn't intervene in time. The ambulance is on the way, my friend."

That's when Kayti saw what Murphy's keen eyes had detected. Though Rob's face was badly beaten, contusions and bruises decorating the skin, what scared her was the small amount of mucus-like blood on his hand from where he'd wiped it after the bout of coughing.

Oh, no! Poor man.

Her pity curled into itself, trying to conceal her sympathy. But Murphy's all-seeing eyes caught it. At first, he shook his head in exasperation, but within seconds, he'd stepped behind her, and she felt his hand groping for hers so he could give it a gentle squeeze.

Lord how she appreciated this simple act of understanding. He gave her what she needed – unspoken kindness rather than censure.

Later that night, she'd take a moment to review the rioting thrills his sweetness created, but now an ambulance and cop cars invaded the area. Rob and three arrests took first consideration.

CHAPTER 36

"You feel like a beer?"

Murphy waited for her answer. He craved rye and coke himself, but that would have to wait until he got home.

By the time they'd overseen the cops' arrests on Somers and his boys, and got Rob comfortably ensconced in a hospital bed with Talin beside him, it was nearing midnight. Finally, they could leave and get back to their original idea to stop at Coopers.

Earlier, Kayti had sat beside a terrified Talin, talking quietly to keep his mind occupied until they'd allow him into his dad's room. Now free of commitments, she turned to him with that lovely warm smile. The one she saved only for him and had been flashing his way all night.

He almost decided the hell with the bar. He'd just take her home with him and show her how she made him feel – like a young kid with his first crush.

"Sure." Her answer didn't surprise him at all. This woman was a pleaser, and he had to admit to being a certified control freak who needed someone able to handle him. If he was in charge, his world sat solid. The few girls he'd tried to get serious with rocked that particular ship so badly, the rot started seeping in within a few weeks.

It's not that he didn't believe in equality for the sexes, and in women's rights. And most certainly, to earn the same as a man if they're doing the exact job. Especially in law enforcement where they took the same risks.

Somehow, he just didn't know why the girls wouldn't let him treat them gently. Like a cherished female creature rather than having to always compete for whose balls were bigger.

In the car, he asked, "Are you sure you're okay? That bastard was squeezing you damn hard."

She laughed. "Not for long after you appeared."

"He's lucky I didn't rip his face off. Hitting a woman. Jesus, there's no limits for these low-lives."

"Murphy, you know you sound like a chauvinist, right?"

"So! It's the way my mom brought me up. The guys I trained with were always going on about how if a woman chose to be in the game, they needed to take the hits without tears. And they're right. But somehow, I still think women deserve just a little more respect – not for how strong or smart they are, but for their capacities to nurture. Not saying some men don't have that gift also, of course they do. But it's not the same. God made males responsive to certain stimuli, or at least he did so with me. I like valuing the femininity in a soft-hearted woman."

"I'm okay with that. More than okay. If that makes me the weaker sex, I'll let you believe it."

"Jesus! See… you're my kind of girl."

"What kind is that?"

"A lady who knows her place."

***

Giggling, Kayti caught on he was pulling her chain. "You said it like that to get a response, admit it."

"Who, me?" The innocence rang false.

"Yes, you. First, you call me a lady and then you try and insult me."

He laughed huskily; a sound so sweet it twisted her insides. And made her want to lean across the seat and kiss the hell out of the teasing devil.

"Busted. Doll, you'd be surprised at how many females take that kind of talk the wrong way and get all huffy about what they consider an insult."

"Not me. If my man wants to treat me like I matter more than anything else in his world, how could I take offense?"

Murphy wheeled into the bar's lit-up parking lot and stopped the SUV near the outdoor tree, lit up for the holidays. Then he leaned across the center console and whispered, "Come here."

She went immediately, and let his mouth find hers in a kiss so mind-blowingly sweet, she knew another spike had just been driven into the gold-lined container where she'd tentatively placed his heart.

Rowdy yelling and drunken slurs shared between friends stumbling to their vehicles brought them back to earth. He held her face away and stared into her eyes. His were big and soft and brown and sultry with passion and... oh God, she didn't want him to ever stop looking at her like that.

"We'll pick this up later, doll. Okay with you?"

"Very okay." When she heard what she'd said, she understood his grinning response. Flustered, she pulled away, got out of the SUV, and headed for the entrance.

Frost had descended and the crisp air warned of the chance of snow. The ground in front appeared slippery and she wondered if it was why he caught up with her, and his arm went around her waist. For seconds he squeezed her hard and then opened the door, waiting for her to enter first.

They found room at the bar, pulled two stools together and ordered their beers. She remembered the smell of the place from the other night, the stink of spilled beer and the stench of smoked weed.

Kayti noticed the old-fashioned Christmas decorations. Fancy cards were taped randomly on the wooden beams separating areas in the large room. Streamers of twinkle lights wound above, draped from space to space.

The Christmas tree in the corner sat high on a raised platform, most likely a temporary stage for when they had live bands. Between its multi-colored lights, droopy ribbons encircled some of the branches and the rather pathetic ornaments. It did give a festive feeling, just no awe for its beauty.

She turned back to Murphy who'd finished checking his messages. "Anything new on Gina or the crime scene? I know there's probably no chance we'd be so lucky, but were there any usable prints?"

"Nope. They have nothing other than she

was brutally choked, and then shoved in the trunk."

"Any DNA under her nails. She must have put up a fight."

"Don't think she could. Her wrists were also bruised as if someone held her for the killer."

Poor, poor girl. Kayti hated to think of her being treated so brutally. "Time of death?"

"All they have is between twenty-four and forty-eight hours."

Gloom settled in and Kayti forced herself to shrug it off. They had work to do. Both surveyed the groups of patrons. Some looked kind of familiar to Kayti. Obviously, those folks would be their best choice of where to begin flashing the photo. "See that couple by the window?"

"Do you remember them?"

"I think I saw them that night. I'll go visit. Be back in a minute."

Kayti strolled over to the middle-aged couple and stopped by their table. "Mind if I join you and ask a couple of questions?"

"You a cop?" The man had an attitude and

wasn't shy to show it.

"Matter of fact." Kayti moved her black leather jacket aside and showed the badge attached to her belt.

"We got nothing to say." He didn't mince words.

The woman's expression went instantly from interested to totally embarrassed.

"I haven't asked any question yet."

"Still got nothing to say."

"Fine, sorry to disturb you." Kayti began to move as if she would walk away and then stopped after a couple of steps. "Do you know any other regulars here tonight I might be able to talk with?"

Before the asshole could act like the royal dictator again, the woman spoke up and pointed to two other tables. "I've seen that couple a number of times, and those men by the door." She ignored the disgusted frown from her partner. Before staring down into her empty beer mug, she accepted Kayti's thanks with a nod.

Kayti headed back to Murphy and shared

what the woman had told her. About the guys by the door, and the couple wearing matching Christmas sweaters showing *I Heart New York* only with an actual heart replacing the word.

"I'll try the couple next." Kayti was on a roll and wanted to get this over with so they could leave.

"Okay. Be careful."

Kayti headed for the table and was roughly pushed out of the way from behind when the first couple was leaving. "Nate!" Shock rang in the woman's voice, and Kayti flashed her a smile and shrugged as if to say no hard feelings.

She felt the woman press something into her hand and opened it to receive a card. Then watched them leave. Of course, Mr. Nasty walked out first without holding the door.

She didn't see Murphy follow the pushy prick out of the bar. Instead, she approached the next couple and could see they were having a good time, joking while holding hands.

"I'm sorry to bother you. Would it be okay

if I asked you some questions?"

Both looked up at her with welcoming grins. The lady answered first. "Sure, what can we do for you, Officer?"

"You knew I was a cop?"

"I saw you show your badge to Marge and Noel before they left."

"I see. I wanted to ask them if they were here on Saturday, but he wouldn't cooperate."

"No doubt. Noel just got released after a DUI and is still pissed at law enforcement for charging him a thousand dollar fine."

"Yet here he is again, drinking highballs. How about yourselves? Were you here on Saturday night?"

"Sorry, honey. We were at my daughter's place. I hear there was a tussle that night, some female fighter broke up the place."

"Actually, that was me. I was trying to stop a young sixteen-year-old girl from getting kidnapped by this man. Do either of you recognize him?" She held her phone out and watched to see if anyone had a reaction.

The man answered first. "I've seen him in here before. He usually sits with that group of guys over there."

He looked at his partner, his voice low, "You remember him too… right, Maureen?"

"Oh yeah, he has a distinct Russian accent, he does. Gets stupid drunk too from what I remember."

"Do you know where he lives?"

"Sorry. Can't help you there."

"No problem. You've been very kind. Thank you." Kayti stood to leave, and the woman's next words stopped her for a few seconds.

"I heard you were dyn-o-mite in jeans, honey, and I just wanted to tell you how grateful we are to having brave law enforcement officers like yourself."

"Thank you, that's very kind."

Kayti left their table and looked around for Murphy who just re-entered the bar, flexing his hand.

Poor guy. He must have really hurt himself while dealing with Somers back at the park. He met up with her and took another slug of beer. "Anything? You look like the sly cat who caught the rat."

"Seriously? How can you talk to a lady that way? Doesn't sound very flattering."

"I've already swollen that pretty head of yours enough tonight. What've you got?"

"The matching sweaters remember seeing him here and say he sat at that group-table most often." She took a sip of her beer, paused for him to head over, and stood to follow him.

"Stay here, okay? We don't want to come on too strong. I'll just cozy up and join them, see if I can't get someone talking."

Not liking being left out, but seeing the sense in his suggestion, she nodded, leaned back, and rested her elbows on the bar.

CHAPTER 37

Holy hell!

It's one thing to be built like a super model but another to flaunt her beauty. Murph had turned his head back for a glance and knew instantly, she didn't do so on purpose. She was just being herself.

Lord save him from his own bullshit jealousy, but he'd seen the glances being drawn her way. When he spotted the avaricious stares, he talked himself down from the green crap eating away at his manhood. *Enough, asshole! Since when did you start being so insecure?*

Once he got closer to the group's table, Murphy looked her way once more, winked and appreciated her lifting her bottle in his direction. He liked that Kayti followed veiled orders without any back talk. He also appreciated that she didn't take offense when he gave them.

He wasn't sure how many regulars might have remembered her from the other night, but figured if any were here, they wouldn't have forgotten. She wowed him. Most likely, she'd have affected the ordinary joe in the same way.

If they could make use of a customer's admiration, he'd do so in a heartbeat.

"Hey fellows, mind if I join you for a beer?"

The four at the table were pretty much in accord, and the guy nearest him kicked over the chair. "Sure. Seat's empty. Help yourself."

Before he sat down, he signaled to the bartender for another beer and swung the chair around so he could straddle it and lean on the back.

"Can I ask you a few questions without pissing anyone off?"

The friendlier fellow who'd welcomed him with the chair asked, "You a cop?"

"FBI. Agent Shane Murphy. It's been a long day and me and Agent Edwards over there figured to come in, grab a beer, and maybe find someone who might know this guy here." He held up his phone and flashed the photo to each of the four men.

The bruiser at the far end had the first response, and it was kind of what Murphy had expected. "Agent Edwards. She was here Saturday night kicking the shit out of Freddie. He's still in the hospital."

"That's right. She's pretty handy with her feet. Do you know who Freddie was working for? Was it Draper?"

"Draper?"

"Yeah, this man in the photo."

"Don't know no Draper. Only know him as Serge."

"Okay. Serge who?"

They all shrugged, then the same fellow piped up, "Just Serge."

The beer arrived and Murphy told the waiter to bring a round, brightening up a couple of the faces who'd looked uncomfortable.

"Don't know if you're aware of what happened the other night. This sixteen-year-old girl," – he held up Misti's photo – "was kidnapped by just Serge. Her father, Senator Steve Bond, is frantic, and her mother's suffered a stroke."

The man on his left nodded and exclaimed, "I saw the news about the kid. You saying they took her from this place on Saturday night?"

"That's right. My partner, Agent Edwards, was trying to stop it from happening."

"Man, can she fight! I took off while it was going on, but I saw her whipping the shit out of Freddie and Hank before I left."

"Freddie and Hank?"

"They ended up in the hospital overnight. Hank's still sore and pissed at letting a girl put him down."

Murphy knew agents working for Kale questioned Hank and his buddy-in-crime that night and got less than nothing from either of them.

Thinking a promise to drop the charges from assaulting a Special Agent to public fighting, a misdemeanor, would sweeten the pie, the officers had gambled.

They believed that if the men knew anything, they'd have spilled the beans in a heartbeat. Seems they had no loyalty to the bastard who'd offered them two hundred bucks for playing bodyguard, and they'd spilled the beans.

Serge has fed them some malarkey about rescuing his sister. And that he had no intention of letting the bastard she'd run away with, or his criminal family, beat on her again. He'd manipulated their soft underbellies about having the right to protect his family.

Using the info he'd been given, Murphy opened the discussion. "So, they purposely attacked Agent Edwards who actually, was trying to stop the kidnapping." Murphy was stringing a line and hoping for a bite. "Are you sure they're not on Serge's payroll?"

Buddy at the end broke in, "Nah. Serge made it seem unlikely there'd be trouble. So, when he offered the deal, they took the cash, thinking it would be the easiest money they'd ever made. Both those dudes needed extra dough what with the holidays only a few weeks away. I bet they're kicking their own asses now though."

Murphy laughed along with the others. "Regretting dumb decisions after the fact is a pretty useless sentiment."

"Yep. Christmas presents be damned. Those fifties cost them bigtime."

"What about the others? There were at least two or three more who jumped in."

"Hey, it's a battle. The guys get a little heated up and a free-for-all takes over. They skedaddled right after it stopped. Can't say I know any of them other than Freddie and Hank."

The rest at the table nodded in agreement. "They're not locals, maybe a biker gang looking for some fun. We get that kind here often."

"So… they wouldn't know Serge any better than the rest of you."

"That's about it. Only saw him around for a couple of weeks before Saturday. He's not an old-timer to the place."

"Not like you, Tiny." The general guffawing

let Murphy gather that the huge man called Tiny spent far too much time around the joint.

"Speak for yourself, ya prick." Tiny spoke softly to the teaser. The smile in his voice showed he didn't take offense but enjoyed the camaraderie.

Murphy waited until the next lull and showed his phone to the table again. "There was another woman involved called Gina Cummings. And, her man, Alex Traver. Did you know this couple?"

Tiny nodded, the only one in the group. "Yeah, I've seen them around. Come to think of it, they cozied up to Serge about a week ago. When they'd arrive, he'd move over to a table with them and buy their drinks. At the time I wondered why, but figured it was none of my business."

Murphy's shrug and nod showed understanding, and Tiny's expression remained comfortable. No way Murphy wanted to make waves.

Tiny spoke again, a shrewd look on his face. "What happened to them?" He watched as Murphy carefully chose his reply.

"Why you asking?"

"Just a feeling. Your face turned cold when you brought them up."

"Probably because they're both dead at the hands of your buddy Serge and his partner. You sure you never saw Serge with another dude in here? We know there's at least one other man involved."

"Nope."

Murphy saw the same denials in all their faces. What pissed him off was they were all believable.

The welcomer voiced what the others at the table were obviously in agreement with. "You figure he might have been setting up Gina and Alex to cooperate in the kidnapping? They were the ones to bring Misti Bond here that night. And it was here where the kidnapping took place."

"Looks like it."

"I liked Gina. One night, she bought me a beer." The fourth guy at the table, who'd sat quietly during the conversation, finally found his voice. Coming across as the group's chump, Murphy paid him the respect of taking him seriously.

"Well, thanks, guys. If you remember anything you think might be helpful, call it in and tell them it's for Murphy."

Again, he signaled the bartender for another round, shook hands, and returned to where Kayti was trying to persuade a stubborn cowboy she wasn't interested.

CHAPTER 38

Kayti understood why Murphy decided to join the group's table alone, but it still rankled. Working undercover, they weren't playing the game strictly as professionals. Admittedly, she preferred this laid-back style rather than the stilted persona they most often used during the regular job. Especially the suits and dress code. She watched Murphy saunter over to the table, his light green shirt sleeves rolled up to show his arms, a style she'd begun to expect from him.

He wore his jeans low and fitting, and he had a swagger to his walk that attracted interested gazes from more than one other female. No doubt his butt was the fascination. It worked for her. The urge to throw her empty bottle at the gawker who tried gaining his attention fled when he ignored her advances and instead turned and aimed a wink

Kayti's way.

The warmth from that tiny action flooded her body. Tightening her muscles in reflex, she wished them at his place – alone, kissing, touching, stark naked... *joined*.

Man, that dude had her number.

Enjoying watching the men interact at the group's table, she didn't pay much attention to the cowboy sidling up to the bar and looking her way. Being ignored probably didn't sit well with him, or he wouldn't have chosen to make a move on a woman who had about as much interest in him as she did in the now empty beer bottle beside her.

"Can I buy you another beer, miss?"

"No, thanks." Her smile was perfunctory, gone as quickly as it had appeared.

"It's a shame for a pretty little filly like you to be here all alone."

The idiot wouldn't take a hint. "I'm just fine, thanks." She spoke in a clipped way that any man whose conceit didn't outweigh his brains would have instantly understood.

Instead, the hero took it to mean he needed to work a little harder with his winning personality. "Aw, honey, I'm really harmless, just lonely is all."

Hating to be rude, but reaching her tolerance limit, Kayti stared him down, her expression closed and unwelcoming. "Not interested. Go find another horse to ride."

Not liking this treatment, the spoiled lover-boy's eyes turned hard, his manner nasty. "Hey, bitch, you need to be taught some manners."

Standing tall and opening her jacket so her shield was in view, she spoke low, "Look, dude, I'm on duty tonight. I don't want any trouble." She'd seen Murphy's approach. The look on his face boded bad for the flirt who wouldn't take no for an answer.

Murphy walked right up to the man determined to get his ass kicked. Moving into his space, the look in his narrowed eyes deadly, she watched as the oaf deflated, apologized, and turned tail.

Then Murphy turned his look on her and

didn't say a word. She figured it was up to her to break the awkward silence. Remembering their discussion on the way to the bar, she knew it was a sensitive moment. Taking the high road, all she said was, "Thanks."

He eased back and suddenly smiled in the way that she especially loved. And all he said was, "Anytime, doll."

CHAPTER 39

The drive home couldn't be over fast enough for Murphy. He itched to get his hands on the warm and willing woman next to him, and the wait was killing him.

Sitting quietly, she continued to smile when she felt his eyes on her. And since he couldn't seem to take them off her, she smiled often.

Finally, shyly, she asked the question, "Did you learn anything new?"

"Nothing we hadn't already figured out. The men didn't know Draper by that name. They called him Serge, which we know was one of his alias's. They couldn't tell me who the other guy was who forced Misti into the car. They only knew two of the fellows that were backing him up the night of the kidnapping. The ones you put in the hospital. And we already have everything they had to share. The stragglers in the battle were most likely just at the place and thought they'd join the fun after the fight started. We have no idea who they are, probably random bikers."

"So, we got next to nothing."

"Right. Seems Draper paid the first two who tried to stop you from following Gina and Misti two hundred cash each. His explanation for needing muscle was to rescue his sister from an abusive boyfriend and his family. Then he basically promised them they'd be getting paid for nothing since he didn't believe they knew about Cooper's."

"And they thought I was family."

"Guess so."

"So… it meant nothing to them when Misti put up a fight."

"No one really saw that. Remember, Gina led Misti out of the place. As you admitted, she argued about leaving Ryan but only put up a real fight outside. The reason they tried to stop you was because Draper gave them the sign to hold you off so they could leave."

"Ah! Now it makes a sick kind of sense."

"Yeah, those guys were decent men in their own way. Not one of them would have played along if they'd have known that the kidnapping of a sixteen-year-old was Draper's ultimate goal."

They pulled into Murphy's driveway, and with a spurt of glee, he noticed the house was dark. Which meant that Talin had stayed in the hospital with his old man. When they'd talked earlier, the kid mentioned the nurses had set up a cot.

But Murphy didn't know what Talin would choose to do. Lately, he'd been losing his cool. Hate had started to replace tolerance for his dad. Murphy had seen it and knew the kid had a right to these feelings. He just didn't know how to offset them with positive comments, since there hadn't been anything encouraging to say.

Tonight, he'd sensed a show of pride in Talin's reaction to what Rob had pulled. A sprout of optimism took root. He hoped this time Rob would let him help. Watching a good man hit bottom wasn't easy.

He left the SUV, made his way over to Kayti, and wrapped his arm around her shoulders. The dark cold seeped into his jacket, and he felt her shivering too. "As the Joker used to say, it's colder than a witch's tit tonight."

Kayti's soft laugh warmed him. "The Joker?"

"My nickname for Dad."

"I wished I'd met him."

"You'd have had his approval. Considering he didn't like pushy women; he'd have loved you and your hidden talents."

"You mean my driving skills?"

"Surely you jest."

"My name isn't Surely, and yeah, I'm just messin' with you."

"See – now that's the wicked sense of humor he liked."

She stopped laughing and looked up at the sky. "I bet it snows again. I can smell it."

He snuggled her closer and replied, "It's not long till the big day. It wouldn't be the first time we have a white Christmas."

"I love Christmas."

"You would." The teasing sneer in his voice made her look at him. She turned in his arms and wrapped hers around his neck.

"No doubt, you don't."

"Well… it's not quite that clear-cut. When my family was together, before Dad passed, it was fine. Mom always insisted on lots of presents. Nothing expensive, just fun things like socks and hoodies, goofy books, and T-shirts. Joker always bought the big stuff. Because he'd been a Supply Manager in Chile for the largest copper mine in the world, he loved finding deals and spent loads on technology items like laptops and cellphones."

"You were spoiled."

"Yep. But all that ended when we lost him. Now, I just get through the day with Talin as best we can. He likes me to cook a turkey and put up the tree, and so I do."

"Of course, you do. And cook a Christmas dinner? What a blessing! Last year, I ordered in.

Opened the present I bought myself, watched movies and ate so much chocolate I had to neutralize it with eggnog."

"Not this year. I'll cook for you, but you'll have to pay for dinner."

"And how do you suggest I do that?"

"I insist on a special currency – sexual favors."

"Ahh, then you've got the right girl. I'm willing to start making a down payment right now."

His rumbling laugh eased through her, causing her to grin up at him. He urged her into the house and helped her off with her jacket. He craved to pick her up, sling her over his shoulder and head straight for the bedroom. Respect stopped him from doing something so classless.

"You hungry?"

"Not for food." Kayti had no idea how she'd become so saucy and comfortable to put herself out there like she did with Murphy. Somehow, she knew he wouldn't hurt her or play with her heart. Somehow, she trusted him more than she'd ever trusted any other man.

His hungry look drilled her, but he still played the host. "Want a drink?"

"What're you offering?"

"My poison is Canadian Club and Coke."

"What's it taste like?"

"It's a rye whisky. I got hooked on it through my dad. He was born in Canada and drank this all his life. Now it's my weakness."

"I'll have one with you. I don't drink a lot of soda but adding whisky will help."

He passed her a tall glass filled with ice, liquor, and Coke. It wasn't until she took the first sip, and the flavor of the alcohol broke through that it instantly became her new favorite drink.

He took a huge swallow and felt his body welcome the treat. *Mmmm, ambrosia.* "Do you like it?"

"I do, very much."

"Good. Are you tired?" *Jesus, did he really ask that? Stupid shit. He hadn't been this nervous since… forever.*

"Is that a leading question?"

Playing the innocent, he replied, "I wouldn't want the lady to feel disrespected by me jumping her bones the minute we entered the house. Even if that was my first inclination. Treating you right won't hurt me."

Shivers of anticipation sensitized her skin. "I wouldn't want to make you suffer."

Their eyes caught, and she stopped breathing. The look in his was pure sexual devilment. With her legs weak, she put down her drink, stood, and approached him slowly.

When he picked her up, she straddled his waist and moaned with anticipation. That did it. He headed in the direction of his room.

While he carried her, she hugged his head, placing kisses along his neck, nuzzling and licking his skin where his beard didn't reach.

"God, woman. Don't make me drop you." He hurried through the door and lowered her to the bed, following her down. "You're too damn beautiful for your own good. I had every intention of behaving myself, treating you with respect, and not attacking you first thing."

She laughed as if he'd made a joke, but he hadn't. He'd seriously planned to behave like a decent guy and not a sex-craved animal. And the fact that she was sticking her tongue in his ear didn't make it any easier. In fact, it made it downright impossible.

"You'll stop me if this isn't what you want to happen."

She pulled back so he could see her face. "If you don't kiss me soon, I'll believe it's you who doesn't want it to happen."

"Oh, baby, that's so far from the truth. I've been aching for you all day, wanting to taste you and hold you. Can't you tell?"

She stared into his eyes. He let her see his need. Within seconds, she melted, reached for him, and whispered achingly, "Murphy, God... quit teasing. Really kiss me before I burst into flames."

Intense desire grabbed hold as he lowered his mouth and took the first taste. Sweet Jesus, the woman could kiss. Her mouth opened, and she welcomed him home.

His lips tingled with hunger as did the rest of his body. Hardening, his pants like a vise around the part of him that crowed with expectation, he moved to release some of the pressure. Plus, he wanted her next to him rather than trapped underneath.

Never would he scare her or imprison her in any way. For some reason, he had the feeling she wasn't sexually active or hadn't been very often.

Not that she was skittish or cold, but rather innocently aroused, more like a playful, loving puppy, willing to do whatever its master wanted.

His hands found the clip holding her hair. He undid it, smoothing his fingers through the mass of silk. He brought some to his face and smelled the essence that could turn his bones to liquid.

He kissed her again, caressing her neck, imprisoning her head. Then he stopped and held her in place.

"You could break my heart, Katherine

Edwards." He didn't know where the sentiment came from, yet he meant every word.

"And you already matter more than anyone else in my world, including myself."

"Come here."

She answered his craving with identical need. They kissed so long; her breathing became as harsh as his. She whimpered for more, and he gave her everything.

***

His hunger shattered every one of her reservations, her protections. He needed her. What woman could resist such a lure? When his hands loosened her hair and brought some to his face, she loved that he liked her smell.

When his tongue invaded her mouth, she welcomed him in every way she knew how.

And when his kisses began to lose control, it shattered her belief that she'd ever been kissed before. This man knew how to draw her very soul through her mouth, and she gave in willingly.

When his warm hands began to undress her,

to open the buttons on her soft wool sweater, she helped him. When they moved to her jeans, she lifted her body to make it easy.

All the while, she stripped him too. Undoing the belt at his waist, her hand accidentally, on purpose, brushed against the bulge she couldn't ignore.

His indrawn hiss let her know his sensitivity. And the delight in her power overheated her own body, discharging waves of wet pleasure.

Soon, he'd kissed every sweet spot on her skin's surface. Some places more than once. From her breasts to her stomach and down to her ankles and back again. Next, he lifted her on top to cover his nakedness, placed his hands on her chest, and urged her to take her pleasure.

"I'm all yours, doll."

By now, she was so wet, he slipped inside easily. Being stretched by his pulsating fullness provided satisfaction for both. Slowly at first, he moved within her, but she couldn't stand the slick gliding pace. Hungrily, she pumped him with her hot needs, and he quickened his tempo.

Intoxicating pleasure built slowly. Temptingly near, yet not quite stimulated for orgasm, she pushed down to deepen his penetration.

Sensitized to the extreme, swells of arousal heightened the passion. Nearing a mind-altering experience, she listened as he encouraged with loving words in a hoarse voice, breaking up with need, "Come to me, baby. Don't hold back. I have you."

She whimpered again. "My God. I'm burning."

"Yes, that's right. Burn for me." His mouth reached up to suck her nipple. His wonderful warm hands grasped her ass in a way so possessive that the spasms began to tease. Straddled over him, impaled by him, she plunged yet again… and again, until waves of explosions, intense and pulsating, forced her head back as she came so powerfully, her mind altered on her visit to heaven.

CHAPTER 40

While Kayti slept, Murphy touched, rubbed, and caressed for as long as he could keep his mind active and sleep at bay. He spooned with her and loved having her nakedness under his control. Her beautiful body, supine and trusting, warm and smooth.

He'd never reached heights of satisfaction such as he'd experienced with Kayti. No other female ever mattered as much, not even close. Wasn't aware such wild emotion could be possible.

Now that he'd made love with a woman solely created for him, he couldn't envision ever wanting or taking another. Which meant, he needed to keep her safe, here in his house under his constant protection... forever.

Jesus! He had it bad.

Keeping her here under his protection might be difficult. If she knew that they'd arrested the asshole who'd stolen her phone, she'd skedaddle back to her own place. And he'd be under constant stress from worrying about her. Just the idea of her being alone ramped up his unease. Another trait no one else knew about him. When he loved someone, their protection became paramount.

But he had her with him now, warm and safe. His eyes closed. He knew nothing until she wriggled against him the next morning and his body's automatic reaction was to swell with delight. She immediately became enthused with the situation, and her kisses proved she was more than willing to carry on where they'd left off the night before.

Only this morning, he took the lead. Within a very short time, they were both aroused from kissing, touching, and rubbing their nakedness against one another.

Murmurs of appreciation were heard as much from her as him. Her breath caught when he entered her, then resumed at a louder pitch, her gasps filled with pleasure.

Within seconds, his control gone, he rose to the same heights he'd reached the night before.

Lost, his rougher side took over… encouraged by her urging, begging for more. "Harder, yes, like that, love me."

Reality floated, his bones overcooked noodles, he cuddled her to him with the thought that he never wanted to let her go.

So much for my wondering if last night was a one-time experience.

CHAPTER 41

She couldn't breathe. Misti broke out of her safe place of foggy disfunction to a nightmare. The man was kissing her, mauling at her body, trying to get inside her clothes.

She yelped, then screamed, only there was little sound. Most of the alarm went off in her horrified mind.

She slapped at him, sobbed, begging him to stop. And when he did, at first, she couldn't believe it. Dimly, she saw another man hauling his body off her, dragging him to the other room. That man's words were rough, angry. "I told you to leave her alone. She's a kid... a fucking kid."

"Draper, I wasn't hurting her."

"You were warned."

"What are you doing? No!"

The gunshot rang through the silence, and Misti flinched before she covered her ears, rolled in a fetal position, and resumed crying… praying.

Not realizing at first, but eventually understanding that she hadn't been given any drugs for long enough that the last fix was wearing off. Hunger clawed at her stomach. It took some time before the scent of the nearby food ate its way past her fear.

A hamburger. In a bag on the floor beside her bed. She reached for it. Ripped at it like an animal, gulping it down in case the man remembered and came back to take it away.

Only that wouldn't happen now. She tried to block the reason why, but it seeped through her disbelief and eased its way into her memory. He couldn't come back.

Her jailer had shot him.

***

"My ear! You bastard. It's bleeding."

"Quit bitching. You have any idea how close I came to saying screw it and shooting to kill? That's a warning, asshole. I won't give you another. Keep your hands off the merchandise."

"Alright. Okay. Jesus… when are we going to get this bullshit over with?"

"I got word from Russia. They said to call in the morning.

CHAPTER 42

Kayti knew she needed to give up the pretense about her apartment being unsafe. Bud had texted her on her new phone the day before that they'd caught the thief and were remanding him for trial. Her place was now risk free.

Seems his last robbery attempt had ended with the loser using his gun. Before they caught up with him, he put a store owner in the hospital. Turns out, it was his kid who snitched on him. Said he did it because of a lady cop who tried to protect him. Then he disappeared, took off from the precinct, and the cops still hadn't found him.

One never knew when something they do might influence another. It made her happy to think she'd had a positive impact. She'd be visiting the kid in juvie as soon as they picked him up.

One thing she knew for sure. It wouldn't be

happening until they got Misti back.

She'd woken up that morning to pure bliss, lying beside Murphy, cuddled close. His warmth, his smell, his arms. God, everything about the dude had her tied up in knots. She never wanted to sleep away from him again.

Now she looked over at him behind the wheel, she wondered how her aunt would react to them in a relationship. If they kept their regular Christmas day appointment, she had a few days to figure out what to say... or not.

During the reprieve, they could keep things between themselves. Not that it sat right with her to lie to the only family she had left. But since she'd kill for the man, she guessed a mere lie didn't warrant this extreme feeling of guilt.

"It's okay for us to show up at Headquarters together?"

"Hey, most know you're under my protection. No one will say anything. If they do, they'll answer to me."

Knowing people didn't approach him

without good reason, she surmised nothing would be said. Certainly, not to their face.

"Did you talk with Bud this morning?" She knew he'd made calls while she was in the shower.

"Yeah. Time's running out. The Bill is up for a vote soon. Kale figures they'll either be calling about the ransom today, or we're completely off the mark."

"But you don't believe we made any mistakes, do you?"

"Not even for a second. I just wish we'd catch a break. We've tried every avenue we could take, even to hanging out at the bar digging for scraps."

Before she could answer, the car phone rang. As soon as she saw the name of the caller, she knew. Pushing the answer button, she listened while Bud exclaimed, excitement obvious in his voice, "He called. You were right, Black. It's the Bill."

CHAPTER 43

When they arrived, it was to find the Senator and Special Agent in Charge, Edna Kale going over a newly constructed plan.

Murphy led the way to the house but stood back for Kayti to enter first. He followed and shook hands with the Senator. "Sir. Looks like the wait is over. They've made contact. Did you ask to speak to Misti?"

"I did, just like you told me to. He said no."

"And…"

"I told him the Bill was scheduled for later today, and it had the votes to pass."

Bud spoke up, "He was believable, Murphy. Went on about his duty to the country. How they'd worked on getting this Bill to the Senate for years, and unless he had absolute proof that his daughter was alive, he wouldn't believe them."

The Senator admitted, "It's from your coaching I was able to stay focused and not blubber like a baby, begging for mercy. Thank God, it worked."

"They let you speak with her?"

"All she said was Daddy, but I'd know my little girl's voice anywhere. Broke my heart. I could tell they muffled her mouth after that."

"What terms did they insist on?"

"A public announcement that because of Linda Nelson's car accident, we would be passing on the Bill during this session in the Senate."

Agent Kale added, "We got word from Boston that Senator Nelson survived her latest operation and will be out of ICU very soon."

Senator Bond's complexion paled. "Thank God. The woman doesn't deserve this treatment. She's been through so much lately, what with her husband's illness for years and then losing him in the spring, she's suffered enough."

"No doubt, Steve. I'll admit that life as a widow takes some getting used to. I'm glad she has a powerful job to keep her busy. My work was my savior when Trevor passed." Edna Kale spoke from experience. Murphy wondered why Kayti didn't appear surprised at the personal information. It was almost like she already knew Kale was a widow.

He'd have sworn Kale told very few people. That he was one, always shocked him, but then a few months ago, he'd caught her in a weak moment. He'd walked into a bar, one of the worst days of his life, took a stool and when the person next to him turned his way, it was Kale.

They'd ended up having drinks together, and when she lifted her glass of ginger ale to toast, she said it had been a year since her husband had died. Not knowing what to say, he'd drank with her and kept quiet. Yet he always had the strangest feeling that she'd been there more as support for him. Weird...

"Bud, can you replay the call."

"Sure, Murph. We've been trying to hear any background noise but there's nothing. They used a voice distorter, so we have no idea if it's a man or woman calling, or if they have accents."

Murphy and Kayti listened closely. The message was brief and the threat basic. "*Call a press conference at three p.m. Explain that Bill 539 has been pushed forward to next year due to Senator Nelson's car accident. Once we see the broadcast, we'll drop off your daughter somewhere safe. She'll call you to pick her up.*"

Kale took Murphy aside. "What do you think?"

"If she's seen their faces, they won't let her go."

"Then let's hope we find them before that. We have five hours."

"That's the son of a bitch. We have no clues to follow. Have there been any legit sounding calls from the general public, anything to follow up on?"

"None that made sense, and I've had agents screening every prank call so far. I've got to head back to the office. Keep me posted. In the meantime, work on that speech with the Senator. He's a mess, and we need him to stay focused. I'll take Agent Edwards with me to Headquarters, and you can meet up with her there."

"Right." Murphy didn't like being separated from his partner, but his boss had the upper hand, and he really had no rebuttal.

***

The minute they were in the back seat of Kale's car being taken to her office; she switched from boss to auntie. "What's this… you sleeping with Agent Murphy?"

Shock burst in Kayti. *Holy hell, the woman knew! How in the world did she find out?* "Who told you?"

"Told me what?"

"That I slept with Murphy."

"You slept with Murphy? Son of a bitch."

"But you knew. You brought it up."

"I knew you'd slept at his place, presumably to keep you safe from the bastard who'd hit you and stole your phone. I did not know you'd been intimate."

Kayti felt her aunt's eyes on her. She met

her angry stare. "Don't you look at me like that. I couldn't help myself."

"Hell, girl. You don't have to yell. The man's magic. I get it. But you're my niece, and it's not sitting well with me. This case is as serious as it gets. There's no time for hanky panky, especially between coworkers. Until we find that poor girl and get her home safe, I need everyone focused."

"I know. And we've done everything possible. Even with all the power behind the FBI, we're still coming up blank for any new leads. Don't think just because I've fallen for the guy, that we're not doing our jobs in as professional a way as you'd expect."

"I didn't say that." Edna started to grin. "You've fallen for him?"

"Well, yeah. I don't sleep around. With him, I couldn't help it. And before you say anything else, I'm kinda in a place where it looks like I'll be suffering from the same condition for the rest of my life."

"Well, now. Does he feel the same? The guy

keeps things pretty close."

"I know. Right now, we're just finding our way to each other."

"Considering the latest threat to your safety is rotting in a jail cell without any chance for bail, you could move back home and give yourselves time. Or if that's not happening, you know I have a spare room with your name on it whenever you want."

"Thanks, Edna. You're right. I need to get back to my place. If for nothing else, to change my clothes and freshen up."

"Want me to drop you there?"

"Sure. We're close by. It won't take long. I'll meet you back at the office."

Within minutes, the car pulled to a stop in front of Kayti's building. Before she could leave, she hugged her aunt, a move they'd started at the end of their Sunday visits. One she now felt an overwhelming need to carry out after Edna's tolerance and understanding of her recent behavior. "Thanks for being supportive, Edna. I'm terrified about this relationship with Murphy. Yet, there's nothing I can do about it." Her weak grin and chuckle said it all. "It's too late to turn off my feelings."

"Then follow them and rely on him to do right by you. The man's all heart. I don't know if you heard the rumors about his past. Why he's been punished and sent back down the ranks."

"Sure. Supposedly, he betrayed his partner, and the man ended up dead. I can't believe it, not after getting to know him. He's too honorable."

"See, you happen to be right. I know for a fact it was the other way around. His partner, Bruce Tarner, was dirty, not Murphy. He'd hooked up with a bad bunch... Mexican mercenaries. Having enough drug money to throw around, they bought a cop. His gambling addiction took precedence over his partner, his job, and worst of all, his family."

"Oh, no. How sad."

"I'm thinking when Murphy appeared on the day Agent Tarner was involved with them receiving payment for a huge shipment, everything started to slide. They believed Tarner had set them up. Murphy drew their fire, trying to get Tarner free. Yet they shot him without any hesitation, judging him as a dirty snitch working undercover."

"Only, he hadn't snitched, had he?"

"On the contrary. He'd been all in. When Murphy found out, he went to try and stop him. When backup arrived, Murphy took the blame for them being caught up in the gunplay and covered for his partner's going rogue."

"Why did they blame Murphy?"

"Word was, there was a dirty cop. Since Tarner died, he became the hero, so that left Murphy looking bad. Thankfully, there was no proof. Based on his exemplary record, the big shots ruled in his favor, kept him on the payroll, but let's just say, they wanted to teach him a lesson by making his life hellish."

Kayti understood now why so many of the office personnel shot dirty looks in Murphy's direction, but only when his back was turned. It was the older staff who kept their feelings hidden and showed him the respect he'd earned. "See, I don't doubt that explanation at all. But why would he take the blame?"

"Because his partner has two kids and a wife who loved and looked up to him. Murphy wouldn't let them suffer the disgrace of knowing their guy was bad."

"So, he wore the sin."

"Uh huh. He never divulged Tarner's role. I only found out from another case where they closed in on an illegal poker game with huge stakes. The man who ran the game liked to talk. He's the one who blabbed about a player he knew was law enforcement. It seems this agent had the worst luck he'd ever seen. When I questioned him with a photo, he corroborated it was Tarner."

"And you chose not to clear Murphy because…?"

"Because he'd made the decision to protect Tarner's family. I respected him for that. Instead, I asked for him to be transferred to my personal team."

Kayti hugged her aunt one more time. All she said was, "It reinforces the instinct I had to trust him completely."

"Hey, that's why I assigned him to work with you. I wanted you to learn from the best. Plus, I knew he'd keep you safe or die trying."

CHAPTER 44

Kayti's thoughts were filled with the story her aunt had shared. With her mind in the clouds, she didn't notice the scuff marks on her welcome mat, nor the faint mud tracks on the floor until she'd entered the apartment and started toward her bedroom.

It was the scent of the person that stopped her, the smell of an unwashed body, and the distinct odor of fear.

She slowed her walk and began using the rest of her senses to distinguish how much danger lay waiting. Her heart raced ahead of her wits, and her stomach took a dive. Clenching her jaw, she slowly began to reach for her weapon. Just as she had it in hand, a whiny voice begged, "Don't be mad."

She whipped around to see a small person

sitting on the floor, his back against the wall, his body outlined by the light filtering in from the window.

Immediately, she recognized the kid who'd had a rubber gun in her back at Vinnie's store. "How did you get in here?" She spoke quietly so as not to spook her visitor.

"My pa taught me how to use a credit card on some locks and it worked on yours."

Seriously? Blasted building was older than silent movies, but you'd think they'd renovate certain outdated thingamajigs such as door locks.

"And you came to me, why? Weren't they going to hold you in juvie?"

"They talked about a foster home. Man, I've been in those places before. As bad as my pa was, some of those joints were worse."

"So, you ran away?"

"No. I came to you. I have your phone. I was bringing it back."

"Except you broke into my apartment."

"The people around here are very nervous

having a black kid like me hanging around outside. The cops showed up more than once. I had nowhere else to go. I had to wait for you to come back, and this seemed the safest place."

"Uh huh…"

"Are you mad?"

"That you brought back my phone? Nope, I'm glad. That you broke into my home? I guess in a crazy way it makes sense. That I could have shot your ass for intruding? Now that scares the bejesus out of me, kid."

"You wouldn't hurt me. I knew you wouldn't."

"How so?"

"You're the only person in my life who's ever stood up for me. You went against my dad. The guy who's twice your size and mean as hell. Yet you took a lickin' to stop him from hurtin' me."

Having said his piece, tears appeared in the kid's eyes, proving the thought of another person concerned about his safety made him emotional.

"Your dad beat you a lot, I saw the bruises

that night. I couldn't let him do it again. Dammit, I see fresh ones on your face now."

"Yeah, he took his meanness out on me all the time. I couldn't fight back."

"Yet you did in the end."

"I did?"

"You got him arrested."

"Only 'cause he'd looked up your address and had plans to come back to git you. First, we was going to hit a 7-Eleven. Then he wanted revenge for you standin' up to him, smashin' him with the Coke cans. That truly pissed him off. You almost got us caught."

"He needed to be stopped. You robbed a hard-working man. Vinnie works long, exhausting hours to keep that store open. It's not fair for people like you and your dad to come along and take what's rightfully his."

Head lowered; the kid nodded. "I know that."

"What happened after he had my phone?"

"I tried talkin' him out of his crazy ideas to

git you. He got mad and beat me, got drunk and passed out. That's when I stole the phone away from him. When he woke up and decided to hit the 7-Eleven, I called 911 and set him up. The police were happy to git him off the streets. That's what they told me."

"You did a good thing. But there's one huge problem."

The boy's chin dropped to his chest like a beaten puppy might do after getting chastised. "I'm in trouble because I'm bad."

"On the contrary. You're a good kid. My problem is, I don't know your name. I could call you what's-his-name, but it seems kind of disrespectful after you saved me from a man who terrified you."

"You ain't mad?"

"Nope. I'm grateful. And, if you want to hang out with me for a while until we can get you settled, I'd be honored to have you."

That did it! Now his eyes filled and overflowed. Shyly, he looked at her and then down again. "You have a-a nice voice, so ahh… so nice. I dreamed of your voice."

Touched beyond measure, Kayti went to sit on the floor next to the kid. At first, she leaned against him, her arm close to his, waiting until he'd gained control. "Don't cry, pal. You and I are going to be good friends."

"I hate crying. I do it a lot. My pa says it's 'cause I'm a puny sissy."

After hearing those words, Kayti couldn't stop herself. She wrapped her arm around him, ignoring his stiffness. "You're no sissy pal, just too full of sadness to keep it all inside." Not caring that she was repeating her promise it slipped out again. "You and I are going to be good friends. But I do need to call you something."

"My dad mostly called me little asshole." A shudder rippled through his slight body. "My real name is Marcel. I don't like it."

"Fine, how about we change it to Mark?" He thought for a few seconds while she waited patiently.

"I like that, it sounds like a name for a strong dude. Mark. Yeah." Very slightly, she felt him yield and lean into her. "I know your name is Katherine Edwards and you're an FBI agent."

"Uh huh. But my friends call me Kayti."

"Can I call you Kayti?"

She felt him draw in a breath and hold it. *He's terrified to be repulsed. It's probably all he's ever known.* "I'd like that, Mark."

He sighed his relief, and she reached out her hand, not in the normal way one would shake another's hand, but as a pal sealing a deal.

Still hesitating, Mark reached out and very slowly let her wrap her fingers around his. She grasped his hand firmly, and then shook as if making a deal. "I'll be good to you, my friend, as long as you remain trustworthy. I expect you to treat me the same, and one day, I'll be dancing at your wedding."

She heard him chuckle, and it made her happy. But what made her heart sing was the tightening of his fingers clinging to hers. It made her wonder if it was the first time in his life where someone had treated him gently.

Suddenly, the doorbell rang. She had to get up to answer it. With a last squeeze of his hand, she rose and did so. First, she checked the peephole and then stood back after swinging the door open.

"Hey, Mr. Baldwin. What's up?"

"I just wanted to warn you about a black kid hanging around here lately. I caught him inside the building, near your door. When I asked him what he wanted, he said he had business with you. I figured more'n likely monkey business. I shooed him away. I hope that's okay."

"Actually, Mark came a long way to find me, but he's here with me now. He's a very good friend, Mr. Baldwin. I'm happy to have him visit. Fact is, he'll be around for a while."

"Oh, man, I'm sorry, Agent Edwards. I guess I took it for granted he was up to no good by his appearance. Kid looks disreputable, you know what I mean?"

"As I said, it's been a long journey for him,

leaving behind his old life for a new one. We'll get him fixed up in no time. Thanks for your courtesy and checking with me. Merry Christmas, Mr. Baldwin."

"Merry Christmas to you too, Agent Edwards."

Kayti thought about her words to the building manager and knew them to be true. "You can come out, Mark. Don't worry about Mr. Baldwin. I cleared you with him. What we need to do now is get you cleaned up and fed. How about you go in and take a shower while I get some breakfast ready. All I can do is eggs and toast. That work for you?"

When Mark came close to her, but didn't answer, she knew something was up.

"Tell me."

"I have no other clothes."

She saw the state of the rags he wore and understood. No one would want to get cleaned up and have to dress back in those dirty scraps.

"Will you be offended if I offer some old

sweats I wore in Quantico. Both the men and women wore the same ones during exercises so they're a unisex style. I figure they'll fit you fine. You're almost my size." Not wanting to discuss underwear, she figured he'd manage going commando until they could get him some proper duds. She searched for the gray sweatshirt that went with the pants and handed them over.

His face lit up. He carried them like he'd just been handed an extremely precious package.

Soon, she also grabbed a quick shower in her ensuite. With no time for a major breakdown, a few tears escaped before she could shut off her inner tap.

Having that skinny, scrawny, love-starved kid care enough about her to go against his wicked father, made her thank God she'd tried to stop the punishment.

Once tidy, she met up with him and headed to the kitchen. The kid was quite a looker under all that grime and bruising. His eyes were slightly slanted, elongated enough to create a dreamy appearance the girls would one day go crazy over.

His hair, though long and shaggy now, once trimmed, the natural curl would show off a nicely shaped face.

Surprisingly, her shrunken clothes fit him good enough for now. The faded light gray gave them the appearance of sweats well used… which they were. The only label showing was the Quantico emblem.

Once the food was on the table, she watched as he tried eating with manners. Seeing this hungry kid holding back, trying to impress her, almost opened the taps again.

"Mark, I have to get back to Headquarters. We're on a case right now, a kidnapping of a sixteen-year-old girl who we need to find as soon as possible, Her time's running out."

"Okay." He sounded whipped, the sad tone clear.

"I hate to leave you here alone, but I have no choice."

This time his eyes swung her way. Shock

made the pupils huge. "You want me to stay *here*?" The emphasis on the last word was telling.

"Of course, where else would you go? Back to the streets? It's freezing out there, and it's been snowing a bit. If the phone rings, answer if my name shows in the caller ID. I'll call and check in with you."

"Kayti. You really think you should leave me here alone?" The apprehension in his voice soothed any misgivings she had.

"Yes. That's if you're okay with being left."

"Why are you trusting me?"

"Is there any reason I shouldn't? Will you do something that'll make me regret this?"

"Hell, no! I just don't understand."

"What don't you understand?"

"Why you're being so nice to me?"

"Because you saved me from having to deal with your asshole of a father. He might have hurt me or worse, killed me… if you hadn't come to my rescue."

"So, it's 'cause you owe me?"

"A bit. Mostly it's because I like you… so I trust you."

Tears again globbed in his eyes before he turned away and muttered, "I won't let you down."

Moved and not wanting to embarrass the boy, Kayti pulled on her jacket, making sure her holster wouldn't be noticeable. Then she tucked her cellphone into the pocket and felt something inside.

Pulling out a strange card, she remembered the woman at the bar the night before shoving it into her hands before she left with her husband. A kind of awareness hit her. She had no doubt this mattered.

Excitement blasted through her. She turned to Mark and before he knew she would, she gave him a quick hug… released him as quickly. Waving, she headed for her car and privacy to make a call.

CHAPTER 45

"Hello."

"Hi, this is Agent Edwards calling. You passed me your card last night. I got the feeling you wanted to talk."

"Have you found Misti yet, the girl on TV who was kidnapped?"

"No, and time is running out. If you have any information—"

Interrupting Kayti, the other woman's voice meant business. "We have to talk. Can you meet me at a restaurant near the bank I work at?"

"Of course, where is it?"

Once Kayti realized it was only a few miles away, she arranged to meet with Roni Johnston, the name showing on the bank's business card in ten minutes.

"My lunch break just started so I'm on my way."

"Good, me too. See you soon."

Recognition hit them both at the same time. Kayti entered to see Roni craning her neck, watching so she could wave her over. She slipped into the booth across from the middle-aged woman, held out her hand and smiled.

"I'm Special Agent Katherine Edwards. Thank you for reaching out last night."

"Katherine? That was my mother's name. It's a good sign. I've been hoping you might not call, but I knew what I have to say might help get that poor girl home, so it needed to be shared. Then after your man had words with my Nate last night and punched him in the stomach – though he had it coming, he swung first – I almost decided that if you called, I'd flip you off. Now, I'm glad we're meeting."

Her man punched Nate? Huh!?

Concentrating on what was important, Kayti started right into the subject at hand. "If you have anything that might help us find Misti, you'll be doing the right thing. You know that. Senator Bond has posted a reward for any information that might lead to her rescue."

"A reward. I didn't know. That's not why I gave you my card."

"Makes your statement all the more valuable. Thank you for reaching out."

While Kayti waited impatiently, Roni gathered her thoughts. "Okay, so I was at that bar a few weeks ago with some lady friends. Nate doesn't know we stopped there for a beer; he wouldn't approve."

"Then I won't tell him."

Roni's relief shone through her embarrassment. She took a sip of her coffee that arrived with the menus and started, "You know the area where they have that small hallway before you enter the washroom?"

Kayti thought for a minute and the memory of her being there came to mind. "Yes."

"Well, I'd just gone to the toilet, and the zipper on my pants let go. While I fiddled with it, I was behind there and heard two men talking. They were sitting at the table nearest the wall. At first, I thought they were describing a TV show, they sounded like a couple of crazies. They said how they would hold the girl in the bathroom, then keep her high so she didn't give them any trouble."

All ears, Kayti stopped her and asked, "Can I share this conversation, Roni, kind of like what folks do on WhatsApp?"

"I don't know what that means."

"It's a business app on my phone where we can have more than one person on a call."

"You have to?"

"I want to include my partner."

"Oh! Okay."

Kayti inwardly glowed when Murphy answered on the first ring. "Where are you, Kayti? Tell me you weren't in another car accident."

"Seriously? No. I'm calling because I have something important. You need to listen now." Kayti couldn't help the pissy tone. She looked across at Roni and jokingly raised her eyebrows and smiled when Roni rolled hers in sympathy.

"I'm here with one of the women from the bar last night, Roni Johnston. She gave me her card so I could contact her. I want you to hear her testimony."

Kayti smiled reassuringly at Roni. "Can you start again where you overheard two men talking?"

"Okay. They both had accents, one was more distinct than the other. Russian, I'm thinking. They said as how they would hold the girl in the bathroom, then keep her high so she didn't give them any trouble."

"I bet that caught your attention."

"Like I said, I thought it was a script for a play. One of the men talked like the boss, giving orders. He told the other fellow he'd be sending along one of his own men to help look after the place in case they had any trouble."

"Is this the boss?" Kayti opened to Draper's photo… his mug shot.

"No, that's Serge. I took a quick peek. The guy I saw with him was much more polished, looked rich, lots of gold on his fingers and a crazy expensive watch."

"Did they say anything about where they would be holding her?"

"That's just it. They talked about the cabin. It had everything, plus privacy."

"A cabin? Like at a lake?"

"I got the feeling that yes, it would be near a lake because the one guy, Serge I think, sounded disgusted. Talked about there being nothing to do but fish while they waited for things to kick in."

"You say they mentioned keeping the girl in the bathroom."

"Yes, that they could hold her in there and she'd look after her own ahh... toilet needs, my words, their meaning." Roni sneered at whatever was actually said. Kayti had no doubt it was crude.

"That means there'd be two bathrooms, so not too small a cabin. Did he give any directions or addresses? Anything?"

"The boss said it was only an hour from there, which I took to mean where they were at the time... the bar. Then Serge complained, saying, *yeah - right into the wilderness where they'd gotten dumps of snow.*"

"Snow. Northern Virginia had a dump of snow last week. I saw it on the news."

Murphy answered, "Okay, I'll get the guys here working on lake areas about an hour's drive from the bar. Maybe they can come up with some locations we can start researching."

"Is there anything else, Roni. Anything else they mentioned?"

"Yes, the boss said as how they were to keep the girl safe. They wanted the job done quickly and cleanly. No accidents, no messing with the girl. He wanted to walk away without complications." Roni stopped there and the look on her face let Kayti know she was thinking back to that night. "Then someone started to push away from the table. I came out so I could get a look at the kind of man who talked like that. Clothes can tell a lot about a person and this man looked like a professional, you know, suit and tie. Expensive."

Murphy spoke, his curiosity apparent. "You

said *they* wanted the job done cleanly? Must mean he had orders from someone over him. I'm sending you the photo with Viktor Baranov and Serge having lunch. Maybe this is the person Ms. Johnston saw that night."

Seconds later, the photo arrived, and Kayti held up her phone. "Is this the other man?"

"I think so. I only got that quick peek at his profile. When he walked away, I mostly saw his back. I can't be sure."

"Don't worry. You've been a tremendous help. I just have to ask what you would have done with this information if I hadn't come up to you in the bar?"

"That's what me and Nate were arguing about when you approached. He wanted me to keep my mouth shut and stay the hell out of the situation. He hates cops and wanted nothing to do with the law. But I don't agree. You couldn't see what was happening, but when you came to over to us, he had my hand under the table, squeezing it, warning me to shut up."

Kayti didn't try to hide the disgust she felt. "He's your man, your choice, but I'm thinking a nice lady like you could do better. Sorry. None of my business. Anything else?"

Looking thoughtful, Roni shook her head. "No. I've been thinking about the conversation so I wouldn't forget it. That's pretty much everything. After the boss left, Serge went over to the men's table and joined them like he usually did."

"Do you remember the exact date." Murphy's voice came clearly through the speaker.

"Yes, it was December 15th, the night of the bank's Christmas party. They had a live band that night and one of the girls heard it was better than most. It's why we were there."

Murphy spoke again. "Agent Edwards, do you want me to pick you up at the restaurant?"

"No. I think I'll head out to Fairfax County. I believe they suffered the worst of the storm. I'll meet you there. I'll let you know when I arrive." She closed off the call before he could argue.

"Thank you, Roni. For your help and for

being a conscientious citizen. You might be instrumental in saving a young girl's life."

CHAPTER 46

Kayti called Mark the minute she got back to her car to warn him she'd be out of town for a while and to make sure he'd settled in.

"Hi, Mark. How's everything there?"

"Yo, Kayti. I'm good. I'm watchin' TV."

"If you get bored, I have a Samsung tablet in the kitchen you can mess around with. There's nothing personal on it, haven't had time to set it up yet. I figured if you could get into my phone, you must have some skills."

She heard him chuckle. "Yeah, I have a knack with those things. A foster mother taught me some stuff."

From the disgust in his voice, Kayti had to suspect she'd taught him more than working with a computer. "I'm calling because I'll be heading to Fairfax County for some time. Just wanted to make sure things were cool there."

"Fairfax County. I have an uncle lives there. We spent some time with him last summer, till he kicked us the hell outta there when my old pa kept drinkin' all his booze."

Interest flared and Kayti broke in, "Do you know the lake district up there?"

"Sure, Uncle Sid owned a fish and tackle shop. It's a run-down old store where he makes his own lures and sells incidentals and convenience food to the cabin owners. He had rooms in the back."

Thinking quickly, Kayti asked, "You up for a ride to Fairfax with me. I have reason to believe that a sixteen-year-old kidnapped girl I was telling you about might be held in a cabin somewhere in Fairfax County, somewhere near a lake."

"You mean Misti Bond? The Senator's daughter they talkin' 'bout on TV?"

"Yes. I'm ten minutes away from you, and I'm leaving now."

"I'll be waitin' for you outside."

At first, when Kayti pulled up in front of the

apartment building, she didn't see Mark. Not until she stopped, and he popped out from behind the bush in front of the building. He jumped into the front seat beside her, his ragged old jacket looking cleaner than the last time she'd seen it.

As if he saw her surprise, he lowered his head and admitted, "Hope you don' mind. I used your washer and dryer so's I could clean my jacket."

"Mind? Of course not. You did good thinking about it. I'm glad."

"Me too. It stunk bad from my pa spillin' his whiskey on the sleeve. Then he got sick all over me. I washed it twice."

"Good thinking. As soon as we get time, I think Santa might come early and take you shopping for some new clothes,"

"Look out!"

Kayti slammed on her brakes and stopped two inches from the bumper ahead of hers.

Mark waved his hand toward the front of the car. "I know that guy stopped fast, but you almost hit him."

"Sorry, I shouldn't be watching you when I'm driving in so much traffic. There's a lot of crazies on the road. Lately, it seems to be worse."

Mark sucked in his breath. "Kayti, that guy has his turn signal on. He wants to cut into traffic… Kay-ti!" The second Kayti sounded loud. Very loud. "Okay, so he'll have to come behind us."

"I'm sorry, Mark. I get nervous driving when there's so many aggressive drivers on the road."

"Maybe, it's because you're not going the speed limit. Here's the turn-off. If we go this way, we'll be on side streets away from the main highway."

The little screech he made when she turned might have seemed funny if the boy hadn't curled into a fetal position with his hands over his head.

"Are you messing with me?" Kayti's short fuse lit. Her nerves were kicking in. She didn't appreciate Mark's antics. His yelp really messed with her. She started feeling strung out. "What are you doing?"

"Hiding my eyes. You cut that guy off."

"What guy?"

Mark stared at her strangely. "The guy in the left-hand turnin' lane who had the right of way. The guy who cussed you out and gave you the finger."

"Oh."

"You didn't see him."

"Of course, I did."

"Not in time."

"What're you trying to say?"

"You need glasses."

"Me? Glasses?" Like a motion picture reel unwinding, Kayti saw incident after incident where she got into situations, ending in accidents with everyone accusing her of wrongdoing. Could it be as simple as getting a prescription for glasses?

"You figure?"

"Kayti. It's so obvious, I don't understand why you never figured it out yourself."

"Because, if there's a problem, I think it's a peripheral thing. I believe I can see fine if I look straight ahead."

"No, you can't. You tailgate so you don't see how close you are to the cars in front of you. Like right now, you're just two feet off the guy's bumper, and he's gettin' mighty pis-mad about it."

"Damn. Am I really? He looks further ahead to me." Shaken, she pulled to the side of the road and put the car in park. "I'm sorry, Mark. You're the only person who's been in my car… who noticed it."

"How many people drive with you and keep their eyes open?" Mark's voice could be teasing, she didn't know for sure.

"You messing with me?" She smiled to take the sting out of the question.

"Yeah. A little." Weakly he added, "But we still have a ways to go, and I can't drive. I guess you're stuck behind the wheel."

"How about if you warn me when you see a possible problem?"

"Will you freak out?"

"No! God, no. Your life's at risk here too.

Okay, you be my co-pilot, and I'll back off more to compensate. We'll get there safely."

In no time, they pulled into the outskirts of Fairfax and headed north to the area past Great Falls where they'd recently suffered a big snowfall. As they neared the town where Mark's uncle lived, vehicles driving toward them were still packing snow.

"How long has your Uncle Sid lived here, Mark?"

"This is where my pa's family grew up. I figure he's been here most of his life."

"Would you want to live here with him while your dad's incarcerated?"

"I'd rather crawl naked through a high school hallway."

Laughing, pleased to find that Mark had a sense of humor, she said, "Okay, no mention of him taking you in."

"Thanks. But you won't have to worry about that. He'd as soon kick my black ass into the river than have me live with him."

"Good thing I don't feel that way. Not yet anyway. Until we get you settled where you're safe and happy, we'll stick together."

"I'm happy when I'm with you." This time his voice came out so low, she had to strain to hear the words. When she did, her heart skipped a beat, and she started picturing her life with the boy in it.

Funny thing, it didn't look weird or seem wrong. The car phone rang. Hearing Murphy's voice gave her a thrill, a warm feeling that spread all over her body. "Kayti, did you get there okay?"

"Yes. I'm fine. Anything new?"

"Not really. The Senator's conference is set for four-thirty. Who's in the car with you?"

"How did you know?"

"I can hear someone sniffling."

"It's Mark. He has a cold from sleeping outside last night."

"Mark?"

"The kid whose dad held up Vinnie's. It's a long story. Did you figure out where they might be holding Misti? The time is running out. It's after two."

"Tell me about it. We broke down the snowed-in-area to a radius of about forty miles but have no specific spot for us to focus on. I'm almost at Fairfax. I've reached out to the Fairfax Police Department, and they will be collaborating with us. Why did you bring the kid?"

"He showed up at my apartment to return my phone. I brought him here with me because his uncle owns a fishing store nearby. It's in a small town north of Great Falls, which is where they had the worst of the snow. I wanted to question the man. See if he might have any idea about a cabin close to the lake that's secluded. I'll show him Draper's... I mean Serge and Viktor's photos. Maybe we can catch a break. It shouldn't take me long."

"Keep me in the loop."

"Will do."

"I mean it. Don't go rogue."

"Why would you say that? You're my partner."

"Don't you forget it, doll."

CHAPTER 47

Murphy hated being separated from Kayti. His protectiveness kicked in and knowing she was driving; his nerves were rattled. He'd give anything if she was next to him in his car… safe, even yapping.

How the fuck that girl hadn't killed herself behind the wheel must be pure luck or good karma? He had to get her to see the reality of her incompetence. Suffering from being a realist, he figured it was only a matter of time. And the thought of her being hurt, or worse, dead, made the bile rise. It was unthinkable.

Unwilling to continue being negative, he switched his mind to ponder something else. Automatically, his thoughts flew to where they'd spent quality time.

Waking up in the morning with her naked, snuggled in his arms had been the sweetest moment in his life. The way she had of giving her all, holding nothing back was magical and drew a sigh from him.

He remembered when they first met, nicknaming her the Yapper. A grin formed. She'd stopped that aggravating bullshit, thank God. Must be she knew him now and figured out it irritated him.

Deep into the feel of her satin skin, her thick sexy-smelling hair, and her soft lips, he almost ran off the road himself. Words slapped at him that had him chuckling. *Jesus, and you're worried about Kayti's driving?*

He pulled into the Fairfax County police parking lot and headed inside to meet up with a detective the Chief had assigned to work with him, Detective Simmons. Walking toward the huge red brick structure, he appreciated the stunning white pillars in front.

Inside the large building, he noticed the swirling wooden upper balconies, and the spaciousness that added to the feeling of this being anything but a police station. Heading toward the uniformed man close by, he asked where he could find Detective Simmons.

Following directions, he knocked on the office door and was told to enter. A mid-thirties, good looker stood to shake hands and offered him a seat.

Not too surprised to find a woman in the office, he nevertheless became annoyed when she wavered on his questioning her for information.

"Hey, my boss, Special Agent in Charge, Edna Kale phoned ahead to Chief Shale. He said you'd be more than happy to assist in this situation."

"And I am helping you with any material that seems useful. I asked around for knowledge of the lake districts, and my officers all admit that without more facts, your cabin could be found in a number of places. We're at a disadvantage here. You haven't given us much to go on."

"Hell lady, if I had more, you'd be the one I'd share it with. It's all we know. Surely, there are lakes that are more popular fishing spots, full of enthusiastic fishermen. Those wouldn't be interesting to us. We're looking for secluded areas, cabins on lakes that are off the main roads. That should rule out some regions."

"Of course, let's head into the main office where we've set up some maps we can study."

When they stopped in a big room filled with desks, uniformed men and women all busy, computers on desks piled high, the Chief appeared to welcome Murphy.

"Chief Philip Shale, happy to be of assistance. Anything you need, Agent Murphy. Edna explained the timeline to me, and I agree that poor girl is in terrible danger. We have to move as quickly as we can."

"Thanks. You're right. I was just explaining to Detective Simmons that we can rule out areas more populated and focus on places off the beaten track. One thing I do know, it's not a shack. The cabin has two bathrooms. I doubt if there's any cable or Wi-Fi. In a discussion that a witness overheard, she said the man holding Senator Bond's daughter was disgusted because according to him, all they could do for entertainment was fish."

"Well, using those parameters, we still have many areas to investigate. I've sent patrol cars out to a number of the places, but so far, no luck."

They continued discussing their options, and Murphy could almost feel the seconds ticking by as if they were entwined with his heartbeats.

The fact that Kayti hadn't called back also irked him. She'd promised to keep him in the loop. An hour had streaked by since they'd talked. He could kick himself for not getting more of an explanation from her of where she was heading. At least the name of the town.

He tried her number again and got upset when it went to voice mail for the second time. "Call me, Kayti." It was all he could say without his voice wavering with worry.

They continued to rule out areas on the map until there were only three left. Unfortunately, they were large and would take a lot of time to search each area for solitary cabins that might fit the flawed description.

His phone's buzz produced relief he hadn't imagined he'd ever feel. The satisfaction lasted only a few seconds after he saw the caller ID and it wasn't Kayti's.

"Yeah, Murphy here."

"Is Kayti with you?" Agent Kale's abrupt voice meant business. "I'm trying to reach her. She must have shut her phone off. My message is going to her voice mail."

"No, she's checking out a lead. She arrived before me."

"Not sure I like the sound of that."

"What?"

"The worry I hear in your voice."

"Jesus, Boss, she drives like a maniac. Just knowing she's behind the wheel scares the crap out of me. What's up?"

"Did you know she sent in a mud sample from the vehicle where they stashed Gina's body?"

"No. I didn't. They'd have sent it to the lab

as protocol, right?"

"Sure. Of course. But Kayti asked for a rush on it, and the results came through. This specific mud has a lot of clay and isn't found just anywhere. I know the approximate location of the cabin. There's a town called Bantam. It's north from where you are, past Great Falls."

"I'm on my way."

Murphy headed for the doorway giving instructions to Chief Shale as he hurried. "The place we're looking for is Bantam. I'm on my way there now. Send me any information you come up with for a cabin by the lake that fit's our description."

"Okay. We'll be right behind you."

Murphy drove like a madman, his heart thumping so hard, it scared him. Taking deep breaths, he concentrated on keeping his cool.

He hoped Kayti had been heading anywhere but there. Just the thought of her in danger made him physically ill.

A call came through. Thanking God when he saw her name, he pushed the button on his navigation system and heard a strange voice, young and scared with tears making it hard to hear.

"Mark? Is that you?"

"Yeah. I done what Kayti said. To call you after she left to explore, to see if she could find Misti. I couldn't get any signal for a long time. She's still not back. I heard them yellin' from the cabin. I—I'm scared for her."

"Look, kid. Just give me directions. Where are you?"

"North of Bantam. My uncle calls it the main artery from the lakefront. It's about 2 miles in from the highway. Go through town on the main street and keep going until you see the sign on the left for Holiday cabins. Turn in there. We checked out the first two, and they was empty, but the last one had people stayin' there. Kayti went to investigate."

"I'll be with you in a few minutes, Mark. I need to call in these directions. I'll phone you back right away. Stay hidden, you hear me?"

"Sorry. Gotta go. There's more screamin'.

This time, I think it's Kayti."

CHAPTER 48

Kayti couldn't believe that such a miserable character ever made enough sales to keep his store afloat. She'd have driven miles out of her way just so she didn't have to deal with the bat-shit crazy old prick. No wonder Mark wouldn't want to move in with his uncle.

"Look, we're not here to make trouble."

"Trouble follows that boy and his father like shadows. I don' want nothing to do wit them no more. My own brother, he stole from me when they left the last time. No way I'm having them back to do it agin."

"Well rest at ease. Mark's living with me now, and he won't be moving here. All we need from you is some information."

"You want him living in your house? He's a sneaky little shit, all eyes, never says nothing, creeps around the place… gave me the willies."

"Blame his father for that. Have you seen the story on TV about a young teenager, sixteen to be exact, who was recently kidnapped?"

"I got no TV. Wouldn't watch the idiot box even if I had me one. I listen to the radio, so yeah, I heard."

"I have reason to believe she might be near here, held in a cabin close by this lake." Kayti opened the photos showing Draper and then Viktor. "Ever seen either of these two men?"

Sid held the phone real close until it almost brushed his scraggly gray beard.

Kayti pulled it away and with a swipe of her fingers enlarged the image. "Is this better?" She handed it back to him and watched the recognition light up his beady, bloodshot eyes.

"Yep, that's the one." He pointed at Draper. With a sneer in his grumpy voice, he admitted, "That's the bastid who took one of my best lures and refused to pay the price. Said as how they wasn't worth more'n five bucks. That's all he left."

"When did this happen?"

"What's it to you?"

Kayti had enough of the vile creep's nonsense. She moved her jacket aside and showed him her badge. "I'm Agent Edwards and if you don't cooperate, I'll make it my mission to get you placed in a cell next to your asshole of a brother for obstruction of justice. So fuckie, don't mess with me, not when there's a young girl's life hanging in the balance."

Kayti saw the shock on Mark's face before the grin showed up that he turned away to hide. She also saw the disgust on Sid's face before he shrugged.

"I ain't messin with no cops. He's in one of the Holiday cabins on the right side of the lake, a ways back to town."

"Do you know which cabin?"

"Nah. All's I know, the guy's a thief. If you see him, arrest him and you can tell him Sid sent you."

Kayti headed back to the car with Mark trailing. "Did you see a sign back there for Holiday cabins?"

"Sure, didn't you?" He looked her way and added, "Forget I asked. Of course, you didn't. Just return to the main road and go back about a mile. I'll let you know when it's close so you can turn in."

They parked at the main entrance and decided to walk in from there. The first place looked vacant, as if no one had been living there for some time. She went back to get the car, and they proceeded further until they saw the outline of another dark building.

Again, she parked a short walk from the place. "Stay here. It looks empty, but I'll go check to make sure." As she walked closer, she noticed the night closing in and knew that time was no longer on their side.

Glancing at her phone, she saw it was four thirty-five. The trees blocked whatever daylight was left and made it seem later.

Good Lord! She prayed she'd find Misti in the final cabin on this lane because this place was also deserted. Returning to the car, she drove a few miles further. Through the trees, they saw the lights.

She purposely turned the car to face the exit, scraping the front fender against one of the trees. Ignoring Mark's hiss of concern, she passed him the keys. "Keep these in case you need to make a run for it. You can drive enough to get away, right?"

"I guess. What are you going to do?"

A female scream rang out and chilled her to the bone. "I'm going in. Call Murphy and tell him where we are."

CHAPTER 49

Kayti knew fear when she heard it, especially when it rang out in a voice filled with terror. Her senses knew it too because every nerve in her body flashed to full alert. The pulse in her throat throbbed due to her heartbeat's pounding. And her mouth felt like the Sahara.

But the gun in her hands stayed steady. As she closed in on the cabin, keeping low, she crept up the steps and peeked into the window.

What she saw made her sick. A man was dragging young Misti's body on the floor. Her face looked raw, as if he'd hit her, probably to stop her screaming.

He threw her toward the couch and followed with every intention of hurting her. Loosening his belt and undoing his zipper made those intentions clear as hell.

Kayti did a swift reconnaissance of the front

yard, to be sure there was no one else coming. Then she pulled her pick from her pocket and used it on the lock. All the while, she heard the sick bastard inside while Misti whimpered her fear.

"Come on, little one. Be nice to me. Serge is fishing so we only have a few minutes for fun before he comes back. Your time's up now – Daddy came through for you. But you know we can't let you go. You know that, right? Look, if you're nice to me and stop all that yelling, I might be able to let you slip away."

"I'd rather die than have you touch me," Misti screamed the words, and Kayti knew it would be the last time she'd get slapped by that evil prick.

Opening the door, she came up behind him and stood with her gun out in front, held firmly in both hands.

"Let her go, you fucking pervert, or I'll shoot you and aim to kill."

Misti saw her and almost fainted. The rapist clutched his pants closed and slowly turned, his other hand reaching out as if to stop her from shooting. "Where'd you come from?" The Russian accent strongly defined his growly voice. The man was an ugly specimen... scary ugly.

"From FBI Headquarters, Washington. You're under arrest. Get your hands behind your head and kneel on the floor. Do it. Now."

Cruelty stared her in the face. She saw him weigh his options before he began to follow her directions. It was the slight appearance of satisfaction first and the warning scream from Misti that saved her from the barrel of the gun powering down toward her head.

Swiveling, she sensed the weapon before she saw it. Missing her by inches, she tried to step back and keep control of the room, her gun being the weapon she'd prefer to use.

But no luck. The asshole on the floor jumped to his feet and grabbing her arm, he viciously forced it above her head, so her firearm fell to the floor.

Purposely, she screamed her anger in his face, saw him hesitate, and that gave her the opportunity to knee him, unfortunately in the upper thigh. His swerving away in time saved his precious jewels from a shitload of pain. Without missing a beat, her elbow connected to his neck at the same moment that she whirled away so she could aim her foot to his face.

Only that didn't happen because Draper's threatening voice stopped her cold. "One more move, lady, and this sweet little girl won't be seeing her precious daddy again."

Kayti stopped.

"Get over there on the couch and keep her quiet, or I swear I'll let this animal at the both of you."

Hysterical, crying as if her heart was breaking, like a baby seeking protection, Misti tried to crawl on top of Kayti. Frantically, she clung, panic making her irrational.

"Calm down, honey." She peeled away Misti's clinging body. "It's going to be okay." Kayti needed to be able to move quickly. She couldn't if the girl held onto her.

She saw Draper pistol whip the other man and follow that with his foot slamming into the writhing body. "Didn't I tell you to leave her alone? I warned you that I'd kill you, moron."

Thinking to take his mind off killing anyone, Kayti interrupted. "Look here. Senator Bond did as you asked. Bill 539 has been buried. It's no longer on the calendar for this year. Leave us here, and you guys take off. Get to an airport and go back to where you came from."

"It's too late for that. Fucking imbecile here's psychotic. Can't help himself. Likes to kill people. Now we're up to our necks in deep shit." Suddenly, he aimed his gun and fired a bullet into the groveler's chest. "I warned him."

Just then Viktor Baranov burst into the room, a string of fish hanging from his hand. "What the fuck are you doing?" Shock showed by the flare in his dark eyes. He appeared livid. Spitting out another angry fuck, he repeated it a few more times, with each rant his voice growing louder until at the end, he threw the fish away and screamed his fury.

Draper didn't flinch. Cold, sharp... clear-minded, he answered, "You brought that sicko here. He couldn't keep it in his pants. Bah! Now he can. Done!"

"We need to get out of here. Nothing was supposed to happen. I told you no violence. The Kremlin will be furious. We're dead men."

The two were so involved in their plight, neither noticed the boy squirm past them and slide behind the couch, heading straight for the gun lying there.

Kayti noticed. When she felt Misti stiffen, then saw her eyes darting toward Mark, Kayti grabbed her hand to gain her attention.

Her hard look meant business. *Say nothing.*

Misti closed her eyes, tears pouring down her face, but she didn't move.

Draper spoke to Viktor, his voice deadly, his attitude full of disgust for the other's performance. "There's one chance to beat this. I kill everybody, make it look like you fired the gun, and then shot yourself. I'd be a free man."

"You wouldn't."

"And why the hell not."

"We're partners. I'm paying you a lot of money."

"You know what? There's some things money can't buy."

Slowly, Draper turned to aim the gun at Kayti who quickly forced herself in front of Misti. "You don't want to do this, Draper."

"You're right. But there's no choice."

Kayti saw the boy with the gun appear before anyone else. But they heard his shaky, hesitant voice threaten." Drop the gun, mister. You ain't shootin' my Kayti."

When Draper turned to fire in Mark's direction, Kayti launched herself from the couch and tackled the son of a bitch, bringing him to the floor.

That's when Viktor decided he needed Draper's gun and got into the tussle. Two grown men against one small woman, she fought for her life. Mark dropped his gun, tried to help her, and got body slammed against the wall for his trouble.

A roar sounded from the doorway. Murphy, the man making the hideous noise, blasted into the pileup like a mad dog. First, Draper went flying, ass in the air before he landed on his face.

While that happened, Kayti twisted out from under Viktor and used her elbow to get him off her. Next thing she knew, Murphy had Victor in his clutches. The maddened agent picked up the cowering loser like a rag doll, punched him in the stomach, then the face, and watched as the bastard deflated like a pricked balloon.

Meanwhile, Kayti dashed to Mark, the boy lying on the floor who'd stayed out of Murphy's way. Only now he was the only one who saw what was about to happen.

Shocking Kayti who'd leaned over him, he pushed her out of the way and angled himself to cover where she'd been. It was his small body that caught the bullet meant for her. And it was Murphy who shot the man on the floor that had picked up Kayti's fallen gun.

"Mark! My God, Murphy. Mark's been shot."

Murphy grabbed her first and made sure the blood on her face wasn't her own before he gently put her aside and crouched by the boy. "It's a shoulder wound, Kayti. Stop crying. He'll be fine."

"I'm not crying." Kayti swiped at her face and cleaned up the mess. "I'm an FBI agent. We don't cry." She took back her place next to Mark and removed her jacket to take off her T-shirt. She'd use if as a bandage and stop the bleeding.

Folding the soft white material, she placed it over the wound and pressed down carefully. Gently, she caressed his forehead, moving the hair away so she could put a kiss there.

"I suppose FBI agents don't kiss their snitch's either?"

Furious, she glared at the man. "Mark's no snitch."

"He is if you want to clear his record and get the law to give him an honorable discharge from his old life."

Kayti grinned, catching on. "You're a sneaky devil."

"Damned rights I am. How's Misti?"

Kayti suddenly remembered. She turned around only to see the girl out cold, lying across the couch.

"She passed out. Poor kid. It's too much for her to handle. Almost getting raped, then seeing a man killed and a kid get shot." Kayti shuddered and spoke her thoughts outloud. "It's too much for me too. I'm thinking to change my career."

Murphy lifted her to her feet, his hands framing her face. "I've got an offer you might be interested in, but this is neither the time nor the place." He pressed a hard kiss on her lips, and another before he added, "You might want to cover yourself. I need to keep my mind on the job. And with you showing off that gorgeous body, even a saint would be in trouble."

She gave him a behave yourself push, and he smiled before moving over to Draper who showed signs of coming to. The unexpected punch he landed put Draper back to sleep. And with a satisfied grunt, pulling zip ties from his pocket, he wrapped one around the man's hands and yanked it closed. Then he did the same to Viktor who hadn't moved. Next, he checked to make sure the third dude was dead.

Sirens blasted through the night's quiet, coming closer every second… a sign of help on their way. Holding out his hand, Murphy wiggled his fingers. "Can I have your keys? I need to move your car."

Kayti, back fussing over Mark who'd begun to revive, reached into his pocket, found them, and handed them to Murphy.

That seemed to bring Mark fully awake. "Kayti, you okay?"

"Only because you stole the bullet meant for me. Now you're my hero."

Tears flowed from his beautiful eyes as he tried valiantly not to scream from the pain. "Heros aren't terrified all the time like me. I'm a sissy like my dad says." His voice broke from an overabundance of emotion.

"Then I'm a sissy too, my friend. What happened here tonight scared the poop outta me."

A grin almost made it. Then as if a thought came to him, he added, "Probably when you're driving too."

"Hey, not fair. I can't retaliate when you're injured."

This time, the grin appeared before it became a grimace. He saw Murphy step back inside the cabin and nodded toward him. "*He* scares the hell outta me."

"Who, Murphy? Why he's a pussy cat."

"Good thing I like dogs."

"What's so funny you two?" The pussy cat reached out to hold Mark's head gently. His gruff male voice purred. "Kid, you have my deepest appreciation for what you just did. Anything you want that I can give you… it's yours."

Looking shocked but crafty, biting his lip, Mark answered, "I want Kayti."

CHAPTER 50

The ride in the ambulance was tight. Both Misti and Mark had to be sent to the hospital in the same vehicle so the other ambulance could take in the prisoners.

On the only stretcher, Mark took up a fair space while they'd made Misti as comfortable as possible on a wheelchair type apparatus. With Kayti between them, and the attendant at the front dealing with hooking Mark up to IVs and properly bandaging his wound, the vehicle was full.

Thinking back to when the paramedics had first arrived, Kayti had to admit, it had been tough. Misti had begun to recover, and her first reaction shocked everyone. Screams of terror, the whites of her eyes grotesquely protruding, she started hyperventilating, unable to catch her breath. Flailing around on the couch, falling to the floor, like an animal at bay fighting off the enemy, her hands became claws.

They rushed to her side which made everything worse. It wasn't until she heard Kayti's voice and saw her approach that she settled down. Arms lifted like a baby reaching to be picked up by it's mama, Kayti slid in and gathered her close. The girl settled instantly, clinging, crying rather than the horrible screams, her gasps slowing to almost sounding normal.

Kayti whispered words of comfort. "It's okay, Misti. I'm here, honey."

Misti looked into Kayti's eyes, hers all cloudy, appearing as if she'd suffered an illness. Recognition mingled with relief suddenly and the stiffening of her muscles relaxed.

Kayti spoke low so as not to alarm the girl. Holding her close with one arm, she used her other hand to caress Misti's face. Ignoring the stench of body odor Misti reeked of, she kissed her cheek and petted her like one would do for a person they cared about.

"Misti, these people are with the police and want to help you. We need to get you to the hospital and back to your parents. Will you let them?"

"Daddy?" The girl's voice broke. "I want my daddy."

"Yes, baby. He's on the way to the hospital right now and will probably meet us there. But we need to let this nice lady here settle you into this chair for the ride back to town."

Misti looked at the paramedic and then back at Kayti who nodded her approval. "Come on, sweetheart. Come with Kayti."

Slowly, very carefully, they settled Misti into the chair they would use to transport her to the hospital.

Now, with both Mark and Misti safe, and their needs being taken care of, Kayti held on to Mark's hand while he drifted from the pain medication they'd injected.

Misti also dozed, and Kayti had a feeling it wasn't completely a normal sleep. Before leaving the lake, the attendants had searched the cabin for drugs, and Kayti knew they'd found a stash. No doubt crap they'd been feeding the teen to keep her sedated and less bothersome.

The nurse finished her duties and sat back, smiling at Kayti then reaching for a clipboard where she began to fill in some forms. Using the quiet moment, Kayti relived the earlier nightmare. The chain of events leading up to Murphy arriving at the exact moment she needed him still baffled her. How had he known where they were?

Dealing with the police had kept him at the scene and would probably tie him up for some time. She'd have to wait to catch up with him at the hospital. Hopefully, they'd have time to share their experiences.

A new image formed and started a warm glow throughout her entire body. Together… There was no other place in the world she'd rather be than with him – in his bed, naked and wrapped around his warm body.

The right to touch him and love on him would bring her joy for the rest of her life.

The lights of the hospital woke her from her fantasizing.

CHAPTER 51

Kayti sat beside Misti, keeping her calm for the nurses while they bathed her. They'd taken Mark to surgery to remove the bullet and intended to bring him back to the same room. Due to a staff shortage and knowing their time in the hospital would be short, the administration had agreed to keep them together.

A movement at the door heralded Misti's parents. Senator Bond flew to the bed and gathered his girl close while she clung, hysterical at seeing him again. "Daddy! You're here. I never thought I'd see you again."

"Oh, baby. We came as soon as they told us where you were." Misti's mom seemed to hesitate, looking toward Kayti for reassurance to approach the bed. Kayti sensed there hadn't been a close relationship between mother and daughter, but the girl needed her mother now more than ever.

She stepped toward the closed-in woman and whispered a lie she hoped would be overlooked because of her good intentions, "She called for you, ma'am. She needs you more than ever right now to forgive her."

That did it. Mrs. Bond's face disintegrated into a mass of pain. Tears gushed. Her lower lip wriggled, unsuccessful in holding back her emotions as tiny whimpers escaped. She rushed to the bed and Misti turned to see her coming. "Mama!" Her voice held only delight.

Wanting to give the family some privacy, Kayti moved to the chair in the hallway. Delight filled her when she saw Murphy striding toward her, his wonderful face alight with happiness when he saw her there.

Just before he reached her side, the elevator doors opened, and her Aunt Edna rushed forward. Seeing Kayti, she swept the girl up in a hug that felt wonderful.

"Kayti, this is the last time you can be mixed

up in such a violent case where there're deaths involved. I forbid it. I think I've aged ten years since I got word you'd entered the cabin. Then screams followed and shots were fired and… dammit girl! My old heart can't take it. Either you need to change departments, or I need to take early retirement and join a knitting class."

Kayti laughed as she hugged her aunt back. "You knitting, Aunt Edna? Seriously? I'd love to see that."

She gazed back towards Murphy who'd come to a full stop. The look of shock on his face made her smile. She'd never divulged her relationship with her aunt. Not that she'd purposely concealed the fact from him after they'd gotten close, it just never seemed a good time to share her surprise.

Shaken, he stood back with his arms crossed and his reactions hidden. Wearing a look she'd come to love most, the one where he hid his emotions from everyone. But not from her. For her… he winked, and she knew all was well.

CHAPTER 52

Murphy didn't get surprised by much. Being a realist, a people watcher, and a fairly good judge of character, he often closed cases because of his common sense and practical nature. He understood people followed routines and not often did he get surprised.

So, finding out that Kayti was Kale's niece did a number on him. Watching them interact, he saw the affection and kind of liked knowing Kayti had yet one more person in her world who mattered.

As much as he respected Kale, having a family relationship with the hard-assed woman might be something he'd have to work on. With Kayti's happiness on the line, he'd bloody well do it; take the high road and put up with what he couldn't change.

He backed away from the pretty scene and headed off the doctor who'd looked after the boy.

"Hey, doc. How's Mark?"

"Mark? Oh, the boy in 302. Williams. Right." He opened a page on the tablet in his hands and scrolled down through the information. Then a narrow-eyed look drilled into Murphy and a hard glean appeared. "You family? Maybe his stepdad?"

"Nope, I'm Agent Murphy. I was with the boy earlier when he got shot."

As quickly as the vitriol appeared, it faded, and tiredness returned to the doc's expression. "I gotta tell you, officer. That kid's taken some beatings and not just recently. I've called Social Services. If they don't get him away from his father… says here he's the only family member, that kid won't make it to high school."

"His old man's in jail and won't be coming out for a long time. Guess the kid will be a ward of the court."

"Good. Let's hope they find him a good family. Kid needs a break."

"Yeah, I agree. He was a hero tonight. We need to protect special people like him." Murphy waved to the doctor and carried on to Mark's room when he spied the social worker heading his way. "Hey, Claudine. You here to see about Mark Williams?"

"How did you know? I was here on another case when they called to say the boy was brought in."

"Just a hunch. Look, he's under my custody for now. It's a delicate situation. Any chance you could just leave him with me until the new year. Then I promise I'll get legal foster papers started."

Claudine, a motherly type with a heart of gold and a mind like a legal file cabinet, shook her head. "Come on, Murphy. You know that's not the way we do things. It's not legal."

"Legal schmegal! It's Christmas in two days and the kid just got shot."

"And… the doc says his wound wasn't critical, and they'll release him tomorrow. Because of overcrowded wards and a shortage of nurses, they'll need this room."

Murphy flashed his winning smile, the one that always got him tail whenever he put it to work for him. "You gonna make me beg, doll?"

"Blasted all to hell, Murph. You know I can't take it when you turn on the sweetness. If you hadn't of given my Toby a second chance when you busted him with marijuana, I wouldn't be in this beholden pickle."

"He's a good kid, just ran with the wrong bunch. You straightened him out."

Claudine looked beaten. "Fine. Take the kid. I'm only agreeing because we haven't any foster homes available now anyway. Juvie's a mess, and the shelters are overrun with sad cases. You give that boy a good holiday, then come and see me in January." She reached to give him a hug and Murphy, hating hugs of any kind unless they were from Kayti, sighed and let her close in.

"Thanks, Claudine. Merry Christmas."

Once he had Mark's future settled, he needed to gather all the pertinent information to close this case. But before he did anything, he went to the second floor to check on Talin and Rob.

Approaching the room, he heard something he hadn't for a very long time. Rob, together with Talin, was laughing over some show they watched on TV. He stood in the doorway and let the wash of good feelings happen. His well-protected soft heart couldn't be anything but thrilled seeing them enjoying being together.

Talin spotted him and grinned. "You should see this episode, Murph. Sheldon is making up a rental agreement for Rog to stay for one night."

"Hey, Batman, me and canned laughter ain't happening. Told you that the last time you tried to suck me into watching The Big Bang Theory with you. That's more your dad's style."

Rob chuckled. "Hey, Black. They say I can go home Christmas Eve. Is it okay with you?"

Murphy saw the fear hovering within the pleading look and turned it back to Rob. "What do you want to do?"

"I want you to set me up with that rehab

place you been yammering on about. But could we take me there in the morning on Boxing Day? I'd really like to spend Christmas with my kid. Kinda like it used to be."

Thrilled to the bone, Murphy hid his elation and gruffly added, "Yeah, sure. You just want another one of my home-cooked turkey dinners. Well, that's fine with me. Having Talin as a houseguest is also fine with me. But it looks like I'll be needing some support in the future when I foster a homeless kid called Mark Williams. The kid's close to Talin's age. You guys up for helping?"

Both father and son appeared curious as hell, but knowing Murphy well, they refrained from pestering him with the questions he'd be answering in his own time.

Rob spoke first. "Sure, not a problem. Now I need to ask your advice. The hospital administrator, an old pal of mine from way back, stopped by this morning. He says they need more security people around this place. Seems the company they hired is always on the lookout for retired cops or Private

Eyes. Figures I'd get a job with no trouble, especially if he put in a request, which he's willing to do. Whaddaya think?"

"They willing to wait until you break loose from rehab?"

"Damn sneaky way of asking if I told him about my problems with booze."

"And yet you caught on. Go figure. Maybe you haven't pickled that keen brain of yours."

"Seriously, Black. I need you to tell me." The pained look in Rob's eyes revealed his fear of failure and his need for affirmation.

"Tell you what? Can you do it? Sure you can… with your eyes closed, man. You're one of the best cops who ever worked the beat. Whether you want to do it is another thing. Or if you're well enough to take it on is something you need to answer for yourself."

Rob looked uncomfortable. Then words poured out. "I had an almighty scare recently, even had a checkup. Turns out, I had a chest infection. The right dose of antibiotics, and I'll be fine. I figure it's my last chance at a decent life. For me and my boy. You're fucking right I want this."

"Then we'll help you make it happen. I'll be here to pick you up tomorrow. That'll give you one day to get ready for Christmas."

CHAPTER 53

It seemed to take forever before Kayti saw Murphy again. He finally strolled into Mark's room – his alone now since they'd air-vac'd Misti to Washington. The man leaned over and kissed her like he meant it, and then he turned to Mark. "Hey, kid."

Was he like a dog marking his territory? She loved it no matter why he chose to openly acknowledge their relationship. It tickled her silly when she looked at her guy and knew in her heart of hearts, he'd let her in.

"You're the cop from the cabin. The one who shot the nutcase trying to kill Kayti."

"And the only reason he didn't succeed was because you took her bullet."

"She's my friend." Mark looked sad. "Kinda like my only friend."

"And now you have two."

"Yeah?" Mark appeared skeptical.

"Yeah." Murphy stared him down until she saw the kid accept his word.

"She told me she likes you."

Kayti cut in. "Mark, that's not true."

"Fine, she told me she loves you."

"Mark! You monster. I told you I admired him more than any other person I've ever met is what I told you." She turned to Murphy in time to see him wink at Mark and then see Mark's wide grin in return.

Murphy took her hand and made his sexy voice soothing. "Settle down brat, I admire you in the same way."

Mark piped up, "That's not very romantic, guys. You're supposed to kiss."

Murphy ruffled his head teasingly. "Yeah, well we'll keep that for later when we're alone. For now, I have something to share."

Kayti saw Mark's distress and prayed the news was good. They'd argued earlier when Mark warned her that officials would be after him, and he'd have to go along with them.

Murphy's tone became serious, and he started with words that broke her heart. "Claudine from Social Services was here looking for you."

Mark's eyes filled. He turned her way with a clear message… I told you so.

"I sent her away with the promise that you'd be hanging out with me and Kayti until after the new year. Then I'd be filing foster papers to make that legal. You okay with that arrangement?"

Kayti's heart burst wide open, and joy flooded through the breach. She didn't know who kissed who more – her all over Murphy's face, or Mark on their clasped hands and then shyly her cheek.

Once the excitement settled, Murphy stood and beckoned her to come to him. "You okay here until tomorrow, Marko? I believe they'll be releasing you after lunch. I'll be here to pick you up."

"Sure. I'll be waiting."

Kayti watched Mark's gleeful expression.

Her eyes took in the bandages on his shoulder and the IV where they were feeding him antibiotics. Pride filled her for the boy who'd gone along with everything they'd done to him, no whimpering, no complaining. Just a good kid with a big heart who'd decided she was his.

Well, he was hers now too. And so, when she leaned over to kiss his cheek goodbye, she whispered what was in her heart. "I love you."

From the shining look of adoration and the mouthing of, "Me too," she knew they'd bonded, and it was solid and forever.

CHAPTER 54

After Murphy and Kayti left him, Mark let out the groan he'd been keeping in. The pain in his shoulder had intensified. But he hadn't wanted them to think him a sissy.

In his almost thirteen years, he'd prayed for a woman to look at him with the same softness that Kayti did. When his pa had kicked him that night at Vinnie's, the store he made Mark rob, and had treated him like a dog who didn't matter, Mark took it. Same way he'd taken it all his life. What else was he to do?

The few times he'd run away had been worse. The people on the streets watched for kids like him. They used them and made them do terrible things. At least his pa only beat him, and that wasn't every day. Most times he ignored Mark, which worked just fine.

He'd make himself as small as possible and

try his hardest to stay out of the mean bastard's way. He'd even go to school whenever he could sneak out.

Child Services, the folks who caught up with his dad at the hospital after one of his punches dislocated Mark's shoulder, told his dad he needed to go every day. It wasn't a hardship. He liked learning. He just didn't like the bullying about his clothes, his hair, and most of all, his gutless spine.

But then something happened. The lady saw *him*. She cared. About him. He knew it. The look he'd waited for all his life. The same look he'd seen some of his schoolmates get when their moms came to pick them up.

She even took a beating for him. No one had ever done that before. Tried to get between him and his dad. Tried to save him. His heart, thrashing in agony from fear for her safety, had fallen to her feet that night. He'd spent time imagining the if onlys.

After they ran for it, his pa had started in about finding her address, paying her back for interfering. He'd opened the phone and damned if he hadn't gotten into her contacts. There was her photo next to her own information.

The rotten son of a bitch laid plans for revenge, and for the first time in his life, Mark thought 'hell no'.

Now, laying in the hospital bed, the pain he had to endure was routine, just another day for him.

It was her last words that had swept him away on a wave of bliss. *I love you.* No one had ever said that to him… ever. She made him feel so much he couldn't contain it. The overwhelming emotion caused the tears.

When the nurse came in and saw him crying, she spoke briskly. "It'll be better as soon as the Tylenol kicks in, Mark." She'd given him a box of Kleenex and had even patted his hand before leaving him alone.

She couldn't know these weren't tears from pain. He'd suffered through so much physical pain; he'd rate this a four. They flowed because of the happiness he didn't know how to deal with. He'd never experienced it before, and it was… it was beautiful.

Kayti made him feel like he mattered. His small needy heart had found a home. She was his lady. *Thank you, God. She cares.*

Now Murphy, the man who said he'd be fostering him, he scared Mark… a little. That dude would be no man's fool. Thinking back over the night, Mark sighed and snuggled down. As his tear-filled eyes closed, a last thought snuck in.

Murphy makes me feel safe.

CHAPTER 55

Murphy needed to concentrate on his shopping list for tomorrow's dinner. After bragging as much as he'd done, he'd better make sure they were fed a Christmas meal showing off his best efforts.

After all, it wasn't just a drunk and his kid around the table this year. The next day, he'd be hosting his boss, his new foster son, as well as the woman he couldn't wait to make his own.

Thinking of Kayti, remembering the naked little devil teasing him with her kisses, using her sexy body so he'd let her drive his car to go Christmas Eve shopping, it was all he could do to tell her – and mean it – "not a hope in hell."

Her pout drew kisses that led to more kisses, until he put an end to that nonsense. "Stop taking advantage of me, woman. I have a lot to do today… that's if you want to eat a turkey dinner tomorrow."

She'd quit her provoking immediately and tried to keep a serious face. Then she'd shared her conversation with Mark, about how she might need glasses, which made him extremely happy. Relief bombarded him, which went to prove how much he'd worried about her behind the wheel.

Holding her down on the bed and teasingly brushing his morning beard against her cheek, he got serious for long enough to say, "Darling, go shopping. I'll pay for as many Ubers as you need to use, just be safe and have fun. That's all I ask."

She'd reached up and gently sifted her fingers through his chest hairs before she'd arched upwards to blow at them teasingly. Letting her hand go in order to scratch was not a good move.

That's when she'd flipped them over, coming on top and taking control. Her questions turned him to mush. "Are we always going to be this happy?"

"Always."

"And stay together?"

"Together forever, doll. I'll always do the

best I can to make you as happy as you are right now."

"Me too. Whatever it takes."

"If you're serious, how about looking into a less dangerous career? You'll most likely save me from a heart attack due to stress overload."

She wrapped her arms around him and hugged. "What I said before, I was serious. As for this career, I'm not a tough-ass like you, and that's a job requirement. Being so easily manipulated isn't the best way for an agent to behave. Edna says she's got just the right place for me to switch to within the agency, so you won't have to be a Mr. Doomsday about me anymore."

Unable to express his delight with words, he showed the best way he knew how… of what she meant to him. Which left it later than he'd anticipated for getting his shopping started.

***

He picked up the crew at the hospital and left them in the mall to do their own present buying, slipping Mark a fifty so he wouldn't be left out.

Seeing the joy in the kid's face set his mood up to suffer good-naturedly through his least favorite pastime… shopping. A jewelry store for Kayti, a sportswear shop for Mark and Talin, and the bookstore for Rob finished off the hard stuff.

Touring the supermarket was his secret passion. While enjoying the spree, his thoughts turned to the morning, and he had trouble wiping the silly grin off his face.

Hours later, when he'd returned from the shops loaded with parcels, he got the shock of his life. Kayti had created miracles in his house.

Not only had she given their poor Charlie Brown tree a makeover, so it hung with pretty ornaments and glowed with extra lights, she'd arranged fresh flowers, chocolates, and an amazing number of presents under the tree all wrapped in fancy paper and bows.

The place had never looked so good.

Talin and Rob agreed with him when they all settled in for a night of pizza and movies. Mark just looked stunned and quietly followed Talin's lead. The boys had hit it off, Talin making a concerted effort to be a pal.

Murphy appreciated the way he and Rob sought out Mark's views, including him in everything going on. The kid veered to Kayti less and less as the evening wore on.

Once the pizza arrived and the smells of cheese, pepperoni and mushrooms filtered through the room, he watched everyone fill their plates and was glad he'd made the decision not to cook that night.

He had the big meal to prepare the next day. He wasn't about to be imprisoned in the kitchen tonight. Not when all he wanted to do was sit in his chair with Kayti nestled in his lap. And sneak looks of approval to the Christmas tree.

CHAPTER 56

The incredible smells emanating from the kitchen drew Kayti in there to see a multitude of delicious dishes and a golden bird stacked the island, waiting for the company to arrive.

When they all piled in, the boys headed straight for the food. Murphy laid down the law, threw them some chips and dip to keep them until suppertime and yelled, "Out. No kids allowed in the kitchen. Only beautiful women."

Picking up on his serious tone, Rob ushered the boys in the living room for a game of cards. And he was there to answer the doorbell when Edna arrived.

Flushed, her face red from the stolen kisses Murphy had given her in the kitchen, Kayti rushed out to join the much more presentable old man in welcoming her aunt. "I'm so glad you agreed to share this day with us, Edna." She hugged her warmly. "You can't know how much it means to have my only family around me today."

"It's special for me too Kayti." The sincerity in Edna's shaky voice had Rob offering to take her bakery boxes so he could escape, leaving the two weepy women together.

They chuckled at his obvious getaway which formed a shared moment of humor and made Kayti reach yet again to hug Edna one more time.

Guiding Edna to the room where Murphy was seen wearing a goofy kitty-with-a-gun Christmas apron, a shared gift from Talin and Mark, she approached and stared.

"Don't say it." Murphy's tone was serious yet teasing.

"I was only going to wish you a Merry Christmas and tell you it smells heavenly in here." The fake innocence in her eyes belied her comment.

"That, you can say." Murphy grinned, accepting her retreat.

He poured virgin drinks for the women, Edna already in the picture about their nonalcoholic celebration. And he wasn't at all surprised when the woman's droll voice commented on the ring Kayti flashed around.

After they'd oohed and aahed sufficiently about his good taste in buying three big diamonds rather than one, he agreed that he was in fact a genius and urged them to go to the other room and leave him to finish the meal. They could set up the table.

Once there, Kayti, overcome with emotion, admitted something to Edna she'd never shared with another soul. Somehow it seemed right, and she didn't feel as if Edna would judge her. After all, she knew Kayti's mom too. They had been sisters.

"I thought about my mom a lot recently, Edna, and there's something I need to ask you."

Edna stiffened but her voice was soft. "Sure, what is it?"

"When Mom was sick, dying in fact, I begged her to tell me about my father. As many times as I questioned her, she'd never talk about him. Said it made her sad, and she didn't want to go there. And I could see that it did have that effect on her. Once when I had pushed for more information, she became hysterical, and I backed off. She said she couldn't even think about him. And she added something that made no sense. She said it wasn't her story to tell."

Edna's face turned pale, but she said nothing.

Continuing, Kayti's voice lowered. "I-I caught her with a woman once. Oh, she didn't know I saw her. It was a friend she'd made in the apartment building where we lived. They were kissing, and as young as I was, I knew it wasn't a casual kiss. The woman moved away soon after, and Mom took a long time to be herself again."

"I'm sorry you had to see that. It must have confused you. Did you tell her what you saw?"

"No. But I knew then that she was most probably raped. If she didn't like men, and I never saw her with one, how else would she have gotten pregnant?"

Edna swiftly came to Kayti and wrapped her

arms around her. "Oh no, Kayti. You were created from love, a young girl's love with a young boy who hadn't even started growing a beard yet. Never, ever believe you weren't wanted. Norma knew she couldn't ever be with a man, but she did want a family. Baby, when we lost our parents, I lost my way. I was sixteen and the boy I loved was as mixed up as I was, but he had a big heart and bigger dreams. He's been dead for years, killed while on a mission in Afghanistan, but he cared as much as I did about you."

Kayti felt stunned. "You're my mother."

"Yes... Yes, I am."

"That's why you sent us money and supported us all those years."

"Even then I knew Norma couldn't hold down a good job. She was a bit of a scatterbrain, had no skills... but she was lovable. She'd make a good mom. Not like me, all messed up and no future until you came along. That's when I promised myself to make a good life, have a career. Be smart and get ahead. I knew I had to look after you and Norma both."

Kayti stared at the woman who'd just announced the biggest news she'd likely hear in her lifetime and waited for the pain to hit her. Except there was only huge relief and a lot of joy.

"Why didn't you come forward and share our lives?" Kayti brushed the sudden tears away and waited for the answer she already knew in her heart.

"Because Norma wouldn't stand for it. We made a deal. She made me sign a paper promising to stay away and never, ever tell you the truth."

"Even after she died… You couldn't tell me even then?"

Edna's words burst from frustration mixed with anger. "I was afraid to. You seemed happy with your memories. And if all I could be was your aunt, then, baby, I was willing to take those crumbs and be thankful to have you in my life. But don't ever think I didn't keep tabs on you and know you were happy. You were always on my mind, always."

Suddenly, Murphy appeared with the golden

turkey arranged on a platter, and he stopped dead. His eyes zoomed to Kayti and his manner stiffened. "You okay, doll?"

She looked into her aunt's – mom's – eyes while she replied, "I've never been better."

***

Soon they were sitting at the beautifully decorated table Kayti had arranged... all the people who'd become most dear to her. The festive air made her heart sing, and she reached for Murphy's hand, "Together forever, right?"

He lifted her hand to put a kiss in her palm, and then closed her fingers over the spot. "You got it, doll!"

~*~*~*~

If you enjoyed reading this book, you might like to try the next in the series called *Special Agent Sophia*. I wrote this story for a dear friend who battled stage four cancer, the death of her husband (and years earlier that of a beloved son), and still had enough spirit to come to Rhodes with me for a month's vacation.

Her grit and determination to overcome all obstacles is highlighted in my heroine, Sophia Dunne. It was a privilege to use the same setting we spent so many happy days in, wandering the markets and enjoying the Greek hospitality.

International Amazon Link:

http://mybook.to/specialagentsophia

See Prologue & Chapter One below.

(FREE in Kindle Unlimited)

Prologue

She couldn't breathe.

Every second he ground his body into hers, his savageness destroyed her faith in mankind. Rank breath, scratching beard, and the disgusting panting increased the crushing revulsion and fear she couldn't get past. Shock began to overwhelm her. His hurting hands ripped at her clothes, and the inevitable moment came closer.

Then she saw the whites of his eyes. Delight at the violence of his actions widening them in the darkness. Her brain charged… a memory or a voice, or maybe just the fighting spirit she'd been born with kicked in. Acting in pure desperation and without thinking, she screamed in fury, worked her hand free and struck… gouging claws ripping at his eyes.

When the creep lunged off her to grab at his face, she shoved him aside, shot to her feet and ran for freedom.

So close. So… so close.

As she ran, lungs bursting for air, snot mixed with tears pouring down her thirteen-year-old face, she made a promise to herself. One day she would do something about other girls forced to suffer this kind of treatment.

For those who endured because *they* couldn't get away.

Chapter 1

Isabella Mendez had put in a full day's work as an FBI agent, working out of the field office and hating every minute. Hunger and weariness joined forces, tempting her to drive straight to her apartment complex and call it a day.

Opening her hidden stash, she slid her hand into to the bag she kept on the floor in the back seat that contained her goodies. Being a car slob, she had empty cans, chocolate bar wrappers, and crumpled candy packages everywhere. Since she seldom drove her own vehicle to work, she kept her secret stash well hidden from everyone. Not that she gave a damn if her bad habit became known… okay, maybe she did. But not enough to clean up the mess. Considering everything else in her life had to be immaculate, she decided early on, she was allowed one shameful trait.

Rubbing her forehead, she imagined releasing her hair from the roll she pinned it up in every morning so the escalating headache would release its grip.

Then she'd take a swim in the pool in her building, go upstairs to shower, and catch up on the latest series she'd been binging on for the past week. Anything to keep her mind from revisiting her suddenly boring days.

But… she didn't drive in that direction. Instead, she headed to Fulton House to help Demi with the bunch of teens staying there tonight. The call she'd gotten an hour ago had determined this choice. Demi had been offhanded, not like herself at all. She'd enquired as to whether Bella would be coming later. Again… not like herself.

Isabella never met anyone more independent. Private about all things, Demi asking for help happened so seldom. And yet, her foster sister had called. So, now, Isabella would try to find out exactly why.

As she drove to the building that housed the homeless youths, ones that only had the streets to live on, but who came to Fulton to be safe, she wondered about the call and what it meant.

Demi had given her a few details about a hopped-up dopie called Hewie who'd arrived at the door the night before, stumbling, cussing, screaming insults, and demanding entrance.

Unable to talk him down, Demi had stood up to the kid, going into details about what she'd said. "I told him, don't come here stoned out of your mind or falling-down drunk. Being rude and aggressive and expecting to be welcomed isn't going to happen. If you can't be respectful to everyone, and that includes the staff, then don't come back till you can be."

Normally, Bella knew no one was turned away if they truly had a need. But there had to be some limitations. Like carrying a weapon. The law in Arizona had a restriction on anyone under the age of 18 possessing or owning a firearm. Therefore, it was also the firm rule in this downtown Phoenix Fulton House.

Not that there should be a problem at this address because the Fulton House residency at this location only served those under eighteen. Other places were available for the older ages – sixteen to twenty-four. But rules make no difference when a messed-up youth is involved, as Bella knew from experience. Mostly, they dance to their own sick music. Especially those like the described Hewie, whose pickled mind cared only about the crap it craved.

Demi did say she'd gotten away from the creep, thanks to the other teens kicking in and getting the lawbreaker to leave. Otherwise, who knew what might have happened? Isabella felt her nerves tighten. She knew from experience, kids like the described Hewie were lightning rods, and could lash out with no restraints. Demi had been lucky. She might have been killed.

Waiting at the door to be let in, Isabella witnessed the cracked window and her leashed anxiety stirred. For months now, she'd been after Demi to get a security guard for the night hours, but she'd refused. Said it would scare off the kids if they saw anything like that.

In minutes, Demi unlocked the door, her expression agitated. As she stood aside, she kept her face turned away. But Bella saw the bruises on her cheek where her eye had been blackened and rage ignited. This young woman's civic conscious knew no bounds when it came to helping kids and the thought of her being injured while trying to do that work seemed unconscionable.

"Hey, Bella. I'm glad you came."

"Sure, no problem. You call. I come. As simple as that."

Demi's smile blossomed, not something seen very often and Bella's urge to hug her foster sister had to be restrained. She knew how it would be received. Demi would stand like a stick and basically bear having someone touching her. Not wanting to stress her sister out any more than necessary, Bella just held out a hand that Demi gratefully took to lead her inside her small cubby-hole office.

"So, what's happening?" Bella pointed significantly at Demi's face.

"Bossy-boots." Demi chuckled. "Always the cop. Can't you give me time to offer you a coffee or even a sandwich?"

Bella laughed at herself and added sheepishly, "Sorry. It's just that you seldom call me to come in if we had no arrangements for the night. And when you do, I know it's because something happened outside your expertise. Usually something to do with a lawbreaker. I can see my hunch was right."

"Stop looking at my face like your examining a victim. It's fine. Like I told you on the phone, one of the kids came to the door in a mess and wouldn't behave. He got a bit physical."

"Right. You sugar-coated the incident. Tell it to me straight, or I'll ask Nora."

"Nora's a big worrywart. She'll enlarge the whole scene until it's like an invasion by the devil himself. Like I told you, a kid called Hewie got temperamental, then confrontational, and wouldn't take no for an answer. Eventually, some of the other kids convinced him to come back when he knew his own name and could speak English rather than gibberish."

"And you're worried he'll be back tonight?"

"I know he will. He's been hovering around the front. I noticed the skinny punk earlier. When he saw me at the window, he pulled up his t-shirt and showed me a gun tucked into the waistband of his jeans. Look, I don't want anyone to get hurt. Yet I didn't want to freak them out by sharing my concern and calling in the cops."

Bella smiled with little humor. "You knew I'd understand and keep it to myself."

"Of course, You're my angel, always here when I need you." Demi's shy grin placated.

"And… what's his name… your bro Tanner, was he busy tonight?"

"Couldn't get a hold of him." Demi's eyes lit up at the mention of the man who also came running when she needed help. He too had a sincere wish to be involved. "He goes off the radar sometimes. This couldn't wait."

"Hey, don't worry. He'd only piss me off and call me Izzie. I'm glad you reached out. How many times have I told you to? Both of us are here to help, you know that."

"Yet you're never here together. It's like you do everything you can not to be in the same vicinity as Tanner. Why?"

Unable to explain her reasons, not wanting anyone to know of her secret dislike she'd been nursing for years, Isabella just laughed slightly and answered. "Even though we're both employed by the Feds, we're in completely different sectors. He works as a field agent mostly in homicide and after that last undercover operation where we had the drug crackdown, they've been keeping me busy in the office."

"You almost died during that raid."

"But I didn't. We stopped the pipeline of drugs from Mexico, and I survived. Story over. And quit stalling. What happened after you saw the creep's gun?"

"He mouthed the words "later bitch". I figure he's got it in for me because I wouldn't allow him to come inside to look for some guy he was searching for. Not only was he drunk and abusive; he meant to hurt the kid. Who, by the way, wasn't here. But Hewie wouldn't listen."

"So he got punchy."

"Right, until Nora got some of the kids to step in

and get rid of him."

"But not until after he put his stinking hands on you." Bella felt anger course through her body at the thought that anyone could hurt Demi. "See… it's times like this you really need to call the police."

"You know what happens when they come around. The kids fade away and many never come back. I just hate to force the issue to that extreme."

"Instead, you let the assholes use you as a punching bag."

Suddenly, they both heard the ruckus outside the front door and stood quickly. Demi looked at Bella and didn't have to say the words, "he's back." She didn't need to.

Bella already knew.

She walked over to peer out of the window and saw an unwashed youth in ill-fitting dirty clothes, brandishing a weapon. His drunken calls for Demi to show herself were menacing.

Knowing he could hurt someone who might inadvertently appear around the corner, or even one of the kids inside who were curious and looked out of an upstairs window, Bella said quickly, "Let me out the back door and don't answer this idiot."

In minutes, she came around from the side of the building and saw that Hewie had ramped up his feelings of injustice and was screaming stupidity toward the building. His vile words mixed with threats and gibberish were out of control. And Bella knew just how dangerous this made him. There'd be no talking him down. All she could hope for was a distraction so she could attack unseen.

Just then a man looked out from behind a vehicle that had been parked in front, and he yelled something at the teen. Hewie turned in that direction.

It was all she needed. Bella bolted from her hiding spot and attacked, settling on Hewie's back to bring him to the ground. Her hand forced the gun up to be sure he'd lose control. When Hewie landed on his stomach, she drove the same hand down hard on the cement, intending for him to release the weapon.

Hoping to immobilize him, she soon realized the reality of the situation. He had the strength of a wild animal, all doped up, feeling no pain. The rebel flipped her over and came back at her like a crazed beast.

Applying her training, she sprung to her feet. Using a low roundhouse kick, she stopped his forward drive. Then she followed with a knee strike that again put him down. But only for a few seconds. He came back at her, punching, slashing, until she'd had enough. Driving her hand into his throat as a last resort didn't work either. The punk didn't seem to feel anything. They fought hard, him screaming cusswords in her face, spit flying from his mouth, and his fists trying to connect.

Suddenly, his hands grabbed at her throat, and she couldn't block his hold. She brought her own arms up to dislodge his, but the steel bands held strong. Just as she intended to drop to the ground to force him down so she could use the movement in her defense, a man approached out of the dark.

If it wasn't for the gun muzzle pushed into Hewie's forehead, she didn't believe he'd have stopped squeezing even if her intended move had worked.

Tanner gave the order in a threatening voice filled with menace. "Let her go now, you little bastard, or I'll shoot. And… I won't lose a moment's sleep."

~*~*~*~

If you enjoyed this preview into Special Agent Sophia and would like to continue reading, click here to go to Amazon:

http://mybook.to/specialagentsophia

AFTERWORD

Thank you so much for reading *Special Agent Murphy*.

I loved writing this story, and I hope you'll enjoy reading it too. If so, I would ask you for a favor. Wherever you purchased this book, please take a few minutes and leave an honest review. Authors enjoy hearing from folks who like their stories, and hopefully, others will read your words and choose to buy this work because of your sentiments.

My website at http://mimibarbour.com now has all my books listed with links to the various publishers to make it easy for you to return to where you bought the book and to find my other work.

While you're there, I'd really appreciate it if you would sign up for my newsletter so I can keep in touch. http://bit.ly/MimiBNewsletter. I only send out newsletters approximately twice a month. It's usually full of giveaways, contests, and freebies along with my personal news. (You have my word that your address will never be shared.)

Hugs, Mimi

ABOUT THE AUTHOR

MIMI BARBOUR: New York Times & USA Today Best-selling, award-winning romance author has written nine series, many single-tiles and is involved in a huge number of box collections.

She lives on the beautiful East coast of Vancouver Island and writes her books with tongue-in-cheek and a mad glint in her eye. The fans all agree that it's the fascinating characters she creates which makes her writing so entertaining and brings them back for more of her magic.

"The favorite part of my job is meeting the characters from each new book. Designing them the way I want and having them act however I think they should. It's thrilling, especially when most of my make-believe folks are people I would love to interact with in reality."

Contact me:

My website: http://www.mimibarbour.com/

or

Mimi Barbour

Write to me anytime. I love to hear from my readers
xo

www.ingramcontent.com/pod-product-compliance
Lightning Source LLC
Chambersburg PA
CBHW020459260626
47156CB00006B/1787